The Complete Aristotle Collection (Vol. 1)

Nicomachean Ethics & Rhetoric – Masterworks on Virtue, Character and Persuasion

A Modern Translation

Adapted for the Contemporary Reader

Aristotle

Translated by Tim Zengerink

Table of Contents

Preface - Message to the Reader

What If You Could Help Rebuild the Greatest Library in Human History?

Thousands of years ago, the Library of Alexandria stood as the crown jewel of human achievement — a sanctuary where the collected wisdom of every known civilization was gathered, preserved, and shared freely.

And then, it was lost.

Through fire, conquest, and the slow erosion of time, humanity lost not just books — but ideas, dreams, discoveries, and stories that could have changed the world forever.

Today, the Library of Alexandria lives again — and you are invited to be a part of its restoration.

Our mission is simple yet profound:

To rebuild the greatest library the world has ever known, and to translate all timeless works into every language and dialect, so that no seeker of knowledge is ever left behind again.

By joining our movement to rebuild the modern Library of Alexandria, you become part of an unprecedented mission:

- **Unlimited Access to the Greatest Audiobooks & eBooks Ever Written:**

  Instantly explore thousands of legendary works—Plato, Shakespeare, Jane Austen, Leo Tolstoy, and countless more. All instantly available to read or listen, placing a complete literary universe at your fingertips.

- **Beautiful Paperback & Deluxe Editions at Printing Cost**

  Own any title as an elegant paperback, deluxe hardcover, or stunning collectible boxset—offered to you at true printing cost, delivered straight to your door. Build your personal Library of Alexandria, crafted for beauty, built for durability, and worthy of proud display.

- **Fresh Translations for Modern Readers—in Every Language & Dialect**

  Enjoy timeless masterpieces reimagined in clear, contemporary language—no more outdated phrases or obscure references. Alongside the original versions, we're tirelessly translating these classics into every language and dialect imaginable, ensuring accessibility and understanding across cultures and generations.

- **Join a Global Renaissance of Literature & Knowledge**

  You directly support expanding our library, publishing deluxe editions at true cost, translating works into all global languages, and bringing humanity's greatest stories to people everywhere. By joining today, you're not just preserving a legacy of masterpieces; you set in motion a powerful wave of literary accessibility.

Become a Torchbearer of Knowledge.

Join us for free now at **LibraryofAlexandria.com**

Together, we will ensure that the light of human wisdom never fades again.

With gratitude and a shared love of knowledge,
The Modern Library of Alexandria Team

Visit:

www.libraryofalexandria.com

Or scan the code below:

Introduction

Virtue, Character, and Persuasive Wisdom

The Complete Aristotle Collection (Vol. 1) presents two of the most influential and enduring works in Western philosophy—Nicomachean Ethics and Rhetoric. Together, they form the moral and intellectual foundation of Aristotelian thought on how human beings ought to live, act, and communicate. These texts speak across millennia not only to scholars and politicians, but to anyone seeking to develop character, lead others wisely, and understand the complex dance between ethics and influence.

In Nicomachean Ethics, Aristotle explores the nature of the good life—what it means to flourish as a human being, and how one cultivates virtues that lead to true happiness. In Rhetoric, he offers a systematic analysis of persuasive speech, showing how character, emotion, and reason intersect in the art of communication. Far from being separate disciplines, these two works complement each other. One concerns the inner architecture of the good person; the other explains how such a person speaks effectively to others.

This introduction provides a guide to the central themes and enduring relevance of each text, demonstrating how Aristotle's integrated vision of virtue and persuasion continues to shape contemporary discussions in ethics, leadership, psychology, education, and politics.

Nicomachean Ethics:
The Architecture of a Flourishing Life

Aristotle's Nicomachean Ethics is perhaps the most influential work ever written on moral philosophy. Composed in the 4th century BCE, likely as lecture notes for his son Nicomachus or his students at the

Lyceum, the work presents a comprehensive inquiry into the highest human good—eudaimonia, commonly translated as "happiness" or "flourishing."

But eudaimonia for Aristotle is not mere pleasure or wealth or honor. It is a life of rational activity in accordance with virtue. Human beings are rational animals, and the good life is one in which we realize our potential through ethical choice, self-discipline, and thoughtful action.

Key teachings of the Ethics include:

- The Function Argument: Every being has a function; the human function is rational activity. The good life is the excellent performance of this function.
- The Doctrine of the Mean: Virtue is a mean between extremes. Courage lies between cowardice and rashness, generosity between stinginess and waste.
- Moral Virtue as Habit: We become just by doing just things. Virtue is not innate but cultivated through repetition and practical wisdom (phronesis).
- The Role of Friendship: Friends are mirrors of the self and essential to moral development. True friendship is based on mutual virtue, not utility or pleasure alone.
- Contemplation as the Highest Good: While ethical activity is essential, the most divine life is one of contemplation—reasoning in accord with eternal truths.

Aristotle sees ethics not as a set of rules, but as a practice. It is less about knowing than about becoming. The goal is not perfection, but harmony—a life that integrates reason, emotion, and action. In a world that often separates ethics from effectiveness, Aristotle insists they are two sides of the same coin.

His ethics are teleological: everything aims at some end, and the highest end for humans is to become fully human—rational, virtuous, fulfilled. The Ethics is thus both a personal map and a political manual, offering insights into education, citizenship, and the nature of justice.

Rhetoric:
The Science and Soul of Persuasion

While Nicomachean Ethics outlines the character of a good person, Rhetoric explains how that character communicates effectively in public life. In Aristotle's view, rhetoric is not the art of trickery or emotional manipulation—it is the art of discovering all the available means of persuasion in a given case. It is the interface between reason and community, between truth and the forum in which truth must be defended.

The Rhetoric is divided into three main books:

- Book I outlines the different kinds of rhetoric (deliberative, judicial, and epideictic), and establishes the foundational elements of persuasive speech: ethos (credibility), pathos (emotion), and logos (reason).
- Book II explores human psychology and emotional states, offering insights into how audiences respond to fear, anger, shame, joy, and other passions.
- Book III examines style, delivery, and arrangement—how clarity, tone, metaphor, and rhythm shape the impact of a speech.

Aristotle's approach is empirical and analytical. He studies real human behavior to understand how persuasion works in practical life. He teaches that:

- Ethos is central: The audience must trust the speaker. Character is not just claimed—it is demonstrated through consistency, respect, and moral seriousness.
- Pathos is powerful: Emotions are not enemies of reason; they are part of human decision-making. A good speaker understands how to stir emotion responsibly.
- Logos is foundational: Persuasion without reason is manipulation. Clear arguments, evidence, and logical structure ground rhetoric in truth.

In a democratic society, Aristotle argues, rhetoric is essential—not because truth needs dressing up, but because people must be moved to act. Rhetoric enables justice to be defended, laws to be debated, and values to be shared. It is a tool for collective reasoning in a pluralistic world.

Importantly, Aristotle sees a deep connection between ethics and rhetoric. A speaker who lacks virtue may sway the crowd, but cannot offer lasting wisdom. True rhetoric arises from a virtuous life—it reflects not performance, but presence.

Aristotle's Legacy: Uniting Moral Clarity and Civic Engagement

Read together, Nicomachean Ethics and Rhetoric form the twin pillars of Aristotle's moral and political philosophy. One explores the internal formation of the soul; the other, the external expression of that formation in community. Aristotle teaches us that to live well is to live with purpose and integrity—and to lead well is to communicate that purpose with clarity and care.

For the modern reader, these texts remain vital:

- In education, they shape character formation and critical thinking.
- In leadership, they promote moral clarity and communicative power.
- In civic life, they guide responsible discourse and collective flourishing.
- In personal growth, they offer a path of self-mastery through practical wisdom.

Aristotle does not offer perfection—he offers practice. His ethics and rhetoric are dynamic disciplines, grounded in the realities of human limitation and the possibilities of human excellence. He teaches us not just how to think, but how to live and speak in a way that honors truth, cultivates virtue, and serves the common good.

Translated by Tim Zengerink

Welcome to The Complete Aristotle Collection (Vol. 1). May these texts not only inform your mind, but shape your character, refine your voice, and guide your path toward the enduring art of living wisely and leading well.

Nicomachean Ethics

Aristotle

Book 1

Every art and every study, as well as every action and choice, is believed to aim at some good. For this reason, the good has been rightly described as what everything seeks. However, there is a difference among these goals: some are activities, while others are products that come from these activities. When there are goals separate from the actions, the products are naturally seen as better than the activities. Since there are many types of actions, arts, and sciences, their goals are many as well. The goal of medicine is health, that of shipbuilding is a ship, that of strategy is victory, and that of economics is wealth. But when different arts are connected under one skill—like bridle-making and the other arts related to horse equipment fall under the skill of riding, and this, along with all military activities, falls under the skill of strategy—it is clear that the goals of the master skills are better than those of the subordinate ones. After all, the subordinate actions are done for the sake of the higher goals. It doesn't matter whether the activities themselves are the goals or if they lead to something else, as is the case with the sciences mentioned.

Now, if there is one ultimate goal of everything we do, something we desire for its own sake (and not for the sake of something else), and if we don't choose everything for some other reason (which would go on forever, making our desires pointless), then this ultimate goal must be the greatest good. Knowing this should have a huge effect on our lives. Wouldn't we, like archers aiming at a target, be more likely to hit the right mark? If this is true, then we must try to figure out what this goal is and which of the sciences or abilities it belongs to. It seems to belong to the most authoritative art, the one that truly leads all others. Politics appears to be this type of art because it decides which sciences should be studied in the state and which subjects different classes of citizens should learn and how much they should learn. We see that even the most important skills, like strategy, economics, and rhetoric, fall under politics. Since politics uses the other sciences and makes laws about what we should and should not do, its goal must include the goals of all other sciences. This means the goal of politics must be the good for humanity. Even if the greatest good is the same for one person as it is for a state, the good of the state is greater and more complete. Whether we are trying to achieve or preserve the good, it's better to do it for a whole nation or for city-states than for one person. These are the goals our study focuses on since we are discussing political science in one sense of the term.

Our discussion will be enough if it is as clear as the topic allows. Precision shouldn't be expected the same way in every discussion, just as it's not expected in every craft. Fine and just actions, which political science studies, can vary greatly and be seen differently by different people. This leads some to think they exist only because of custom, not nature. Goods also vary in this way because they can sometimes bring harm to people. For example, people have been ruined because of their wealth, and others because of their courage. So, when speaking about such topics and using such ideas, we should be satisfied with indicating the truth roughly and in general terms. When discussing things that are only mostly true and starting with similar ideas, we can't expect perfect conclusions. Therefore, each statement should be accepted in the spirit it is given. It is the mark of an educated person to look for precision in each subject only as far as the topic allows. It is clearly foolish to expect mathematical certainty from a speechmaker and to demand scientific proof from a storyteller.

Each person judges well what they know, and they are good judges of the things they are familiar with. So, the person who is trained in a subject is a good judge of that subject, and the person with a well-rounded education is a good judge in general. This is why a young person isn't the best audience for lessons on political science. They are inexperienced in life's actions, which are the starting point for these discussions. Also, since young people tend to follow their emotions, their study will be useless because the goal is not knowledge but action. It doesn't matter whether they are young in years or young in character. The problem isn't age but living in a way where they pursue each passing desire as their emotions guide them. For such people, as with those who are lacking self-control, knowledge brings no benefit. But for those who want to live and act based on reason, knowledge about these subjects will be very useful.

These thoughts about the student, the kind of treatment to expect, and the purpose of our study can serve as our introduction.

Let's return to our study and, considering that all knowledge and every pursuit aims at some good, ask what we say political science aims at and what the highest good achievable by action is. In words, there is broad agreement: most people and those of higher understanding say that it is happiness. They agree that living well and doing well are the same as being happy. But they disagree about what happiness is. Many people don't agree with the wise on this. Most think it's something obvious like pleasure, wealth, or honor. However, they often change their minds—thinking happiness is health when they're sick or wealth when they're poor. Still, knowing they don't know, they admire those who speak of great ideas beyond their understanding. Some believe that there is another good beyond these obvious ones, something that exists on its own and causes the goodness of all other things. It may not be necessary to examine every opinion ever held, but it is enough to look at those that are most common or seem worth considering.

Let's not forget, though, that there's a difference between arguments from first principles and arguments toward first principles. Plato was right to ask whether we are coming from or going toward first principles. It's like a race where you either run from the starting line to the turn or from the turn back to the starting line. We must begin with what is known, but knowledge can mean two things: what is known to us and what is known without conditions. We should begin with what is known to us. So, anyone who wants to understand what is noble, just, and generally related to political science must have been brought up with good habits. The facts are the starting point, and if these are clear enough to him, he won't need the reasoning right away. A person who has been well brought up has or can easily gain these starting points. As for someone who neither has them nor can get them, let him listen to the words of Hesiod:

"Best of all is the one who knows everything for himself;
Good is he who listens to wise advice from others;
But he who neither knows nor listens to others
Is a useless fool."

Let's now return to the main point of our discussion. Looking at how people live, most people—especially those of lower desires—seem to equate the good, or happiness, with pleasure. This is why they love a life of enjoyment. There are, we might say, three main types of life: the life of pleasure, the political life, and the contemplative life. Most people are quite base in their tastes, preferring a life suitable for animals, but they get this idea because many powerful people share the same desires.

Looking at the main types of life, people of higher refinement and active nature tend to identify happiness with honor. Roughly speaking, this is the goal of the political life. However, honor seems too shallow to be what we are truly looking for, as it depends more on those who give honor rather than the one who receives it. But the good we seek should be something that belongs to a person and can't be easily taken away. Furthermore, people seem to seek honor to be assured of their goodness. They seek honor from wise people who know them and value their virtue. Clearly, then, virtue is better than honor, at least according to these people. One might even say that virtue, rather than honor, is the true goal of the political life. Yet, even this seems incomplete because having virtue is compatible with being asleep or inactive, and it can even exist alongside great suffering and misfortune. But no one would call a person happy if they were living like that unless they were just stubbornly defending their argument. But enough about this—it has been discussed at length in other debates. The third type of life is the contemplative life, which we will discuss later.

The life of money-making is one pursued out of necessity, and wealth is clearly not the good we are searching for. Wealth is useful for getting something else. So, we might instead say that the earlier-mentioned things (like pleasure and honor) are true goals because they are loved for themselves. But it's clear that even these aren't the ultimate goals. Many arguments have been made to support them, but we should now move on from this subject.

Next, we should consider the idea of the universal good and carefully examine what it means. This inquiry is made difficult by the fact that the idea of Forms has been introduced by friends of ours. Still, it is better—and indeed our duty—to pursue the truth even if it means criticizing ideas that are dear to us, especially since we are philosophers and lovers of wisdom. While both truth and friends are important, piety demands we honor truth above our friends.

Those who introduced the idea of Forms did not propose Ideas for categories that included levels of priority and order. For this reason, they did not suggest there was an Idea for all numbers. But the term "good" is used in different ways in different categories, such as substance, quality, and relation. Substance is more fundamental in nature than relation because relation is like an offshoot or an accident of being. So, there cannot be one common Idea of good across all these categories. Furthermore, "good" has many meanings, just like "being" does. It is used for substances like God and reason, for qualities like the virtues, for quantities like moderation, and for relations like usefulness. It is also used for time, like the right moment, and for place, like the right location. Clearly, it cannot be one thing present in all cases. If it were, it could not be used in all these different categories. Also, since each science studies one thing, there would be one science of all goods, but instead, we see many sciences studying things within the same category. For example, strategy studies opportunity in war, and medicine studies opportunity in illness. Medicine also studies moderation in food, while gymnastics studies moderation in exercise.

One might also ask what is meant by "the thing itself," as when we say "man himself" or a particular man, the definition of man is the same. If they are both men, they don't differ in that respect. The same should be true of "good itself" and particular goods—they shouldn't differ as far as their goodness is concerned. Furthermore, something doesn't become better just because it lasts longer. Something that lasts a day isn't necessarily less good than something that lasts forever. The Pythagoreans seem to give a better explanation of the good when they place "the One" in the column of goods. This is the view that Speusippus seems to have followed.

But we should discuss these things elsewhere. However, we should consider that the Platonists haven't been talking about all goods. They say that the goods we pursue for themselves are good in relation to a single Form, while things that produce or preserve these goods, or prevent their opposites, are only secondarily called good. Clearly, then, goods must be spoken of in two ways: some are good in themselves, and others are good because they lead to these. Let's separate goods that are good in themselves from those that are useful and see if the former are all good because of one Idea. What kind of things would we call good in themselves? Is it things we pursue even when they are not connected to other things, like knowledge, sight, and certain pleasures and honors? Certainly, even if we pursue these for something else, we would still place them among things that are good in themselves. Or, is nothing good in itself except the Form of good? If that's the case, the Form would be empty. But if the things we've mentioned are good in themselves, then there must be some common quality that makes them all good, just like there is something common in both snow and white lead that makes them white. But when we consider things like honor, wisdom, and pleasure, their goodness seems to come from different sources. So, the good is not one single thing that applies to all these different cases.

Then, what do we mean by the good? It's not like things that only have the same name by chance. Are goods one because they come from one good or because they all contribute to one good? Or are they one by analogy? Certainly, reason is in the soul just as sight is in the body, and so on in other cases. But maybe we should leave these subjects for now. Perfect accuracy about them belongs to another area of philosophy. The same goes for the idea of the universal good. Even if there is one good that applies to all goods or exists on its own, it clearly can't be achieved by humans. But right now, we're looking for something that can be achieved. Still, some might think it's worth recognizing this idea of the universal good as a way to better understand the goods we can achieve. If we know the universal good, we can use it as a guide to help us achieve the goods that are good for us. This argument sounds reasonable, but it seems to go against the methods used in the sciences. All sciences aim at some good and try to supply what is missing, but they don't start by studying the universal good. It's hard to believe that experts in different fields don't know about such a great help as the universal good. It's also difficult to see how a carpenter or a weaver would benefit in their craft by knowing about the universal good, or how someone who understands the Idea of the good would be a better doctor or general. A doctor seems to study not general health, but the health of a particular person. After all, it's individuals that doctors treat. But we've said enough about these topics for now.

Let us once again focus on the idea of the good we are trying to find, and ask what it could be. It seems to vary depending on different actions and skills. For example, in medicine, strategy, and other arts, it differs. So what is the good in each case? Surely, it is the thing for which everything else is done. In medicine, it's health; in strategy, it's victory; in architecture, it's a house; and in other areas, it's something else. In every action and effort, it is the end goal, because it is for this goal that people do everything else they do. So, if there is one goal for everything we do, this goal will be the good we can achieve through action. And if there are more than one, these will be the goods we can achieve through action.

This reasoning leads us, in a different way, to the same point. But we should try to explain this more clearly. Since there are clearly multiple goals, and we choose some of them (for example, wealth, flutes, or tools) for the sake of something else, it is clear that not all goals are final ends. The highest good is clearly something final. So, if there is only one final end, that will be what we are looking for. If there are more than one, the most final of these will be what we are searching for. We say that what is worthy of being pursued for its own sake is more final than something pursued for another reason, and what is never desired for something else is more final than things desired both for themselves and for another reason. Therefore, we call "final" without any limits that which is always desired for itself and never for something else.

Happiness, more than anything else, seems to be this kind of thing. We always choose it for ourselves, not for something else. But honor, pleasure, reason, and every virtue we choose for themselves (because even if nothing else came from them, we would still choose each one of them), yet we also choose them because they lead to happiness. Happiness, on the other hand, no one chooses for the sake of these or for any other reason.

From the perspective of self-sufficiency, the same result appears. The final good is thought to be self-sufficient. Now, by self-sufficient, we do not mean something that only one person needs, like someone living alone, but also something for their family, friends, and fellow citizens, because humans are social beings. But we must set a limit to this, because if we include our ancestors, descendants, and friends' friends, we will be dealing with an infinite chain. Let us leave this for another time and now define self-sufficient as that which, when alone, makes life desirable and complete, lacking nothing. We believe happiness to be like this. We also think it is the most desirable thing of all, not just one good thing among others. If it were one of many, even the smallest addition would make it more desirable, because the added good would make it better, and greater good is always more desirable. So, happiness is something final and self-sufficient, and it is the goal of action.

However, saying that happiness is the highest good might seem obvious, and people might still want a clearer explanation of what it really is. We could explain it more clearly if we could first figure out the function of a human being. Just as for a flute-player, sculptor, or artist, and generally for all things that have a purpose or activity, the good is thought to reside in that purpose, so it seems to be with humans, if they also have a function. Do the carpenter and the leatherworker have specific functions or tasks, but not humans? Were we born without a purpose? Or, just as the eye, hand, and foot have functions, does humanity, too, have a specific role apart from these? What might it be? Life itself seems common to both plants and animals, but we are searching for what is unique to humans. Therefore, let's rule out the life of nutrition and growth. The next possibility is a life of perception, but this also seems to be shared with horses, oxen, and every animal. What remains is the active life of the part of us that has reason. One part of reason follows principles, and the other part has and exercises them. Since "life of reason" has two meanings, we should clarify that we mean life in the sense of activity because that seems to be the truer meaning of the term. If the function of a human is an activity of the soul that follows or implies a rational principle, and if we say that both a person and a good person share the same function—like a lyre and a good lyre-player—and if, in all cases, the function is the same but excellence makes it better, then we must add to this definition the idea of performing that function well. For example, the function of a lyre-player is to play the lyre, and the function of a good lyre-player is to do so skillfully. If this is the case, and if the function of a person is a kind of life, this life will involve actions of the soul that follow a rational principle, and the function of a good person will be to perform these actions nobly and well. Since any action is performed well when it is done in line with its excellence, human good turns out to be activity of the soul in accordance with virtue. If there are many virtues, the good follows the best and most complete ones.

But we must add "throughout a complete life." One swallow does not make a summer, nor does one day. Likewise, one good day or short time does not make someone blessed and happy.

Let this be a rough outline of the good. We should first sketch it out roughly, then fill in the details later. It seems that anyone can carry on and explain something that has been well outlined, and time is a good helper in such tasks. The growth of the arts happens this way— anyone can add what is missing. We should also remember what has been said before and not seek the same level of precision in all subjects. Instead, in each area, we should aim for the kind of accuracy that fits the topic. A carpenter and a mathematician study the right angle in different ways. The carpenter looks at how useful it is for his work, while the mathematician is interested in what it actually is. We must act the same way in all subjects, ensuring that our main task does not get bogged down by minor questions. Nor should we always demand to know the cause of everything. Sometimes, it's enough that the facts are well-established, especially in the case of first principles. First principles are the most important thing. We come to know them in different ways—some by induction, others by observation, habit, or other methods. But we should try to understand each principle in the right way, putting effort into explaining them clearly, as they greatly influence everything that follows. The beginning is said to be more than half of the whole, and many of the questions we ask are cleared up by it.

We must also consider this matter in light of both our conclusions and what is commonly believed. When our view is correct, all the facts fit together, but when it is wrong, the facts start to clash. Goods have been divided into three types: some are external, some are related to the soul, and some to the body. We consider those related to the soul as the truest goods, and we classify actions and activities of the soul in this category. Therefore, our argument must be correct according to this view, which is an old one agreed upon by many philosophers. It is also correct because we define the goal in terms of certain actions and activities. This places it among goods of the soul, not among external goods. Another common belief that fits our account is that a happy person lives well and acts well because we have basically defined happiness as living and acting well. The traits that are usually associated with happiness all seem to match our definition of it. Some people say happiness is virtue, some say it's practical wisdom, while others believe it's a kind of philosophical wisdom. Some say it's one or all of these things, either with or without pleasure. Others include external prosperity. Many of these ideas have been held by both ordinary people and important thinkers, and it's unlikely that all of them are completely wrong. Instead, they are probably right in at least one way, or even in most ways.

Our account fits with those who say that happiness is virtue or a specific virtue, because virtuous activity belongs to virtue. However, there is an important difference between putting the highest good in having virtue or in using it, in the state of mind or in the action itself. The state of mind might exist without leading to any good results, like when someone is asleep or otherwise inactive, but action cannot. If someone is engaged in virtuous activity, they will act, and act well. Like in the Olympic Games, it is not the most beautiful or strongest people who win crowns, but those who actually compete. It is some of these who are victorious. Likewise, it is those who act that win the good things in life.

Their life is also naturally pleasant. Pleasure is a state of the soul, and to each person, what they love is pleasant to them. For example, a horse is pleasant to someone who loves horses, and a spectacle is pleasant to someone who loves sights. In the same way, just actions are pleasant to someone who loves justice, and virtuous actions are pleasant to someone who loves virtue. For most people, their pleasures conflict with each other because their pleasures are not naturally pleasant, but for lovers of the noble, the things that are naturally pleasant are also pleasant to them. Virtuous actions are like this. So for them, these actions are pleasant in themselves, and also naturally pleasant. Therefore, their life does not need any extra pleasure to make it enjoyable—it is already pleasant. Also, a person who does not enjoy doing noble things is not truly good. No one would call someone just if they didn't enjoy acting justly, or call someone generous if they didn't enjoy generous acts. This applies to all other virtues as well. If this is true, then virtuous actions are naturally pleasant. They are also good and noble, and have all these qualities to the highest degree, because a good person judges them to be so. Their judgment is as we have described. So happiness is the best, noblest, and most pleasant thing in the world. These qualities are not separated from one another, as in the old inscription at Delos:

The noblest is what is most just, the best is health, but the most pleasant thing is to get what you desire.

All these qualities belong to the best activities, and we believe that one or all of these activities are connected with happiness.

But as we said, happiness also needs external goods. It is either impossible or difficult to do noble deeds without the proper resources. In many cases, we use friends, wealth, and political power as tools, and there are some things that, if missing, take away from happiness. For example, good birth, good children, and beauty. A person who is very ugly or poorly born, or who is isolated and without children, is unlikely to be very happy. A person would be even less likely to be happy if they had very bad children or friends, or if they lost good children or friends to death. So, as we said, happiness seems to need a certain level of good fortune. This is why some people connect happiness with luck, while others link it with virtue.

For this reason, people also ask whether happiness is something we learn or develop through habit or some other kind of training, or whether it comes from divine intervention or luck. If it is a gift from the gods, it would make sense that happiness is something they give, as it is the best thing a person can have. But this question might be better for another discussion. Even if happiness is not a gift from the gods but instead comes as a result of virtue or some kind of learning or training, it still seems to be one of the most godlike things. The reward and goal of virtue seem to be the best things in the world, something divine and blessed.

According to this view, happiness will also be widely shared because everyone who has the potential for virtue can achieve it with the right study and effort. If it is better to be happy because of our actions rather than because of chance, it makes sense that this is the way it works. Everything that depends on nature is as good as it can be, and the same goes for anything that relies on art or reason. This is especially true when it depends on the best cause of all. It would be a very poor arrangement if the greatest and most noble thing in life were left to chance.

The answer to this question is also clear from the definition of happiness. We said that happiness is a virtuous activity of the soul, of a certain kind. Of the other goods, some must exist beforehand as conditions for happiness, and others are helpful and useful as tools. This agrees with what we said at the beginning. We said the goal of political science is the best end, and political science focuses on making the citizens good and capable of noble actions.

It makes sense, then, that we do not call an ox, horse, or any other animal happy because none of them can take part in this kind of activity. For this reason, a boy is not happy either, because he is not yet able to act this way due to his age. When we call boys happy, it is because of the hopes we have for their future. As we said, not only is complete virtue needed for happiness, but also a complete life, because many changes and chances happen throughout life. The most fortunate people may experience great misfortune in old age, like Priam in the Trojan story. No one would call someone who ended their life in misery happy.

Should we not call anyone happy while they are still alive, as Solon says, and wait until they die to judge? But even if we accept this idea, does that mean someone is happy only when they're dead? Isn't that an odd thing to say, especially since we believe that happiness involves activity? If we don't call a dead person happy, and Solon didn't mean that, maybe what he meant is that once someone dies, we can safely say they were blessed because they are no longer at risk of misfortune. However, this raises another question. We think good and bad things can still happen to a dead person, just like they can happen to someone who is alive but unaware of them—like when children or descendants experience good or bad fortunes, or receive honors or dishonors.

This creates a problem. What if a man lived a happy life and died in a way that honored his life, but later his descendants faced many hardships or some did well while others did not? The closeness of the relationship between the man and his descendants can also vary a lot. It would seem strange if the dead person's happiness changed based on what happens to their descendants—sometimes being happy and other times being sad. But it also seems strange if their descendants' fortunes had no effect on the dead person's happiness.

Let's go back to the main problem. Maybe looking at it again will help us solve this issue. If we must wait until a person dies to call them happy, not because they are happy now but because they were happy before, this seems like a paradox. How could we not call someone happy while they're alive, if happiness is something that belongs to them at that time? We might hesitate to call living people happy because life is full of changes, and happiness seems like something that should be stable and not easily altered. One person might experience many ups and downs in life. If we judged them based on every turn of events, we might call them happy at one moment and unhappy the next, making happiness seem as changeable as a chameleon. But maybe it's wrong to let a person's happiness depend so much on their changing fortunes. Happiness doesn't depend on things like wealth or power but on a person's virtuous actions, which define happiness.

This discussion actually supports our definition of happiness. No part of a person's life is as lasting as their virtuous actions. These actions are thought to last even longer than knowledge of the sciences.

Among these actions, the most valuable ones last the longest because happy people tend to live their lives consistently in line with virtue. This may be why we don't forget them. So, we can say the happy person will remain happy throughout their life because they will always or most often be engaged in virtuous activities and contemplation. They will handle life's ups and downs with nobility and grace, especially if they are truly good and morally strong.

Many things in life happen by chance, but these events differ in importance. Small strokes of good or bad luck don't affect life much, but if many big events turn out well, they can make life happier. Not only do they add beauty to life, but the way a person handles these events can show their nobility and goodness. On the other hand, if these events go badly, they can harm happiness because they bring pain and can stop people from doing many things. Even then, a person's nobility can still shine through when they endure great misfortunes with dignity—not by ignoring the pain, but by showing greatness of soul.

If, as we said, a person's actions define their life, a truly happy person can never become miserable. They won't do things that are disgraceful or mean. We believe that a truly good and wise person will handle whatever life brings in the best possible way, like how a good general uses the army he has or a good shoemaker works with the leather he's given. The same goes for all other craftsmen. If this is true, a happy person cannot become miserable, although they may not reach the highest level of happiness if they face extreme misfortunes like those of Priam.

A truly happy person is not constantly changing in their happiness. They won't lose their happiness easily or because of ordinary bad luck. Only a series of very great misfortunes could shake their happiness. Even if they do face many great misfortunes, they won't regain their happiness quickly. If they regain it at all, it will only be after a long period of time and after they've had many great successes.

So, should we not say that someone is happy if they live according to complete virtue and have enough external goods—not just for a short time, but for their entire life? Or should we add that they must also die in a way that reflects how they lived? The future is unknown to us, but happiness, as we've said, is the final goal and something complete in every way. If this is true, we will call happy those among the living who meet these conditions and who will continue to do so, but we will only call them truly happy once their life is complete. That settles these questions.

The idea that the fortunes of a person's descendants and friends don't affect their happiness at all seems a bit harsh and goes against what people generally believe. But since there are many events, and these events can vary greatly in how much they matter, it would take too long to go through each one in detail. A general outline should be enough. Just as some of the misfortunes a person experiences have a bigger impact on their life than others, the same is true for the misfortunes of their friends and descendants. It also makes a difference whether these misfortunes happen to people who are alive or those who are already dead. For example, in a tragedy, it matters whether horrible deeds happen on stage or are just talked about. Whether or not the dead are affected by the fortunes of the living is something people still debate. It seems that if good or bad things do reach the dead, the effects are weak or small, or at least not enough to make a happy person unhappy or change the situation of someone who is blessed. The fortunes of friends and descendants may have some impact on the dead, but only in a way that doesn't make the happy unhappy or cause any major change in their state.

Now that we've answered those questions, let's consider whether happiness is something to be praised or something to be valued. It's clear that happiness isn't just a potential thing. Everything that is praised seems to be praised because it's a certain kind of thing and is related to something else. For example, we praise a just or brave person because of their actions and what they do. We praise someone strong or fast because they are good at something important. This is clear when it comes to the gods, too. It seems strange to compare the gods to human standards, but we do this in praise because praise involves comparing one thing to another. However, we don't praise the best things, we value them more highly. Instead of praising the gods and the most godlike humans, we call them blessed and happy. The same goes for good things like happiness. No one praises happiness in the same way they praise justice. Instead, they call it blessed because it's more divine and better than things that are praised.

Eudoxus seems to have been right in arguing that pleasure is the highest good. He believed that the fact that pleasure, though good, is not praised shows that it is better than the things that are praised. He thought that God and the good were similar because all other things are judged in comparison to them. Praise is fitting for virtue because virtue leads people to do good deeds, but we celebrate virtuous acts themselves. This might be something that those who study praise and celebration focus on, but for us, it's enough to understand that happiness is something to be valued and complete. This seems clear because happiness is the first principle. It is the reason we do everything we do, and we consider the first principle of anything to be the most valuable and divine.

Since happiness is an activity of the soul according to perfect virtue, we need to examine what virtue is. Maybe this will help us better understand the nature of happiness. The true student of politics is thought to study virtue above all things because they want to make their fellow citizens good and obedient to the law. This is shown by lawgivers like those in Crete and Sparta, and others like them. If this inquiry belongs to political science, then it fits with our overall plan. But clearly, the virtue we need to study is human virtue because the good we are looking for is human good, and the happiness we are concerned with is human happiness. By human virtue, we don't mean bodily virtue but virtue of the soul, since happiness is also an activity of the soul. If this is true, the student of politics must know something about the soul, just as a doctor must know about the body if they are to heal it. And politics is more important than medicine. Even the best doctors spend much time learning about the body. So, the student of politics must study the soul, but only enough to answer the questions we are discussing. Going deeper would require more precision than our purpose demands.

Some things about the soul are already discussed well enough in other works, and we can use them here. For example, people say that one part of the soul is irrational, and one part follows reason. Whether these parts are physically separate, like parts of the body, or only separated in how we define them, doesn't matter for our current discussion.

Of the irrational part, one part seems to be shared by all living things and is responsible for nutrition and growth. This is the power of the soul we find in all plants and animals, including humans. It's more reasonable to think of this as a common power than to assign different powers to different creatures. The excellence of this part of the soul seems to be shared by all living things, not just humans. This part of the soul seems to be most active during sleep, and since goodness and badness aren't obvious during sleep, there's a saying that happy people are no better off than unhappy people for half of their lives. This happens naturally because sleep is when the soul is inactive in the part where it can be good or bad. However, perhaps some movements of the soul happen during sleep, and in that case, the dreams of good people might be better than those of others. But let's leave this topic aside for now, as the nutritive part of the soul has no part in human excellence.

There seems to be another irrational part of the soul that, in a way, listens to reason. For example, we praise the rational part of a person who has self-control and the person who lacks it. We praise the part of their soul that listens to reason because it guides them in the right direction toward the best things. But we also find another part of the soul that seems naturally opposed to reason and fights against it. Just as paralyzed limbs may move in the opposite direction when we try to move them, so it is with the soul. The impulses of those who lack self-control often pull them in opposite directions. In the body, we can see what goes wrong, but in the soul, it's less visible. However, we must assume that the soul, too, has something that goes against reason. Exactly how it is distinct from other parts of the soul doesn't concern us right now.

Even this part of the soul seems to listen to reason in some way. In a person with self-control, it obeys reason, and in the brave and temperate person, it listens even more closely to reason. In these people, the irrational part and the rational part speak with the same voice.

So, the irrational part of the soul seems to have two parts. The part responsible for nutrition doesn't follow reason at all, while the part responsible for desires and appetites does, in a way, listen to and obey reason. This is the same way we talk about following the advice of a father or a friend, not in the same way we discuss following a mathematical rule. The fact that the irrational part of the soul listens to reason is shown by how we give advice, reproof, or encouragement. If we say this part of the soul listens to reason, then the part of the soul that follows reason and the part that doesn't will each have two parts. One part follows reason strictly, while the other part follows reason like a person follows the guidance of their father.

Virtue is also divided into two kinds based on this difference. Some virtues are intellectual, and others are moral. For example, wisdom, understanding, and practical judgment are intellectual virtues, while generosity and temperance are moral virtues. When we talk about someone's character, we don't say they are wise or have understanding, but that they are good-tempered or temperate. Yet, we also praise the wise person for their state of mind. States of mind that deserve praise are called virtues.

Book 2

Virtue, as we know, is of two types: intellectual and moral. Intellectual virtue mainly comes from teaching, which is why it requires both experience and time. Moral virtue, on the other hand, comes from habit, which is why the word for moral virtue (ethike) comes from the word for habit (ethos). This shows that none of the moral virtues are naturally within us, because nothing that exists by nature can develop a habit that goes against its nature. For example, a stone, which naturally moves downward, can't be trained to move upward, even if you throw it up ten thousand times. The same goes for fire—it naturally rises and can't be trained to move downward. In the same way, nothing that behaves naturally in one way can be trained to behave in the opposite way. So, virtues don't come to us by nature or against nature. Instead, we are naturally able to acquire them, but they are perfected through habit.

For all things that come to us naturally, we first have the potential for them, and only later do we actually use them. This is clear with the senses: we didn't develop our ability to see or hear by using these senses many times. On the contrary, we had them before we used them. But we develop virtues by practicing them, just like with skills. For the things we need to learn before we can do them, we learn by doing them. For example, we become builders by building, and we become musicians by playing music. In the same way, we become just by doing just acts, temperate by doing temperate acts, and brave by doing brave acts.

This idea is also supported by what happens in cities. Lawmakers make citizens good by forming good habits in them. This is the goal of every lawmaker, and those who fail at this miss their target. This is the difference between a good and bad constitution.

In addition, the same causes that produce a virtue can also destroy it, just like with skills. A person becomes a good or bad musician by playing well or poorly. The same applies to builders and all other trades. People become good or bad at their craft based on how well they practice it. If this weren't true, there would be no need for teachers, and everyone would simply be born good or bad at their craft. The same goes for virtues. By behaving a certain way in our interactions with others, we become either just or unjust. By behaving a certain way when faced with danger, and by getting used to feeling either fear or confidence, we become either brave or cowardly. The same is true for our desires and feelings of anger: some people become temperate and calm, while others become self-indulgent and irritable, based on how they act in different situations. In short, our character develops from our repeated actions. That's why the actions we take must be of a certain kind, because our character reflects the differences in our actions. It makes a huge difference whether we develop good or bad habits from a young age.

Since we aren't trying to gain theoretical knowledge (like in other studies), but instead to become good, we must focus on actions—specifically, how we should do them. The way we act shapes the kind of character we develop, as we've already said. We all agree that we must act according to the right rule, and we'll discuss what this rule is later and how it connects to the other virtues. But for now, we should agree that when we talk about conduct, we are speaking in general terms, and we shouldn't expect exact details. Just like in matters of health, what is good for us doesn't have a strict set of rules. The same goes for specific cases, which are even less precise, as they don't follow any strict laws or rules. It's up to each individual to decide what is appropriate for the situation, just like a doctor or a navigator must do in their work.

Even though this is the nature of our discussion, we can still provide some help. First, let's consider that things can be destroyed by either deficiency or excess. This is true for both strength and health. To better understand this, we can look at things we can sense. For example, both too much or too little exercise can destroy strength, and both too much or too little food or drink can destroy health. However, the right amount of these things will both produce and maintain strength and health. The same is true for temperance, courage, and the other virtues. A person who runs from everything or fears everything becomes a coward. A person who is afraid of nothing and faces every danger becomes reckless. A person who indulges in every pleasure and avoids none becomes self-indulgent. Meanwhile, a person who avoids every pleasure, like someone who is insensitive, also misses the mark. So, temperance and courage are destroyed by both excess and deficiency, but they are maintained by moderation.

The same things that help virtues grow can also destroy them. This is true for all things we can sense. For example, strength comes from eating well and exercising, and strong people are better able to continue doing these things. The same is true for the virtues. By avoiding pleasures, we become temperate, and once we've become temperate, we are better able to avoid pleasures. The same applies to courage. By getting used to facing frightening things and standing our ground, we become brave, and once we are brave, we are more capable of standing our ground in the face of danger.

We can use pleasure and pain as a sign of our character. A person who avoids bodily pleasures and takes joy in doing so is temperate, while a person who is bothered by this is self-indulgent. A person who stands firm in the face of fear and either takes joy in doing so or is not troubled by it is brave, while a person who is troubled by it is a coward. Moral excellence is connected to pleasure and pain because we do bad things for pleasure and avoid noble things because they cause us pain. That's why we should be brought up from a young age, as Plato suggests, to take pleasure in the right things and feel pain for the right things. This is the proper way to be educated.

If the virtues are connected to our actions and feelings, and every action and feeling is tied to pleasure and pain, then virtue must also be connected to pleasure and pain. This is further proven by the fact that punishments use pleasure and pain, and punishment is a kind of cure. Cures work through opposites, so this shows the importance of pleasure and pain in shaping our character.

As we mentioned earlier, every state of the soul is influenced by the things that can make it better or worse. People become bad by chasing the wrong pleasures or avoiding the wrong pains, either at the wrong time or in the wrong way. This is why some people define virtues as being free from emotion and stillness. However, this definition isn't quite right because it doesn't include important details like doing things at the right time, in the right way, and for the right reasons. We assume that excellence in virtue means doing what is best in relation to pleasure and pain, while vice is doing the opposite.

We can also see that virtue and vice deal with these same things through other facts. There are three things we can choose and three things we can avoid: the noble, the beneficial, and the pleasant, as well as their opposites, the disgraceful, the harmful, and the painful. The good person tends to make the right choices in all of these areas, while the bad person makes the wrong choices, especially when it comes to pleasure. This is because pleasure is something all animals experience, and it is connected to all of our choices. Even the noble and beneficial things can feel pleasant.

Pleasure has been with us since we were born, which is why it's hard to remove it from our lives. We use pleasure and pain to measure our actions—some people more than others. For this reason, our whole study must focus on these feelings, because how we feel pleasure and pain has a big impact on our actions.

It's harder to fight against pleasure than against anger, as Heraclitus said, but both art and virtue deal with difficult things. Goodness is even better when it is more challenging. For this reason, both virtue and political science deal with pleasure and pain. A person who uses pleasure and pain correctly will be good, while a person who uses them incorrectly will be bad.

So, we can say that virtue is connected to pleasure and pain, and that it is strengthened by the actions that created it. If these actions are done differently, it can be destroyed. The actions that created virtue are the same ones that maintain it.

Some might ask what we mean when we say that we become just by doing just acts and temperate by doing temperate acts. After all, if people are doing just or temperate acts, aren't they already just and temperate? This seems to be like saying that if people follow the rules of grammar or music, they are already grammarians or musicians.

But this isn't even true for the arts. It's possible to follow the rules of grammar by chance or at someone's suggestion. A person is only a grammarian if they not only follow the rules but also understand them and apply them with knowledge.

The same goes for the virtues. The products of the arts have their value in themselves, so it's enough that they have a certain quality. But if acts of virtue have the right qualities, that doesn't mean they are done with justice or temperance. The person doing the act must also be in the right state when they do it. First, they must know what they are doing. Second, they must choose to do it, and choose it for its own sake. Third, their action must come from a firm and unchanging character. These conditions don't apply to the arts. In the arts, knowledge is enough, but for virtue, knowledge is only a small part. The other conditions are far more important and come from repeatedly doing just and temperate acts.

Actions are called just and temperate when they are the kinds of actions a just or temperate person would do. But just because someone does these actions doesn't mean they are just or temperate themselves. Instead, they must do them in the way a just or temperate person would do them. So it is true that we become just by doing just acts, and we become temperate by doing temperate acts. Without doing these things, no one would ever become good.

Most people, however, don't do these things. Instead, they turn to theory, thinking that by studying philosophy, they will become good. They behave like patients who listen carefully to their doctors but don't follow any of the instructions. Just as these patients will never be healthy this way, people will never improve their character by simply studying philosophy.

Next, we need to consider what virtue is. Since the things that are found in the soul are divided into three types—passions, faculties, and states of character—virtue must be one of these. By passions, I mean things like appetite, anger, fear, confidence, envy, joy, friendship, hatred, longing, and pity—in general, any feelings that come with pleasure or pain. By faculties, I mean the things that make us able to feel these emotions, like the ability to feel anger, pain, or pity. By states of character, I mean the way we relate to our emotions—whether we manage them well or poorly. For example, we manage anger poorly if we feel it too strongly or too weakly, and we manage it well if we feel it moderately. The same goes for all the other emotions.

Virtue and vice, however, are not passions. We are not called good or bad because of our passions, but because of our virtues or vices. We also aren't praised or blamed for simply feeling a certain way. A person isn't praised for feeling fear or anger, nor is someone blamed for feeling angry. Instead, we are praised or blamed for how we manage our virtues or vices.

Also, we don't choose to feel emotions like anger or fear, but virtues involve choice. In respect to our passions, we are said to be moved, but in respect to our virtues and vices, we are said to be in a certain state.

For these reasons, virtues are not faculties. We aren't called good or bad for simply having the capacity to feel emotions. Also, our faculties are natural, but we aren't naturally good or bad. We've already discussed this. So, if virtues are neither passions nor faculties, they must be states of character.

This explains what virtue is in terms of its category.

We also need to explain what kind of state virtue is. Every virtue brings something into good condition and helps it do its work well. For example, the virtue of the eye makes the eye and its work good. The virtue of a horse makes it good and capable of running, carrying its rider, and facing enemies. If this is true in every case, then the virtue of a person is the state of character that makes a person good and helps them do their work well.

We've already explained how this happens, but we can also clarify this by considering the specific nature of virtue. In everything that is continuous and divisible, we can take more, less, or an equal amount, either in terms of the thing itself or in relation to us. The equal amount is a middle point between excess and deficiency. The middle point in the object is equally distant from the extremes, and this is the same for everyone. But the middle point in relation to us is different. It is neither too much nor too little, and this varies for each person. For example, if ten pounds of food is too much and two pounds is too little, the middle point for one person might be six pounds, but that might still be too much or too little for another person. The same applies to running or wrestling. A skilled person will avoid both excess and deficiency and aim for the middle point, not in the object, but in relation to themselves.

If this is true for all the arts, where the best work is done by aiming for the middle point, then virtue must also aim for the middle. We often say that good works of art can't have anything added or taken away, because excess and deficiency ruin the work, while the middle point preserves it. Good artists focus on this in their work, and since virtue is better and more exact than art, it must aim at the middle as well. I'm referring to moral virtue here, which deals with emotions and actions. In both, there can be excess, deficiency, and a middle point. For example, we can feel fear, confidence, desire, anger, pity, and pleasure too much or too little, and in both cases, this is bad. But to feel them at the right time, in the right way, and for the right reasons is to find the middle point, and this is what virtue aims for. The same is true for actions. In all actions, excess is a kind of failure, as is deficiency, while the middle point is praised and successful. Since being praised and being successful are qualities of virtue, virtue is a kind of middle.

It's easy to fail in many ways because evil is limitless, as the Pythagoreans said, while good is limited. It's easier to miss the target than to hit it, which is why excess and deficiency are signs of vice, while the middle point is a sign of virtue.

People can be good in only one way, but they can be bad in many ways.

Virtue, then, is a state of character that involves choice and lies in a middle point, which is determined by reason and by how a wise person would determine it. It is a middle point between two vices: one of excess and one of deficiency. In both emotions and actions, vices go too far or not far enough, while virtue finds and chooses the middle.

However, not all actions or emotions have a middle point. Some are inherently bad, such as spite, shamelessness, and envy. In terms of actions, things like adultery, theft, and murder are always wrong, no matter how they are done. You can't be right with these actions by committing adultery with the right person, at the right time, and in the right way. These actions are always wrong. There is no middle point for unjust, cowardly, or indulgent actions. It would be absurd to think that there could be a middle, an excess, or a deficiency in such things. Just as there is no excess or deficiency of temperance or courage, since the middle point is actually an extreme, there is no middle, excess, or deficiency for the actions we mentioned. They are always wrong, no matter how they are done. There is no middle point for actions that are inherently bad.

We need to apply what we've discussed to specific situations. General statements about behavior apply broadly, but when it comes to actions, specific examples are more accurate since actions involve individual situations. We'll take our examples from our list. When it comes to feelings like fear and confidence, courage is the middle ground. Those who are too fearless don't have a name, while people with too much confidence are called reckless, and those with too much fear and too little confidence are called cowards.

For pleasures and pains (mainly pleasures), the middle is called temperance, and the excess is self-indulgence. People who are deficient in feeling pleasure are rare and don't have a common name, but we'll call them "insensible."

When it comes to giving and taking money, the middle is called generosity, and the excess and deficiency are wastefulness and stinginess. Wasteful people spend too much and take too little, while stingy people take too much and spend too little. (We're giving a summary here and will explain these more precisely later.) When dealing with larger amounts of money, we call the middle magnificence, and the excess is called tastelessness or vulgarity, while the deficiency is called meanness. These are different from generosity, which deals with smaller amounts, and we'll explain the differences later.

When it comes to honor and dishonor, the middle is proper pride. Too much pride is vanity, and too little is humility. Just as generosity relates to magnificence, dealing with small and large amounts, proper pride relates to honors, with some people aiming for small honors and others for large ones. You can desire honor in the right way, too much, or too little. The person who wants too much honor is called ambitious, while the person who wants too little is unambitious. The middle person doesn't have a specific name, but the extreme positions are often labeled ambition. Because these people are at the extremes, they both claim to be in the middle. That's why we sometimes call people ambitious and other times unambitious, and sometimes praise one group or the other. We'll explain this later, but for now, let's continue.

Anger also has a middle, an excess, and a deficiency. Though these don't have clear names, we call the person in the middle good-tempered. The person who gets too angry is irascible, and the person who doesn't get angry enough is inirascible (not easily angered).

There are three other qualities that are similar but slightly different because they deal with how we interact with others. One is about truthfulness, and the other two deal with being pleasant, either through joking or in everyday life. We'll discuss these to show that in everything, the middle is good, while the extremes are bad and deserve blame. Many of these qualities don't have names, but we'll create some for clarity. When it comes to truthfulness, the middle is honesty, the excess is exaggeration, and the deficiency is false modesty. In terms of joking and amusement, the middle is ready-wittedness, the excess is buffoonery (being overly silly), and the deficiency is boorishness (being dull or boring). When it comes to being pleasant in everyday life, the middle is friendliness, the excess is flattery (if done for personal gain) or being overly agreeable (without an ulterior motive), and the deficiency is being quarrelsome or surly (constantly unpleasant).

Some traits, like shame, are not virtues but are still praised. For example, someone who feels shame at everything is overly bashful, while someone who never feels shame is shameless. The middle is modesty. Righteous indignation is the middle between envy and spite, and these traits relate to how we feel about other people's fortunes. A person with righteous indignation is upset by undeserved good fortune, an envious person is upset by all good fortune, and a spiteful person is happy when others suffer. We'll explain these traits more later. When it comes to justice, which has multiple meanings, we'll explore its types and how it relates to the idea of the middle. We'll also discuss rational virtues in a similar way.

There are three kinds of dispositions: two vices (excess and deficiency) and one virtue, which is the middle. They are all opposed to each other in some way. The extreme states are opposed to each other and to the middle, just as something large is bigger than something small, but both are larger and smaller than something equal. For example, a brave person might seem reckless to a coward and cowardly to a reckless person. Similarly, a temperate person might seem self-indulgent to someone who is insensible and insensible to someone who is self-indulgent. The same goes for someone who is generous; they may seem wasteful to someone stingy and stingy to someone wasteful. Because of this, people at the extremes tend to accuse those in the middle of being at the opposite extreme.

Since these states are opposed, the greatest opposition is between the two extremes, not between the extremes and the middle, because the extremes are farther apart. For example, recklessness might seem somewhat similar to bravery, and wastefulness to generosity, but the extremes are furthest from each other, and opposites are defined by how far apart they are.

In some cases, one extreme is more opposed to the middle than the other. For example, it's not recklessness (the excess) but cowardice (the deficiency) that is most opposed to bravery. Likewise, it's not insensibility (the deficiency) but self-indulgence (the excess) that is most opposed to temperance. This happens for two reasons. First, one extreme is often closer to the middle than the other, so we focus on the extreme that's farther away. For example, recklessness seems more similar to bravery, while cowardice seems more different. Second, people naturally tend toward certain extremes, and we oppose the one we tend toward more. Since we're more likely to seek pleasure, self-indulgence (an excess) is more opposed to temperance than insensibility (a deficiency).

So, moral virtue is a middle between two extremes, one involving excess and the other deficiency. It focuses on finding the middle ground in both feelings and actions. This shows that being good is not easy. It's hard to find the middle in everything, just like it's hard to find the exact center of a circle. Anyone can get angry or spend money, but doing it in the right way, for the right reasons, and at the right time is much harder. That's why being good is rare, praiseworthy, and noble.

To aim for the middle, we should first move away from what's most opposed to it, just like Calypso advises in The Odyssey, "Steer the ship away from the waves." Since one extreme is usually more wrong than the other, and hitting the middle is very difficult, the next best thing is to choose the lesser of two evils. The best way to do this is to think about where we tend to go wrong, and steer ourselves in the opposite direction. This will help us get closer to the middle, like straightening a bent stick.

We also need to be especially careful with pleasure, because it's something we don't judge fairly. We should treat pleasure like the elders treated Helen of Troy, blaming her for the chaos she caused. By rejecting pleasure in this way, we're less likely to make mistakes. If we do this, we'll be able to hit the middle.

But this is difficult, especially in specific situations. For example, it's hard to say exactly when and for how long it's right to be angry or whom we should be angry with. Sometimes we praise people for being mild and not getting angry, and other times we praise them for getting angry and being brave. A person who only deviates a little from the right path isn't criticized, but someone who deviates a lot is noticed and blamed. However, it's hard to say exactly where the line is, and that's something that depends on experience. What's clear is that the middle is always praiseworthy, and we should lean toward either excess or deficiency as needed to stay as close to the middle as possible.

Book 3

Since virtue is concerned with feelings and actions, and praise or blame is given for feelings and actions that are voluntary, while those that are involuntary receive pardon or sometimes pity, it is important to know the difference between voluntary and involuntary actions. This distinction is necessary for understanding virtue and is also useful for lawmakers when deciding on rewards and punishments. We consider actions involuntary if they happen due to force or ignorance. An action is considered forced if its cause is completely outside the person, and they contribute nothing to it, like being carried somewhere by a strong wind or by other people who have control over them.

However, there are actions done out of fear of greater harm or to achieve a noble goal (for example, if a tyrant orders someone to do something shameful, threatening to kill their family unless they comply). It's debated whether such actions are voluntary or involuntary. The same question arises with throwing goods overboard during a storm. In general, nobody would throw their goods away voluntarily, but if doing so would save their life and the lives of their crew, any sensible person would choose to do it. These actions are a mix of voluntary and involuntary, but they are closer to being voluntary because they are chosen as the best option at that moment. The decision at the time of the action makes it voluntary. The person acts voluntarily because the source of movement that controls their body is within them, and they have the power to do or not do these things. Therefore, while these actions might seem involuntary in some ways, they are more voluntary when considering the circumstances.

People are sometimes praised for such actions, especially when they endure something bad or shameful for the sake of a noble cause. On the other hand, they may be blamed if they go through terrible things for no good reason. Some actions aren't praised, but people might be excused for them when they are forced to do things that push beyond what human nature can withstand. In some cases, however, there are things that should never be done, no matter how extreme the circumstances, and people should face death instead of committing such acts. For instance, the story of Euripides' Alcmaeon being forced to kill his mother seems absurd. It can be difficult to determine what is worth enduring and at what cost, and it's even harder to stick to those decisions. Usually, people are expected to endure pain, while the things they are forced to do are seen as disgraceful. As a result, people are either praised or blamed for how they respond when faced with force.

So, what kinds of actions should be called forced? We can say that actions are truly forced when the cause comes entirely from outside, and the person does not contribute anything to them. However, actions that are undesirable on their own, but are chosen because they bring about some benefit, and where the cause comes from the person, are in themselves involuntary but are now voluntary because of the circumstances. They are more like voluntary actions because in specific cases, the individual acts voluntarily. It's hard to say what should be chosen and what shouldn't be, as there are many differences depending on the situation.

If someone were to say that pleasant and noble goals have the power to force us, then all actions would be considered forced because people do everything for these goals. But those who act under force do so unwillingly and with pain, while those who act for pleasure or nobility do so willingly and with joy. It would be strange to blame outside circumstances for disgraceful actions while praising oneself for noble ones. It seems, then, that forced actions are those where the cause is outside the person, and the person contributes nothing.

Not everything done out of ignorance is involuntary. Only actions that cause regret or pain are involuntary. Someone who acts out of ignorance but feels no regret about what they did isn't considered to have acted involuntarily, since they didn't know what they were doing, but they also aren't called voluntary, because they don't feel pain over their actions. If someone acts out of ignorance and later regrets it, they are considered to have acted involuntarily. But if they don't regret it, they are not considered involuntary actors, though we might say they acted without knowing.

Acting out of ignorance is different from acting while being ignorant. For example, someone who is drunk or angry is not acting out of ignorance, but they are acting without full knowledge of their actions.

Every wicked person is ignorant of what they should and shouldn't do, and it's this kind of mistake that leads people to become unjust or bad in general. However, the word "involuntary" is not used when someone is ignorant of what benefits them personally, because acting from mistaken judgment doesn't make an action involuntary—it makes someone wicked. Rather, involuntary actions arise from ignorance of specific circumstances related to the action. This is where pity and pardon come in, as someone who is unaware of these particulars acts involuntarily.

It's helpful to understand what specific things someone can be ignorant of. A person can be ignorant of who they are, what they are doing, who or what they are affecting, what tool they are using, or what result they expect their action to bring. Additionally, they might not know how they are doing something, such as whether they are acting gently or violently. No one can be ignorant of all of these things without being mad. It's especially hard for someone to be ignorant of themselves. However, someone might be unaware of what they are doing, like saying something without realizing it or not knowing they were revealing a secret, as Aeschylus did with the mysteries. Or someone might accidentally discharge a weapon while only intending to show how it worked. Someone might mistake a person for an enemy, as Merope did, or think a spear has a safety tip when it doesn't, or believe a rock is light and harmless when it's not. A person might give someone a drink to heal them but accidentally cause harm, or they might try to tap someone in sparring and actually wound them. Ignorance could relate to any of these aspects of an action, and the person is seen as acting involuntarily, especially if they were unaware of the most important details, such as the goal of the action. Additionally, if the action was painful and caused regret, it is considered involuntary.

Since actions done by force or ignorance are involuntary, voluntary actions are those where the cause lies within the person, and they are aware of the specifics of what they are doing. It seems wrong to say that actions done out of anger or desire are involuntary. If that were true, animals and children would never act voluntarily, and we'd have to say that noble actions are done voluntarily while bad actions are done involuntarily. But this doesn't make sense because the same source—anger or desire—causes both types of actions. It would be strange to call actions involuntary when they are driven by desires we should have, like the desire for health or learning. Also, involuntary actions are usually painful, but actions that come from desire are generally pleasurable. There isn't much difference between mistakes made from calculation and mistakes made from anger, as both are considered human traits. Therefore, actions driven by anger or desire are still our actions, and it would be strange to call them involuntary.

Now that we have distinguished between voluntary and involuntary actions, we need to discuss choice. Choice is thought to be closely connected with virtue and is a better way of understanding character than actions are.

Choice seems to be voluntary, but it is not the same thing as voluntary action. Voluntary actions are more widespread. Both children and animals can act voluntarily, but they cannot make choices. We might describe actions done suddenly as voluntary, but we wouldn't say they are done by choice.

People who say that choice is the same as appetite, anger, wish, or a kind of opinion are wrong. Choice is not shared by animals, but appetite and anger are. An impulsive person acts on appetite, but not on choice. A self-controlled person acts with choice, but not appetite. Appetite can be opposed to choice, but not to itself. Appetite is concerned with pleasure and pain, while choice is not.

Anger is even less connected with choice because actions done out of anger are thought to be less deliberate.

Choice is also not the same as wish, though they are related. We can wish for impossible things, like immortality, but we don't choose them because choosing implies a belief that the action can be accomplished. We might wish for something we have no control over, like a particular athlete winning a competition, but we don't choose it. Choice is focused on actions we believe we can achieve ourselves. We wish for goals, but we choose the means to reach them. For instance, we wish to be healthy, but we choose the actions that make us healthy. We wish to be happy, but we don't choose happiness in the same way. Choice is connected to things that are in our power.

Choice is also different from opinion. Opinion deals with all kinds of subjects, even things that are impossible or eternal. It is judged based on whether it is true or false, while choice is judged based on whether it is good or bad.

We don't become good or bad people just by having certain opinions, but we do by making certain choices. Opinions are about what is true or false, while choices are about what we pursue or avoid. Opinion is praised for being accurate, while choice is praised for aiming at the right target. When we choose, we focus on what we know to be good, while opinions are often about things we are unsure of. Some people make good choices but have bad opinions, and others have good opinions but make bad choices because of their character. Whether opinion comes before or alongside choice is not important here. What matters is that they are not the same thing.

So, what exactly is choice, if it's not any of the things we've discussed? Choice seems to be voluntary, but not all voluntary actions involve choice. Could it be something that follows deliberate thinking? Choice involves reasoning and thought. Even the word "choice" suggests that it involves selecting something over other options.

Do we deliberate about everything, and is everything something we can deliberate about, or are there some things we can't? We should probably say that only what a sensible person would deliberate about is something worth deliberating on, not what a fool or madman would think about. For instance, no one deliberates about things that are eternal, like the material universe or whether the diagonal of a square is equal to its side. Similarly, we don't deliberate about things that involve movement but always happen the same way, whether by necessity or nature or some other cause, like the solstices or the rising of the stars. Nor do we deliberate about things that happen differently each time, like droughts or rain, or about random events like finding treasure.

We also don't deliberate about all human matters. For example, no Spartan deliberates about what the best government for the

Scythians would be. These things can't be influenced by our efforts. We deliberate about things that are within our power and that we can actually do. Everything else, like nature, necessity, or chance, is not up to us. People deliberate about things they can do by themselves. For example, there's no need to deliberate about exact sciences, like writing letters of the alphabet—we know how to do that. But we do deliberate about things that involve our efforts and don't always have a fixed outcome, like medical treatment or making money. We deliberate more about navigation than about gymnastics, because navigation hasn't been worked out as exactly. We also deliberate more about the arts than the sciences because we tend to have more doubts about arts.

Deliberation deals with things that usually happen in a certain way but where the outcome is unclear, or things where there is uncertainty. We ask others to help us deliberate on important matters when we don't trust ourselves to make the right decision.

We don't deliberate about ends, only about means. A doctor doesn't deliberate whether he should heal people, nor does an orator deliberate whether he should persuade people. A statesman doesn't wonder whether he should create law and order. They take their goals for granted and think about how to reach them. If there are several ways to reach the goal, they deliberate about which way is best and easiest. If there's only one way, they think about how to use that method and what steps are needed to achieve it. It's like solving a geometry problem—the person who deliberates breaks down the problem into steps. Deliberation is a form of investigation, though not all investigation is deliberation, such as mathematical studies. What comes last in deliberation seems to come first in the process of doing things. If something seems impossible, like if money is needed but can't be obtained, we stop deliberating. If something seems possible, we try to do it.

By 'possible,' I mean something that can be done through our own efforts, and this includes things we can achieve with the help of friends since the source of the action is still within us. Sometimes we deliberate about tools, other times about how to use them. In the same way, we deliberate about the means to achieve our goal and how to use those means. As was said earlier, human beings are the source of their own actions. Deliberation is about the things a person can do themselves, and actions are done for the sake of something else. The end goal is not something we deliberate about, only the means to achieve it. We don't deliberate about basic facts, like whether something is bread or if it has been baked properly. Those are matters of perception. If we were always deliberating, we'd never stop.

The same thing is both deliberated about and chosen. However, the thing we choose is already decided upon because it's what we concluded after deliberating. We stop investigating how to act when we've traced the source of the action back to ourselves. The part of ourselves that rules is what makes the choice. This can be seen in ancient governments, as described by Homer. Kings would announce their decisions to the people.

The object of choice is something within our power that we desire after deliberating. So, choice is a deliberate desire for things that are in our control. Once we've deliberated, we desire things in line with our deliberation.

We've now given an outline of choice, explained what kinds of things it deals with, and shown that it concerns the means to an end.

Wish is for the end. Some people think it's for what is truly good, while others think it's for what seems good. Those who say it's for the good must admit that what a person who doesn't choose rightly wishes for isn't really a wish. If they wish for something bad, then it wasn't a true object of wish. Those who say wish is for what seems good must admit that there's no single natural object of wish—only what seems good to each person. Different things seem good to different people, and sometimes even opposite things seem good.

If these ideas seem unsatisfying, we could say that the true good is the object of wish for everyone, but for each person, their wish is based on what seems good to them. The truly good thing is wished for by the good person, while anything could be wished for by a bad person. This is like the way healthy things are good for healthy bodies, but other things might seem healthy to someone who is sick. The good person sees the truth in everything, while others don't. Different people have different ideas of what is noble and what is pleasant, but perhaps what makes a good person different is that they see the truth in these matters. People often make mistakes because of pleasure, thinking something is good when it isn't. This is why we sometimes choose pleasure as though it were good and avoid pain as though it were evil.

The end is what we wish for, and the means to that end are what we deliberate about and choose. Actions that concern the means to an end must be voluntary and based on choice. The exercise of virtues involves choosing the right means, so virtue is in our control, just like vice. If we can choose to act, then we can also choose not to act. So if doing the right thing is in our power, then not doing the wrong thing is also in our power, and vice versa.

If it's within our power to do noble or base acts and we can choose not to do them, then being good or bad is also in our power.

The saying that "no one is wicked voluntarily or happy involuntarily" is partly false and partly true. No one is involuntarily happy, but wickedness is voluntary. Otherwise, we would have to deny that a person is the cause of their own actions, just as they are the cause of their children. If it's clear that actions come from within us, then the actions whose source is within us must also be in our control and voluntary.

This is supported by individuals and by lawmakers, who punish people for wicked acts (unless they were forced or acted out of ignorance that wasn't their fault). They honor people who do noble acts, as if to encourage them and discourage others. No one encourages people to avoid things that are out of their control, like being hot or in pain. We will experience these things anyway. In fact, we punish people for ignorance when it's their fault, like doubling penalties for drunkenness. The person had the power not to get drunk, and their drunkenness caused their ignorance. We also punish people for not knowing the law when they should know it. We assume they could have avoided ignorance if they had been more careful.

A person might say that all people desire what seems good, but they can't control how things seem to them. The way things appear depends on their character. But if people are responsible for their own state of mind, then they are also responsible for how things appear to them. If not, then no one is responsible for their bad actions, and everyone does bad things because they are ignorant of the true end, thinking they will get what is best. It's like being born with an eye for seeing what is truly good—some people are naturally gifted with this, and others are not.

Whether it's natural or not, virtue is voluntary because the good person chooses the right means voluntarily. Vice is also voluntary because the bad person's actions also depend on themselves, even if not their end goal. If the virtues are voluntary, then vices must be voluntary too, since we are responsible for our character and how we see things.

We've described the virtues in general—they are means, states of character, and involve doing the acts by which they are produced. They are in our control and voluntary, following the right rule. Actions and states of character are not voluntary in the same way, though. We control our actions from beginning to end if we know the facts. But while we control the start of our character, its development is less obvious, just like with illnesses. Because it was in our power to act a certain way, our character is voluntary.

Let's now look at the individual virtues, explain what they are about, how they work, and how many there are. Let's start by discussing courage.

It has already been shown that courage is about how we handle feelings of fear and confidence. Clearly, the things we fear are the terrible things, and these are, without a doubt, evils. That is why people often define fear as expecting something bad to happen. We fear all kinds of evils, like disgrace, poverty, illness, loneliness, and death, but not all of these are what a brave person deals with. In fact, it is right and honorable to fear certain things, and it would be wrong not to fear them—such as disgrace. A person who fears disgrace is seen as good and modest, while someone who doesn't fear it is shameless. Sometimes people mistakenly call a shameless person brave because they don't fear disgrace, and in a way, they seem like the brave person, since a brave person is also fearless. However, things like poverty and illness are not the kinds of things we should fear, and they don't come from vice or wrongdoing. Yet, even someone who is unafraid of these things is not considered brave. We sometimes still call them brave because of a similarity—just as some people who are cowards in war can still be generous and confident when it comes to losing money.

A man is not a coward if he fears his wife or children being insulted, or if he fears envy or similar things. Nor is someone brave just because they stay confident when they are about to be beaten. So, what kinds of terrible things does the brave person face? Surely, it is the most frightening things, because no one is more likely to stand firm against something truly terrifying than the brave person. Death is the most terrible thing of all because it is the end, and once someone is dead, nothing can be good or bad for them anymore. However, even the brave person does not face death in every situation, like at sea or when dealing with illness. In what situations, then? Surely, in the most noble ones. The noblest deaths are those that happen in battle because they occur in the greatest and most honorable danger. These deaths are honored both in city-states and at royal courts. So, a brave person is one who is unafraid of a noble death and of all situations that involve death, especially those in war, which are the most honorable of these situations. Even at sea or in sickness, the brave person is fearless, but in a different way from the sailor, for example. The brave person has lost hope for safety and dislikes the thought of dying this way, while sailors are more hopeful because of their experience. We show bravery when there is a chance to demonstrate skill or when dying is noble, but these situations do not offer either.

What is frightening is not the same for all people, but we can say that there are some things that are beyond human strength and terrifying for everyone—at least for anyone sensible. However, the frightening things that are not beyond human strength vary in size and degree, and the same is true for the things that give us confidence. The brave person is as fearless as a human can be. Therefore, while they will fear things within human strength, they will face them properly and as the rule of honor dictates, because the purpose of virtue is honor. But it is possible to fear these things either too much or too little, or to fear things that aren't actually frightening at all. The mistakes people make involve fearing what they shouldn't, fearing in the wrong way, or fearing at the wrong time, and the same goes for the things that give us confidence. The brave person faces and fears the right things, at the right time, and for the right reasons, while also feeling confidence in the right way and under the right conditions. This person is brave because they act according to what is right and how the rule directs. In everything, the goal is to match our actions to the state of character. This applies to the brave person as well. Courage is noble, and so the goal is noble too, because everything is defined by its goal. Therefore, the brave person endures and acts courageously for the sake of a noble goal.

For those who go to extremes, the person who has no fear of anything has no name (as we've already said, many character traits have no names), but this person would be like a madman or someone insensible if they feared nothing—not even earthquakes or storms, as it is said the Celts do not. A person who is overly confident in the face of real dangers is rash. The rash person is seen as boastful, pretending to be brave. They want to appear brave just like the brave person, so they imitate bravery when they can. Because of this, most rash people are a mix of rashness and cowardice. They act confident in certain situations but fail to stand firm against truly frightening things. The person who fears too much is a coward because they fear what they shouldn't, or they fear things in the wrong way. All these descriptions apply to the coward, who also lacks confidence. However, the coward's excessive fear is especially noticeable in painful situations. The coward is a despairing person, fearing everything, while the brave person is the opposite. Confidence is a sign of hopefulness. So, the coward, the rash person, and the brave person deal with the same situations, but they react to them differently: the first two overreact or underreact, while the third holds the right balance. Rash people are eager for danger ahead of time, but back out when faced with it. Brave people, on the other hand, are calm beforehand but ready when the time comes for action.

As we have said, courage is about finding the right balance between fear and confidence in the situations we've described. The brave person chooses or endures things because it is noble to do so or because it would be shameful not to. However, dying just to escape poverty, heartache, or any other painful situation is not the act of a brave person. In fact, it's cowardly, because it shows weakness in the face of hardship, and such a person faces death not because it's noble, but just to avoid suffering.

Courage is like this, but the name also applies to five other types of behavior.

First, there is the courage of a citizen-soldier, which is most like true courage. Citizen-soldiers seem to face danger because of the punishments they'd receive by law or the shame they'd face if they didn't, and also because of the honors they gain from acting bravely. This is why the bravest nations are those where cowards are dishonored and the brave are rewarded with respect. This type of courage is what Homer describes in characters like Diomede and Hector:

"First will Polydamas heap disgrace on me," and
"For Hector will speak to the Trojans,

'Tydeides was afraid and fled from my face.'"

This courage is the closest to true courage because it comes from virtue. It is based on feelings of shame, the desire for honor, and avoiding disgrace, which is shameful. We might put in this same category those who are forced by their leaders to fight. They are inferior, though, because they do what they do not out of shame but out of fear, and they are not avoiding disgrace but avoiding pain. They are forced by their rulers, as Hector says:

"But if I spy any coward hanging back from the fight,
That man will have no hope to escape the dogs."

The people who assign these men to their positions and beat them if they retreat do the same thing, as do those who put trenches behind the troops to prevent escape. All of these methods are forms of compulsion. But true bravery comes from acting nobly, not from being forced to act.

The second kind of courage is based on experience in certain situations. This is why Socrates thought that courage was knowledge. Different people show this in different situations, but professional soldiers show it in war. There are often false alarms in battle, and these soldiers are familiar with them, which makes them appear brave. Their experience gives them confidence because they know how to use their weapons well and have the best ones for both attack and defense. Therefore, they fight like armed men against unarmed men or like trained athletes against beginners. In these cases, it isn't the bravest who fight best, but those who are the strongest and in the best condition. However, professional soldiers often turn cowardly when the danger is too great and they are outnumbered or outmatched. They are the first to flee, while citizen-soldiers die where they stand, as happened at the temple of Hermes. For the citizen-soldier, running away is disgraceful, and death is better than living with shame. The professional soldiers, on the other hand, always expected to be the stronger ones, so when they realize they're not, they run away. They fear death more than disgrace, which is not how a brave person behaves.

Third, some people act bravely because of passion. They charge into danger like wild animals attacking those who have wounded them, and this is sometimes mistaken for bravery. Brave people also act with passion because passion drives us to rush into danger. This is why Homer uses phrases like "put strength into his passion" or "aroused their spirit" or "hard he breathed panting" and "his blood boiled." All these expressions suggest the stirring of passion. Brave people, however, act for honor, and passion helps them, but wild animals act out of pain. They attack because they've been hurt or because they are afraid. For example, if they're in the woods, they don't approach anyone. Wild animals are not brave because they rush into danger without thinking of the risks—they act out of pain and passion. If that were bravery, even a donkey would be brave when it's hungry, because no amount of beating can drive it away from food. Lust also drives adulterers to take risks. So, being driven by pain or passion doesn't make someone brave. The kind of bravery that comes from passion seems the most natural, and it would be true bravery if it were combined with choice and a noble goal.

Men, like animals, feel pain when they are angry and feel pleasure when they take revenge. Those who fight for these reasons are aggressive, but not truly brave, because they don't act for honor or according to the rules—they act out of strong emotion. They are somewhat like brave people, but not exactly.

Fourth, optimistic people are not brave either, though they seem confident in danger because they have won many times and defeated many enemies. They are similar to brave people because both feel confident, but brave people are confident for the right reasons, while optimistic people are confident because they think they are the strongest and cannot be hurt. Drunk people also behave this way—they become overly confident. However, when things don't go as they expected, they run away. A truly brave person faces dangers that are real and terrifying because it is noble to do so, and shameful not to. This is why it is considered braver to remain calm and fearless in sudden emergencies rather than in situations that are expected. In unexpected situations, actions come more from a person's character, because there is less time to prepare. Expected actions may be planned and calculated, but sudden actions must come from a person's state of character.

Fifth, people who are unaware of the danger may also appear brave, but they are not far removed from optimistic people, except that they lack the same self-confidence. Optimistic people can hold their ground for a while, but those who realize the danger or suspect that things are different from what they thought, flee, as happened with the Argives when they mistook the Spartans for Sicyonians.

So, we have described the character of truly brave people and those who are only thought to be brave.

Although courage involves feelings of both confidence and fear, it deals more with fear. Someone who remains calm and acts as they should in the face of fear is considered braver than someone who simply feels confident. Bravery is about facing what is painful, and because of this, courage is justly praised. It is harder to face pain than to resist something pleasant.

Even though the goal of courage is something pleasant, it is often hidden by the painful circumstances that come with it. This is similar to athletic competitions. Boxers aim for the pleasant outcome—the victory and honors—but the blows they take along the way are painful and exhausting. Because the pain and effort are great, the pleasant goal seems small and insignificant. In the same way, death and wounds are painful and something the brave person does not want, but they face them because it is noble to do so and shameful not to. The more virtuous and happier a person is, the more painful the thought of death will be because life is most valuable to them, and they know they are losing the greatest goods. This is painful, but it makes them even braver, because they still choose noble deeds in war at this cost. So, not all virtues are pleasant when practiced, except in the sense that they reach their goal. The best soldiers may not always be those with the greatest virtue, but those who have nothing else good in their lives. These people are willing to face danger and even sell their lives for small rewards.

This, then, is a summary of courage. It is not hard to understand its nature, at least in outline, from what has been said.

Now that we've talked about courage, let's discuss temperance, since these seem to be the virtues of the parts of us that aren't controlled by reason. We've said that temperance is about finding balance when it comes to pleasures (it's less concerned with pains and not in the same way), and self-indulgence also deals with the same things. So, let's now figure out what kind of pleasures temperance and self-indulgence are concerned with. We can distinguish between physical pleasures and those of the mind, such as the love of honor or learning. People who love these things enjoy them with their mind, not their body. But those who are focused on these pleasures aren't called temperate or self-indulgent. Similarly, those who enjoy other types of non-physical pleasures, like those who love hearing or telling stories or spend their days on random things, are called gossips, but not self-indulgent. The same goes for people who are upset about losing money or friends—they aren't called self-indulgent either.

Temperance is related to physical pleasures, but not all of them. For example, those who enjoy looking at things like colors, shapes, or paintings aren't called temperate or self-indulgent, even though it's possible to take pleasure in them in the right amount, or too much, or too little.

The same goes for things we hear. No one calls someone self-indulgent for enjoying music or acting too much, and those who enjoy these things appropriately aren't called temperate either.

We also don't use these terms for those who enjoy smells, unless it's in a certain way. For instance, we don't call someone self-indulgent for enjoying the smell of apples, roses, or incense, but we do call them self-indulgent if they enjoy the smell of perfume or rich food. This is because self-indulgent people like these smells since they remind them of the things they crave. You can even see other people, when they're hungry, enjoying the smell of food, but it's the self-indulgent person who loves this kind of thing because it's what they crave.

There aren't any animals other than humans who enjoy these kinds of senses, except accidentally. For example, dogs don't enjoy the smell of a hare, but they enjoy eating it, and the smell just tells them the hare is nearby. Similarly, a lion doesn't enjoy the sound of an ox, but enjoys eating it; the ox's sound just tells the lion the ox is near, which makes it seem like the lion enjoys the sound. And it's the same when the lion sees a stag or goat—it's not the sight that pleases the lion, but the meal that's coming.

Temperance and self-indulgence, however, are concerned with the kinds of pleasures that humans share with other animals, which seem more basic and animal-like. These are the pleasures of touch and taste. But even taste doesn't play a big role here, since taste is about recognizing flavors, which is what wine tasters or chefs do. Self-indulgent people don't enjoy making these distinctions; they enjoy the physical pleasure, which always comes through touch—whether with food, drink, or sexual contact. This is why a certain glutton once wished his throat were as long as a crane's, because he wanted to enjoy the contact for longer. So, the sense most connected to self-indulgence is the sense of touch, which is the most common of all the senses. Self-indulgence is rightly criticized because it connects us more to our animal side than to our human side. To love these kinds of pleasures more than anything else is animal-like. Even of the pleasures of touch, the most acceptable ones have been eliminated, like the pleasure that comes from rubbing in the gym or the heat that results from it. The kind of touch a self-indulgent person enjoys doesn't affect their whole body, just certain parts.

Some desires seem to be natural to everyone, while others are unique to individuals and are learned. For example, the desire for food is natural, because anyone who is hungry craves food, and the same goes for drink, and for love, especially if someone is young and strong, as Homer says. But not everyone craves the same type of food or love, and that's what makes personal desires seem more individual. However, these personal desires still have a natural element, because different things are more pleasing to different types of people, and some things are more pleasing to everyone than others.

With natural desires, most people make mistakes in only one way—by going too far. To eat or drink more than necessary until you're overfull is to go beyond what your body naturally needs, since natural desire is about filling a lack. People who do this are called gluttons, which suggests they fill their stomachs beyond what is right. It's people with a very servile character who behave this way. But with personal desires, people make many mistakes in many different ways. For example, someone who is "fond of something" might like it too much, or like something they shouldn't, or like it more than most people do. Self-indulgent people go wrong in all these ways. They either enjoy things they shouldn't because they're harmful, or they enjoy the right things but do so more than they should or more than most people.

Clearly, then, overindulgence with pleasure is self-indulgence and is wrong. But with pain, it's not like courage where you're praised for facing it or blamed for avoiding it. The self-indulgent person is called that because they are more upset than they should be when they don't get something pleasant, even though their upset is caused by the pleasure they crave. The temperate person, on the other hand, is praised for not being upset when something pleasant is absent or when they have to avoid it.

The self-indulgent person craves all pleasant things or at least the most pleasant ones, and they are led by their desires, even if it means sacrificing everything else. That's why they are upset both when they don't get what they want and even while they're still craving it (because desire itself involves pain). But it seems ridiculous to be upset in the pursuit of pleasure. People who don't enjoy pleasure as much as they should are rare, because that level of insensitivity is not human. Even other animals can tell the difference between different kinds of food and enjoy some more than others. If there were someone who found no pleasure in anything, they would be something very different from a human. This type of person doesn't have a name because they almost never exist.

The temperate person, however, takes a balanced approach to these things. They don't enjoy the things the self-indulgent person does, or if they do, they enjoy them less. They also don't crave what they shouldn't, or if they do, they don't crave it too much or feel pain when it's absent, or they do so only to a small degree and at the right times. Instead, they enjoy the things that bring health or good condition, and they do so in moderation. They may enjoy other pleasant things as well, but only if they don't interfere with health or nobility or go beyond what they can afford. A person who ignores these limits loves pleasure more than it's worth. The temperate person, however, is the kind of person who follows the right rules.

Self-indulgence is more voluntary than cowardice because it's driven by pleasure, while cowardice is driven by pain. Pleasure is something we choose, and pain is something we avoid. Pain messes with the person who feels it, while pleasure doesn't. That's why self-indulgence is more voluntary and also more blameworthy. It's easier to get used to the things that lead to self-indulgence because there are many of them in life, and getting used to them doesn't involve any danger. But the opposite is true for terrifying things.

Cowardice seems voluntary in some ways but not others. Cowardice itself is painless, but in specific situations, pain causes us to act, such as when we throw down our weapons or disgrace ourselves in other ways. In these cases, it seems like our actions are done under pressure. But for the self-indulgent person, specific acts are voluntary because they act out of desire, even though the overall state of being self-indulgent is less voluntary. No one desires to be self-indulgent.

The term self-indulgence is also used for childish faults because these resemble the things we've been discussing. It doesn't matter which one was named after the other for our purposes—the point is that childish faults are called after self-indulgence. This comparison isn't a bad one because the desire for what is base and which grows quickly should be kept in check. This is especially true for appetite and children, since children live by their appetites and have the strongest desires for pleasure. If this part of ourselves is not controlled by reason, it can go too far. In an irrational being, the desire for pleasure is never satisfied, even if it tries every source of gratification, and the more it indulges its appetite, the stronger the desire grows. If these appetites are powerful, they can even drive out reason. That's why they should be limited and few, and they should not conflict with reason—this is what we call a controlled state. Just as a child should follow the guidance of a tutor, our appetites should follow reason. In a temperate person, the appetites should align with reason, because both aim at what is noble. The temperate person desires the right things, in the right way, and at the right time. This is what reason tells us to do.

And this concludes our discussion of temperance.

Book 4

Let's now talk about liberality. It seems to be the balance when it comes to wealth. A liberal person is praised not for their skills in war, or for being moderate, or for making legal decisions, but for how they give and receive wealth, especially for how they give it. By "wealth," we mean anything that is valued by money. Prodigality and stinginess are extremes related to wealth. We call someone stingy when they care too much about money, but sometimes we use the word "prodigal" in a more complicated way. We call people prodigal when they lack self-control and spend money on things that are indulgent. That's why these people are considered to have poor character, as they show more than one vice. So, this is not the proper way to use the word "prodigal." A prodigal person has one bad trait: wasting their wealth. A prodigal person is ruining themselves, and since life depends on having some wealth, wasting it is like ruining your own life.

This is how we'll understand the word "prodigality" here. Now, anything that can be used can either be used well or poorly, and wealth is something useful. Anything useful is best used by someone who has the virtue related to it. So, wealth will be best used by someone who has the virtue related to wealth—this is the liberal person. Spending and giving seem to be how wealth is used, while taking and keeping it are about possession. So, it's more important for a liberal person to give to the right people than to take from the right sources, or to avoid taking from the wrong ones. Doing good is more virtuous than receiving good, and doing what's noble is better than not doing something shameful. Giving is clearly a way of doing good and acting nobly, while taking is more about receiving good or avoiding shameful behavior. We feel grateful toward someone who gives, not to someone who simply doesn't take, and we praise givers more. It's also easier not to take than to give, as people are more likely to give too little of what's theirs than to take from others. Givers are called liberal, but those who don't take aren't praised for being liberal—they're praised for being just. Those who take aren't really praised at all. Liberality is one of the most loved virtues because liberal people are generous, and their generosity is helpful, depending on their giving.

Virtuous actions are noble and done for the sake of nobility. The liberal person, like all virtuous people, will give for the sake of nobility and will do it rightly. They will give to the right people, the right amounts, at the right time, and in the right way. They will also do it with pleasure, or at least without pain, since virtuous acts are either pleasant or not painful. A person who gives to the wrong people, or not for the sake of nobility but for some other reason, is not considered liberal. And someone who gives with pain is not liberal either because they value their wealth more than the noble act, and this isn't typical of a liberal person.

A truly liberal person also won't take from wrong sources, as this doesn't fit with someone who doesn't care too much about wealth. They also won't be eager to ask for things because it's not typical of someone who gives to others to want benefits for themselves. They will, however, take from the right sources, like their own wealth, not because it's noble but out of necessity—so they can continue to give. They won't neglect their own property, as they use it to help others. They won't give to just anyone, but will give to the right people at the right time, when it is noble to do so. It's very typical of a liberal person to give too much, leaving little for themselves. This is because a liberal person doesn't focus on their own needs. The term "liberality" relates to a person's resources. Being liberal isn't about the number of gifts but about the character of the giver, and this depends on how much wealth they have. So, someone who gives less can still be more liberal if they have less to give.

People who inherited their wealth, rather than earning it, are often thought to be more liberal. First, because they've never experienced a lack of resources, and second, because people tend to value what they've created themselves, just like parents love their children. A liberal person usually doesn't become wealthy because they're not focused on taking or keeping wealth but on giving it away. They don't value wealth for its own sake but as a way to give. This leads to the common complaint that the people who deserve wealth the most often have the least of it. But it's not surprising because wealth, like anything else, can't be had without effort. Even so, a liberal person won't give to the wrong people or at the wrong time, because that wouldn't be true liberality. If they spent money on the wrong things, they wouldn't have anything left for the right causes.

As we've said, a liberal person spends according to their means and on the right things. A person who goes beyond this is called prodigal. We don't call rulers prodigal because it's hard for them to spend more than they have. Liberality is a balance in giving and receiving wealth. A liberal person will give and spend the right amount, on the right things, whether big or small, and do so with pleasure. They will also take the right amounts from the right sources. Since virtue is a balance between both, the liberal person will do both as they should. Proper giving and taking go hand in hand, while improper giving and taking don't happen together. If a liberal person ends up spending in a way that isn't right or noble, they will feel some pain, but only a little, and as they should. Virtue involves feeling both pleasure and pain at the right things and in the right way.

A liberal person is easy to deal with in money matters because they don't care too much about money. They get more upset if they haven't spent on something they should have, rather than feeling bad about spending on something they shouldn't have. They don't agree with the saying of Simonides.

A prodigal person also makes mistakes here because they aren't pleased or upset by the right things or in the right way. This will become clearer as we continue. Prodigality and stinginess are extremes when it comes to giving and taking. Prodigality goes too far in giving and doesn't take enough, while stinginess falls short in giving and takes too much, except in small things.

The traits of prodigality don't often go together because it's hard to keep giving if you're not taking. Private individuals quickly run out of money if they keep giving, and these are the people we usually call prodigal. Still, a person like this seems much better than a stingy person. Prodigality can be cured with age or poverty, and this can help the person move toward a middle state. Prodigal people have some traits of a liberal person because they give and don't take, even though they don't do these things well. If they learned to do these things properly, they could become liberal because they would then give to the right people and avoid taking from the wrong sources. This is why prodigals are thought to have a less bad character—it's not evil to give too much and take too little, but it is foolish. A person like this is considered much better than a stingy person because they benefit others, while a stingy person benefits no one, not even themselves.

Most prodigals, however, do take from the wrong sources, and in this way, they're similar to stingy people. They take because they want to keep spending, but their resources run out quickly, so they're forced to find money from other places. Since they don't care about honor, they take from any source, however wrong. Their giving isn't liberal because it's not noble, and it's not done properly. Sometimes they give to the wrong people, like flatterers, and neglect those with good character. Because of this, most prodigals are also self-indulgent, spending their money on pleasures instead of living for what's noble.

The prodigal person, if left unchecked, will continue this way. But with guidance, they can become more balanced. Meanness, on the other hand, is harder to cure. Old age and hardship tend to make people stingy. Most people are more interested in gaining money than giving it. Stinginess comes in many forms and seems to cover many different behaviors.

It has two parts: not giving enough and taking too much. Not all stingy people are the same, though. Some people take too much, while others don't give enough. People we call "miserly" or "stingy" don't give much but don't covet other people's property either. Some of these people hoard money to avoid doing anything shameful in the future. Others avoid taking from others because they know that if they do, others will take from them. So, they prefer to neither give nor take.

There are others who take from any source, like people in shady businesses, pimps, or moneylenders who charge high interest. These people take more than they should and from the wrong places. Their love of gain is their main fault. They'll accept a bad reputation if it means they can make money, even if it's just a little. People who make big gains from wrong sources, like tyrants who rob cities or temples, aren't called stingy—they're called wicked or unjust. But gamblers and thieves are considered stingy because they love gain and endure shame for the sake of money. They're both willing to take from wrong sources, making them greedy.

Meanness is considered the opposite of liberality. It's worse than prodigality, and people are more likely to be stingy than prodigal.

This covers liberality and its opposing vices.

It seems fitting to discuss magnificence next. This also deals with wealth, but it's different from liberality. It doesn't cover all uses of wealth but focuses on spending large amounts. As the name suggests, magnificence involves spending on a grand scale. However, the scale depends on the situation. For example, outfitting a ship is not the same as leading a sacred procession. Magnificence is about spending appropriately for the person and the occasion. A person who spends properly on small or moderate things isn't called magnificent, but the person who spends properly on big things is. A magnificent person is liberal, but a liberal person isn't necessarily magnificent. The lack of magnificence is called stinginess, while the excess is called vulgarity or bad taste. These vices don't involve spending too much on the right things but spending extravagantly on the wrong things. We'll discuss these vices more later.

A magnificent person is like an artist who knows how to spend large amounts in a tasteful way. As we said earlier, a person's character is shown by their actions and their goals. The magnificent person spends large amounts appropriately, and the result is fitting. The result should match the expense, or even surpass it. The magnificent person spends for honor's sake, which is true of all virtues. They will do so gladly and generously because careful calculation is a sign of stinginess. They'll focus on making the result as beautiful as possible, rather than on how cheaply it can be done. The magnificent person must also be liberal. A liberal person spends what they should, but a magnificent person does this on a grander scale, creating something even more impressive. Possessions and works of art aren't valuable in the same way. A possession's value is based on its cost, while a work of art's value comes from its beauty and greatness. Magnificence applies to spending on important and honorable things, like offerings to the gods, temples, or public projects. Magnificent people spend their money to support the city or the people, not for themselves.

A magnificent person will also make their house reflect their wealth because even a house is a public symbol. They prefer to spend on things that last because those are the most beautiful. They spend appropriately on everything. What's right for gods is not the same as what's right for humans, and what's right in a temple is different from what's right in a tomb. Each expenditure has its own greatness. What's most magnificent is spending a large amount on something great, but what's magnificent in one case may be small in another. The magnificent person makes sure everything they create matches the size of the expense.

The person who goes too far and is vulgar spends too much on the wrong things, showing bad taste. They might host a dinner party on the scale of a wedding banquet or use purple robes for a comedy, like they do in Megara. They do these things not for honor but to show off their wealth, thinking they'll be admired. Where they should spend a lot, they spend too little, and where they should spend a little, they spend too much. The stingy person, on the other hand, spends too little on everything. After spending a lot, they'll ruin the result by skimping on a small detail. They always try to spend as little as possible and regret even that.

Both vulgarity and stinginess are vices, but they don't bring as much disgrace because they aren't harmful to others or very shameful.

The goods that come from fortune, such as wealth and power, are also thought to add to a sense of pride. People who are well-born, wealthy, or powerful are considered worthy of honor because they are in a better position than others. When someone has something good that sets them apart, they are usually honored more. This is why people with these advantages tend to be prouder since others honor them for these things. However, in reality, only a truly good person deserves honor. A person who has both virtue and good fortune is seen as even more deserving of honor. But those who have wealth and power without virtue have no right to make great claims or to be called "proud" because true pride requires perfect virtue.

People without virtue often become disdainful and arrogant when they have good fortune. Without virtue, it's hard to handle the advantages of fortune with grace. They look down on others because they think they are better, and they act however they please. These people try to imitate a proud person, but they don't really understand what true pride is. The proud person looks down on others in a just way because they know their true worth, while most people look down on others for no good reason.

A proud person does not rush into small or trivial dangers, nor do they enjoy danger for its own sake, because they value only a few things. But they will face great dangers, and when they do, they won't hesitate to risk their life, knowing that sometimes life isn't worth living under certain conditions. A proud person is the kind who gives help to others but is ashamed of receiving help, because giving is a sign of superiority, while receiving is a sign of inferiority. When they do receive help, they tend to return the favor with even greater kindness, making the original giver feel indebted to them, which allows the proud person to stay in control of the relationship. They also tend to remember the help they have given but not the help they've received because the giver is superior, and the proud person always wants to be in a superior position. This is why Thetis didn't remind Zeus of the help she gave him, and why the Spartans didn't talk about how they helped the Athenians but focused on what they had received.

A proud person also doesn't ask for much from others, if anything, but is quick to give help when needed. They act with dignity toward people who are in high positions or who are fortunate, but they are humble toward people of the middle class. It's difficult to be superior to those in high positions, but easy to be above those in lower positions, and it isn't seen as rude to act superior to the powerful, but it would be rude to act that way toward the weak. A proud person doesn't aim for the things that others value or excel in, and they are often slow to act unless something great and honorable is at stake. They don't do many things, but the things they do are great and worthy of note.

A proud person must also be open about their feelings, whether love or hate. Hiding one's feelings or caring more about what others think than about the truth is seen as cowardly. A proud person speaks and acts openly because they are confident and don't need to hide anything. They tell the truth unless they are using irony to mock those who are beneath them. A proud person won't revolve their life around someone else unless that person is a friend because that would be like being a servant. For this reason, flatterers are seen as having no self-respect, and people who lack self-respect often become flatterers.

A proud person isn't easily impressed because nothing seems great to them. They don't hold onto grudges because that's not what proud people do—they overlook wrongs. They don't gossip, either about themselves or about others, because they don't care to be praised, nor do they care to blame others. Similarly, they aren't in the habit of praising others and don't speak ill of their enemies unless out of a sense of superiority.

When it comes to small or necessary matters, a proud person doesn't complain or beg for favors. This is because they don't take such things too seriously. A proud person would rather have beautiful but useless things than useful and profitable ones because this better fits their self-sufficient character.

A slow and deliberate step, a deep voice, and calm speech are all seen as traits of a proud person. Someone who takes few things seriously won't be in a hurry, and someone who thinks nothing is great won't get easily excited. A shrill voice and fast movements come from being in a rush or getting excited.

This, then, is the proud person. The person who falls short of this is overly humble, and the person who goes too far is vain. However, neither of these types of people is considered bad, just mistaken. An overly humble person denies themselves what they deserve, even if they are worthy of good things, and this shows a lack of self-awareness. If they knew their worth, they would seek out the things they are worthy of since these things are good. These people aren't thought to be foolish but rather too shy. However, this attitude can make them worse because people usually aim for what matches their worth, and these overly humble people avoid noble actions and even good things because they feel unworthy.

On the other hand, vain people are foolish because they don't know themselves. They attempt to do honorable things they aren't capable of, and then they fail. They also like to show off with fancy clothes and outward displays, and they talk about their good fortune as if that will make them more honorable. However, being overly humble is more opposed to pride than vanity because it's both more common and worse.

Pride, then, is concerned with great honor, as we've said. There seems to be another virtue related to honor that is like generosity compared to magnificence. Neither deals with the grand scale, but both guide us to act rightly in smaller matters. Just as there is a balance in giving and receiving wealth, there is a balance in seeking honor. Some people want honor too much or from the wrong sources, while others don't seek honor even for noble reasons. Sometimes we praise the ambitious person as someone who loves what is noble, and other times we praise the unambitious person for being moderate and self-controlled.

It's clear that there is more than one way to be "fond of" honor. When we praise ambition, we are thinking of someone who loves honor more than most people, and when we blame it, we are thinking of someone who loves it too much. Since the balance here doesn't have a name, it seems like the extremes compete to take its place. However, just as people can desire more honor than they should or less than they should, it's also possible to desire the right amount, and this state of character is praised. This balanced state doesn't have a name, but it is still virtuous. It seems unambitious compared to ambition and ambitious compared to being unambitious. This is true of other virtues as well.

Good temper is a balance when it comes to anger. The middle state doesn't have a name, and the extremes don't have clear names either, but we place good temper in the middle, although it leans toward the side of not being angry enough. The excess of anger might be called "irascibility" because the emotion involved is anger, but there are many causes for anger.

A person who gets angry at the right things, with the right people, in the right way, at the right time, and for the right length of time is praised. This is the good-tempered person because good temper is praised. A good-tempered person is calm and doesn't act on their emotions. They get angry only as the situation requires, but they tend to lean more toward being too calm than being too angry. A good-tempered person is not vengeful and tends to be forgiving.

On the other hand, those who don't get angry when they should are blamed. People who don't get angry in the right way or with the right people at the right time are seen as foolish because it seems like they don't care or don't feel pain when they are wronged. Since they don't get angry, they are also seen as unlikely to defend themselves. People who endure insults or allow their friends to be insulted are seen as weak.

The excess of anger can show up in many ways. A person might get angry with the wrong people, at the wrong things, too often, too quickly, or for too long. Not all of these traits show up in the same person because too much anger can destroy itself. Quick-tempered people tend to get angry too fast and with the wrong people or for the wrong reasons, but their anger doesn't last long, which is their best trait. They don't hold back their anger, so they express it quickly and then it's over.

People who are choleric, or quick to anger, get angry at everything and everyone, earning their name. Sulky people are harder to calm down and hold onto their anger for a long time. They don't express their anger right away, so it builds up inside them, and they won't feel better until they get revenge. If they don't, they carry the anger with them because no one knows they are upset, and that takes time to process. These people are difficult for both themselves and their close friends to be around. We call people bad-tempered if they are angry at the wrong things, too much, and for too long, and if they can't be calmed down until they have punished someone.

Good temper is more opposed to the excess of anger than to the lack of it because excessive anger is more common (since revenge is more natural to humans), and bad-tempered people are harder to live with.

It's clear from what we've already said that it's not easy to define exactly how much anger is appropriate, with whom, about what, or for how long. It's hard to say at what point right action becomes wrong. We don't blame someone who strays only a little, either toward too much anger or too little. Sometimes we praise people who seem too calm, calling them good-tempered, and sometimes we praise people who seem too angry, calling them strong and capable of leadership. It's hard to say exactly how far someone can go before they are blamed, and this depends on the situation and requires good judgment. However, it's clear that the middle state is praiseworthy— being angry in the right way, at the right time, with the right people. The extremes are blameworthy, either a little or a lot, depending on how far someone goes. Clearly, the middle state is best.

In social life, some people are seen as too eager to please. These people always agree with others and never cause conflict because they think it's their job to avoid upsetting anyone. On the other hand, people who argue about everything and don't care if they upset others are seen as rude and argumentative. It's clear that both of these extremes are wrong, and the balanced approach is better—where someone is pleasant and helpful, but also stands up for what is right. This middle state doesn't have a name, but it is similar to friendship.

The person who holds this middle position is like a good friend, but without the emotional attachment of friendship. This person acts rightly not because they love or hate anyone, but because they are a good person. They act the same way toward both close friends and strangers, though they adjust their behavior to fit each relationship. They don't treat everyone the same but respond to each person appropriately, based on what's right.

This person tries to bring pleasure to others and avoid causing pain when it's honorable and good to do so. But if their actions would bring dishonor or harm to someone, they will choose to cause a little pain instead of agreeing with something wrong. This person will act differently toward those in higher positions and those in lower ones, and they will adjust their behavior depending on the situation.

This balanced person doesn't have a name, but people who are too eager to please are called "obsequious," and those who do it for personal gain, like money, are called "flatterers." People who argue all the time are called "contentious" or "churlish." These extremes seem to be opposites, and the middle state is without a name.

There's also a balance when it comes to boasting. The person who tells the truth about themselves without exaggeration or understatement is in the middle. The boaster, however, claims to have qualities they don't really have or exaggerates what they do have. On the other hand, the overly modest person downplays their qualities or denies them. Both of these extremes are wrong, but the person who tells the truth about themselves is praiseworthy.

Each person acts and speaks according to their character. A truthful person speaks and lives in a straightforward way because of their character, not for some other purpose. Lying is generally seen as bad, and truth is seen as good. Therefore, the truthful person is praised, while both the boaster and the overly modest person are criticized, though the boaster is usually seen as worse.

Now, let's discuss the boaster first. We aren't talking about someone who breaks promises or lies in serious matters—that falls under justice. We're talking about someone who is truthful in everyday life because of their character. This kind of person is seen as fair because they value the truth, and if they avoid lying even when nothing important is at stake, they are likely to be truthful when something important is on the line.

A boaster is seen as someone who claims more than they have, especially when they do it to gain something. The boaster who seeks fame or honor is less blameworthy than the one who does it for money, but both are wrong. A boaster who exaggerates their skills for money, like pretending to be a doctor or fortune-teller, is more blameworthy because they are lying for personal gain.

On the other hand, someone who is overly modest and downplays their good qualities is seen as more likable. This person isn't lying for personal gain but is avoiding showing off. However, if someone downplays their qualities too much, especially things that are obvious, they are seen as deceitful, and this can be a form of boastfulness in disguise.

The person who finds the middle ground—neither exaggerating nor downplaying their qualities—is the one who deserves praise. Both the boaster and the overly modest person are wrong, but the boaster is the worse of the two.

In life, there is also a balance between seriousness and playfulness. Some people are too serious, while others are too eager to joke around. A person who jokes too much and doesn't care if they hurt others is seen as vulgar, while someone who can't take a joke or make one is seen as rude or unapproachable. The person who finds the middle ground is considered witty because they know how to say the right thing at the right time, and their humor is appropriate for the situation.

A well-bred person's jokes are different from those of a vulgar person. You can see this difference in old and new comedies. The old comedies often focused on indecency, while the newer ones rely more on clever humor. This shows the difference between good taste and poor taste.

The person who jokes well does so in a way that is fitting for a well-bred person. They don't seek to hurt others with their humor, and their jokes are enjoyable for the listener. This person will also only make jokes that are appropriate and avoid ones that are mean-spirited.

The person who finds the right balance in humor is praiseworthy. The person who jokes too much and in bad taste is like a buffoon, while the person who can't take a joke is no fun to be around. Relaxation and amusement are important parts of life, but they need to be done in the right way.

So, these middle states in life are three in number, all dealing with how we interact with others in words and actions. They differ in that one is about truth, while the other two are about being pleasant.

Shame, however, is not a virtue. It's more like a feeling than a state of character. Shame is a kind of fear of dishonor, like how people feel fear in the face of danger. For example, people blush when they feel ashamed, just like they turn pale when they are afraid. Both are physical reactions, and this is more characteristic of a feeling than a character trait.

Shame is more appropriate for young people because they live more by their feelings and are more likely to make mistakes. Young people who feel shame are praised because it shows they care about their mistakes. However, we wouldn't praise an older person for feeling shame because we expect them to avoid actions that would make them feel ashamed. A good person doesn't need to feel shame because they don't do bad things, and shame is only felt when someone does something wrong. Feeling ashamed of bad actions doesn't make you a good person. It's better to avoid bad actions altogether.

So, while shame might be a good thing in certain situations, it's not the same as a virtue. A good person won't do anything shameful, so they don't need to feel shame. We'll talk more about continence and other related states later, but for now, let's move on to justice.

Book 5

When talking about justice and injustice, we need to (1) look at what actions they focus on, (2) figure out what kind of balance justice is, and (3) understand what extremes justice lies between. We will follow the same path as we did in previous discussions.

We know that everyone sees justice as a way of thinking that makes people want to do the right thing and act fairly. They also see injustice as a way of thinking that makes people act unfairly and desire what's unfair. Let's start with that. This is different from how we view science and skills. A science or skill can relate to opposite things, but a state of character only leads to one type of result. For example, being healthy means we only do things that are good for our health, like walking in a healthy way.

Often, we understand one thing by comparing it to its opposite, or by looking at the people who show these qualities. For example, (A) if we know what good health is, we can also understand bad health. (B) We know good health from those who are healthy, and vice versa. If good health means firm flesh, then bad health would mean flabby flesh, and something that creates firmness would be considered healthy. If one opposite is unclear, the other usually is too. For example, if the word "just" is unclear, "unjust" will be too.

The terms "justice" and "injustice" can have more than one meaning, but because the meanings are so close, we often don't notice. This is different from words with very different meanings, like how "kleis" can mean a collarbone or the tool to lock a door. Let's look at the different meanings of "an unjust person." We call both the lawbreaker and the greedy, unfair person unjust, so it's clear that both law-abiding and fair people are just. So, the just person is both law-abiding and fair, while the unjust person is both lawless and unfair.

Since the unjust person is greedy, they focus on certain goods— not all goods, but those that affect success or failure. These are always good in general, but they're not always good for a specific person.

People often pray for and chase these things, but they should really pray that these things are good for them, and they should choose what is good for them specifically. The unjust person doesn't always choose the bigger thing, but sometimes they choose the smaller, especially when it's something bad. Since the smaller evil is still considered somewhat good, and greed focuses on the good, the unjust person is seen as greedy. They are also unfair, which is true in both cases.

Since the lawbreaker is unjust and the law-abiding person is just, all lawful actions are, in a way, just actions. The laws, set up by legislators, are considered lawful, and we say each of these actions is just. The laws are meant to benefit everyone or the best people or those in power, depending on the case. So, in one sense, we call those actions just that help create and maintain happiness and its parts for the whole community. The law tells us to act bravely, like not running away from danger or giving up our weapons. It also tells us to act with self-control, like not committing adultery or giving in to every desire, and to be good-tempered, like not hitting others or speaking badly of them. The law does this for other virtues and vices too, commanding some actions and forbidding others. A well-made law does this well, while a hastily made law does it less effectively. So, this kind of justice is complete virtue, but not in every sense—only when it comes to how we treat others. That's why justice is often seen as the greatest virtue, and there's a saying that "justice holds all virtues." It's considered complete virtue because it involves practicing all virtues, and it's complete because the person who has it uses it both for themselves and in their interactions with others. Many people can be virtuous in their own lives but not with others. This is why people say, "power reveals the person," because a ruler has to deal with others and be part of a community.

This is also why justice is called "another's good," since it's about treating others well. The worst person is someone who acts badly toward both themselves and their friends, while the best person isn't the one who's only good to themselves, but the one who's good to others. This is harder to do. Justice, in this sense, isn't just part of virtue—it's the whole of virtue, and the same goes for injustice. The difference between virtue and justice is clear from what we've said. They are the same, but their essence isn't the same. Justice is about how we treat others, while virtue is about the kind of person we are.

What we are studying now is justice as a part of virtue because we believe there is a kind of justice like that. The same goes for injustice in the particular way we're looking at it.

There is this kind of justice, and we can see it when we notice that someone can do wrong without being greedy, like throwing away their shield out of cowardice or speaking harshly out of anger. But when someone acts greedily, they are unjust, even if they don't show these other vices. So, there's another kind of injustice that's just part of the wider idea of injustice, which means "against the law." For example, if someone commits adultery for money and gains from it, they are unjust. But if someone does it because of their desires and loses money or gets punished, they are more self-indulgent than unjust. The person who profits from it is unjust but not self-indulgent, showing that greed is linked to injustice.

All other unjust acts are connected to some other vice. Adultery is linked to self-indulgence, leaving a comrade in battle is tied to cowardice, and hitting someone is linked to anger. But when someone gains from their actions, it's not connected to any specific vice except injustice. So, there's another, specific type of injustice, which is part of the broader kind because it shares the same basic idea. Both forms of injustice relate to others, but the specific one is about honor, money, safety, or all three, driven by the pleasure of gaining something. The general kind of justice involves all the things that matter to a good person.

It's clear, then, that there are different kinds of justice, and that one is separate from full virtue. We need to understand its type and differences.

We divided injustice into lawbreaking and unfairness, and justice into law-abiding and fairness. Lawbreaking connects to the broader sense of injustice, but unfairness is different from lawbreaking, like a part is different from the whole. All unfair acts are lawbreaking, but not all lawbreaking acts are unfair. So, injustice in the sense of unfairness is just a part of the wider idea of injustice, and the same goes for justice. This is why we need to talk about specific justice and injustice.

The kind of justice that covers all virtues and the injustice that covers all vices toward others can be set aside for now. We already know how "just" and "unjust" are used in this broad sense. Most of the laws focus on what's virtuous overall. The law tells us to practice every virtue and avoid every vice. Laws that aim to create virtue overall are those made for the common good. But when it comes to making an individual a good person in general, we need to figure out whether that's the role of politics or something else. It may not be the same thing to be a good person and a good citizen in every state.

When it comes to specific justice and what's just in this sense, (A) one type is about dividing things like honor, money, or anything else that people share in a society, where people can get either equal or unequal parts. (B) The other type deals with making things right between people in transactions. These can be divided into two groups: (1) some transactions are voluntary, like buying, selling, lending, and renting, which are voluntary because they start by choice, and (2) some are involuntary, like theft, adultery, poisoning, bribery, and murder. These can be either done in secret or violently, like physical assault or robbery.

(A) We've shown that both unjust people and unjust actions are unfair or unequal. So, it's clear that there's something in between these two extremes, and that's what's equal. In any case where there's a more and a less, there's also something that's equal. If injustice is inequality, then justice is equality, as people generally think. Since equality is in the middle, justice must also be in the middle. Equality means at least two things are being compared, so justice is both about balance and being equal for certain people. Equality is in the middle of greater and less, and it involves two people and the things being compared. If the people are unequal, they won't receive equal shares, and this is what causes conflicts. People argue when equals get unequal shares, or unequals get equal shares. This is clear because rewards should be given based on merit. Everyone agrees that justice in distribution must be based on some type of merit, though people don't all agree on what kind. Democrats say merit is based on being free, oligarchs say it's based on wealth or noble birth, and aristocrats say it's based on excellence.

So, justice is a kind of proportional equality, and proportion applies not just to numbers but to relationships between things. Proportion means the ratios are equal, and it always involves at least four terms. Continuous proportions can involve repeating terms, like saying, "as line A is to line B, so is line B to line C." Here, B is mentioned twice, so there are still four terms. Justice involves at least four terms, where the ratio between one pair is the same as the ratio between the other. As A is to B, so C is to D, and similarly, as A is to C, B is to D. So, the whole is in the same ratio to the whole. This kind of proportion makes distribution fair, and when terms are matched this way, justice is achieved. This fairness is the balance between the extremes, and injustice violates this balance. Mathematicians call this kind of proportion "geometrical" because it keeps the same ratio between parts and the whole.

So, what's just is proportional, and what's unjust breaks that proportion. When someone acts unjustly, they get too much, and the person treated unjustly gets too little of what's good. In the case of bad things, the reverse is true. The person with the lesser evil is considered to have more good because the lesser evil is better to choose than the greater one, and what's worth choosing is good. Therefore, the lesser evil is considered a greater good.

This, then, is one type of justice.

The other type is about correcting wrongs in both voluntary and involuntary dealings between people. This form of justice is different from the kind that deals with sharing common goods. The justice that deals with sharing is always based on a certain proportion (for example, in dividing up the money of a business partnership, it will be based on the amount each partner contributed). The injustice here happens when someone breaks this proportion. But justice in dealings between people is about equality, and injustice is about inequality— not in the same proportion as before, but in equal parts. It doesn't matter if a good person cheats a bad person, or a bad person cheats a good person, or if a good or bad person commits adultery. The law only looks at the wrong that was done and treats both people as equal—if one person is wrong and the other was wronged, if one person caused harm and the other received it. Since this type of injustice creates inequality, the judge's job is to restore equality. For example, if one person was wounded and the other did the wounding, or one person was killed and the other did the killing, the harm and the act are unequal. The judge's role is to equalize this by giving a penalty, taking away from what the wrongdoer gained. Even if the wrongdoer didn't gain in every situation (like wounding someone), we still call the harm "gain" for the wrongdoer and "loss" for the victim. After the judge determines the extent of the harm, one person is seen as having lost, and the other as having gained. Therefore, justice is the middle ground between gain and loss, and justice will correct things so that both sides are equal.

This is why, when people argue, they go to a judge. To go to the judge is to seek justice because a judge is like a living form of justice. People seek the judge as a neutral party, and in some places, they even call judges mediators because they believe that if they get a fair middle ground, they will get justice. So, justice is a middle point, and since the judge aims for fairness, justice is also a middle point. The judge tries to restore equality, like dividing a line into two unequal parts and taking from the longer part to make both sides equal. When the whole is divided equally, then people say they have what is rightfully theirs. The equal part is the middle point between the larger and smaller parts, according to simple mathematical equality.

This is also why justice is called "sikaion" because it means splitting something into two equal parts. It's similar to calling a judge "sikastes," which means a divider or equalizer. When you take something from one equal part and add it to the other, one part ends up being greater than the other by two units; if nothing had been added to the larger part, it would only be bigger by one unit. So, one part exceeds the middle by one unit, and the middle exceeds the smaller part by one unit. This helps us understand how much we must take from the bigger part and how much we must add to the smaller part. We need to add to the smaller part what the middle exceeds it by, and take from the larger part what exceeds the middle.

Let's say the lines AA', BB', and CC' are equal. If we take a segment AE from line AA' and add a segment Cd to line CC', the whole line DCC' will exceed the line EA' by the segments CD and CF, and therefore it also exceeds the line Bb' by the segment CD. (See diagram.)

The terms "loss" and "gain" come from voluntary exchanges, like buying and selling. To have more than your share is called gaining, and to have less is called losing. When people get neither more nor less than their fair share, they say they have what's rightfully theirs, and that they neither lose nor gain.

Justice, then, is the middle point between gaining and losing, specifically in cases that aren't voluntary. Justice is about having the same amount before and after the event.

Some people think that equality in return, or reciprocity, is always just, like the Pythagoreans believed. They defined justice as reciprocity. But reciprocity doesn't always fit either distributive or corrective justice—though people think Rhadamanthus' justice was based on this idea:

"If someone suffers what they caused, justice is done."

However, reciprocity and corrective justice don't always align. For example, (1) if an official has wounded someone, they shouldn't be wounded in return, and if someone wounds an official, they should be punished more than just being wounded. Also, (2) there's a big difference between acts done on purpose and acts done by accident. But in business, reciprocity works—people exchange fairly based on what's agreed. This proportional exchange keeps society together. People try to give back either good for good or bad for bad. If they can't do this, they feel powerless, like slaves. If they can't return good for good, no exchange happens, and without exchange, society can't function. This is why the temple of the Graces is important—it encourages people to give back favors. Grace means helping someone who helped you, and sometimes taking the lead in showing kindness first.

Fair exchange is based on proportion. Let's say A is a builder, B is a shoemaker, C is a house, and D is a shoe. The builder should receive shoes from the shoemaker and give the shoemaker a house in return. First, there must be proportional equality in what's being exchanged, and then the trade happens. If the work of one person is better than the other, the trade isn't equal, and the agreement doesn't hold. This applies to all professions. For example, two doctors don't trade with each other; instead, a doctor trades with a farmer or another person who provides a different service. Their work is different and unequal, so they need to find a way to balance it.

This is why money exists—it acts as a way to compare everything. It's like an intermediate that measures the value of all goods. It allows us to determine how many shoes are worth a house or how much food is worth a house. The number of shoes that trade for a house depends on the value of the builder's work compared to the shoemaker's work. Without money, there would be no exchange, and without exchange, people wouldn't interact. Proportion can't happen unless things are made equal. So, everything has to be measured by something, and that's why money was created.

In truth, it's not easy to make such different things equal, but they can be made equal enough by looking at how much they're needed.

Money represents demand, and because of this, it allows things to be compared. That's why it's called "nomisma" (money)—because it exists by law (nomos) and can be changed or made useless if people decide. So, reciprocity happens when the value of the goods is equal—when the shoemaker's work equals the builder's work. We don't compare them after they've been traded, but while they still have their goods. This makes them equal partners. If not for this balance, no trade would happen.

Money ensures people can exchange even if they don't need something right now, by acting as a guarantee for future trade. Even though the value of money can change, it's usually more stable than goods. Because of this, everything needs a price so that trade can always happen. If there's trade, people can work together.

Money, as a measure, makes things equal by allowing them to be compared. Without money, there wouldn't be exchange, and without exchange, people couldn't cooperate. Although it's impossible to make such different things truly equal, they can be made comparable based on demand. Money acts as this comparison because everything is measured by money.

Let's say A is a house, B is ten minae, and C is a bed. If A is worth five minae, the house is half of B. If C is a bed worth one-tenth of B, then it's clear how many beds are worth one house—five. It didn't matter if people exchanged five beds for a house or the value of five beds in money.

Now, we have defined what is just and unjust. It's clear that just action is a middle point between acting unjustly and being treated unjustly. One person gets too much, and the other gets too little. Justice is a balance, but not in the same way as other virtues—it relates to an intermediate amount, while injustice is about the extremes. A just person does what is fair by choice and will share fairly with others, giving neither more good to themselves nor more harm to others. This fairness follows a proportion. Injustice, on the other hand, involves either taking too much or too little of what's good or bad, which leads to imbalance.

Justice helps create equality by making sure everyone gets what they deserve. Injustice causes either excess or lack, and just action is about finding that middle ground.

Acts done out of anger are rightly judged not to be done with evil intent. It's not the person acting in anger who starts the wrongdoing, but the person who made them angry. Also, the argument isn't whether the action happened or not, but whether it was fair. It's the clear unfairness that causes the anger. People don't argue about whether the act occurred, as they might in business disputes where one of the two parties must be dishonest—unless they forgot. But they agree on the fact and argue about who is in the right. A person who deliberately hurts another knows they've done so, so one person believes they were wronged while the other disagrees.

If someone harms another on purpose, they act unjustly. These are the actions of an unjust person if they violate fairness or equality. Likewise, someone is just when they act fairly by choice, but they act fairly if they simply act voluntarily.

Some involuntary actions are excusable, and others are not. Mistakes that people make because they don't know any better or due to ignorance are excusable. However, mistakes made not because of ignorance, but because of an unnatural or uncontrollable passion, are not excusable.

Since we have defined what it means to suffer and do injustice, we can now ask if Euripides' strange words hold any truth:

"I killed my mother, that's my story in short.
Were you both willing, or both unwilling?"

Is it really possible to be treated unjustly on purpose, or is suffering injustice always the opposite—something involuntary—just as doing injustice is voluntary? Is suffering injustice always involuntary, or can it be voluntary at times? The same question can be asked for being treated fairly: all fair actions are voluntary, so it seems reasonable that both being treated unfairly and being treated fairly could be either voluntary or involuntary. But it seems strange, even in the case of being treated fairly, that it could always be voluntary, since some people are treated fairly against their will.

Another question we might ask is whether everyone who suffers something unjust is being treated unjustly, or if it's like taking action. In both doing and receiving, it's possible to experience justice or injustice by accident. Doing something unjust isn't the same as acting unjustly, just as suffering something unjust isn't the same as being treated unjustly. The same is true for acting justly and being treated fairly. It's impossible to be treated unjustly if the other person isn't acting unjustly, or to be treated fairly if they aren't acting fairly.

Now, if acting unjustly means deliberately harming someone, and 'deliberately' means knowing the person you're acting on, the tool you're using, and how you're doing it, then someone who harms themselves because they lack self-control does it voluntarily. This means they can also be treated unjustly on purpose, which raises the question of whether someone can treat themselves unjustly. A person may harm themselves on purpose due to a lack of self-control while being harmed by someone else who also acts deliberately, so it's possible to be treated unjustly on purpose.

Or perhaps our definition is wrong. Should we add to 'harming another on purpose' the idea that it must also be 'against the will of the person being harmed'? In that case, a person may be harmed on purpose and suffer an unjust act on purpose, but no one is treated unjustly on purpose, because no one wants to be treated unjustly— not even the person who lacks self-control. They act against their own will since no one wants what they don't think is good, even though the person without self-control does things they believe they shouldn't.

Also, a person who gives away their possessions, like how Homer says Glaucus gave Diomede "armor of gold for bronze, worth a hundred oxen for nine," is not treated unjustly. Though giving is within his power, being treated unjustly isn't, because someone else must treat him unjustly. So, it's clear that being treated unjustly is not something done willingly.

Two questions still remain: whether it's the person who gives someone more than their share who acts unjustly, or the person who gets too much, and whether it's possible to treat yourself unjustly. These questions are connected. If the first case is true—that the one who distributes unfairly is unjust but not the person who receives too much—then if a person gives another more than they give themselves, knowing and choosing to do so, they treat themselves unjustly. This is what modest people seem to do, since the virtuous person tends to take less than their share. Or is this view too simple? Maybe they receive more of some other good, like honor or dignity. We can solve this by applying the same rule we use for unjust action: the person isn't treated unjustly if it's what they wanted, so they don't suffer injustice, though they may suffer harm.

It's clear that the one who distributes unfairly acts unjustly, but not always the person who gets too much. Injustice belongs to the person who deliberately acts unfairly, not the one who receives the unfair share. The responsibility lies with the person who makes the decision, and in this case, that's the distributor, not the recipient. Also, the word 'act' has different meanings: lifeless objects, a hand, or a servant carrying out an order can be said to 'kill,' but it's not really them acting unjustly, even though they carry out an unjust action.

If the distributor made their judgment in ignorance, they don't act unjustly according to the law, and their decision isn't legally unjust, though it may be unjust in another sense (since legal justice and natural justice are different). But if the distributor knowingly makes an unfair judgment, they are trying to get something extra, either gratitude or revenge. In this case, they get too much, just like if they had taken part of the spoils. It doesn't matter if what they get is different from what they distribute; for example, if they give out land but aim to receive money from it.

People think that it's easy to act unjustly, and so being just must be easy too. But it's not. It's easy to sleep with someone else's wife, hurt someone, or take a bribe. But doing these things as part of a bad character is neither easy nor within everyone's control. Similarly, people think it takes no great wisdom to know what's just and unjust, because understanding the laws isn't hard. But how actions should be done and goods divided fairly—that's harder to know than what's good for health. Even though knowing that honey, wine, or medicine can help is easy, knowing how, to whom, and when to use them requires the skill of a doctor.

For this reason, people think that being unjust can come as easily to a just person as it does to an unjust one. The just person would be even better at unjust actions because they know what to do. For example, they could sleep with someone or harm their neighbor, and the brave person could throw away their shield and run from danger. But to act cowardly or unjustly isn't just doing those things—it's doing them because of a bad character, just as being a doctor doesn't mean simply using or not using a knife, but knowing how to heal in the right way.

Just actions occur between people who share good things and can have too much or too little of them. Some beings, like the gods, can't have too much of them, and to others, like those who are beyond help, not even a little share is good—it harms them. But to others, these goods are helpful up to a certain point, so justice is a human concept.

Next, we'll talk about fairness and what it means to be fair. Fairness and justice seem to be neither entirely the same nor completely different. We sometimes praise fairness and fair people, so we use the term to praise other virtues as well. But when we think about it, it seems strange that fairness could be different from justice yet still praiseworthy. If they are different, then either justice or fairness can't be good. If both are good, they must be the same.

These thoughts give rise to questions about fairness. All of them are somewhat correct and not in opposition. Fairness is better than one type of justice, but it's still a kind of justice. Fairness isn't different in kind, just better in a certain way. The same thing can be just and fair, and while both are good, fairness is better. The reason we face this problem is that fairness corrects legal justice. All laws are general, but sometimes it's impossible to make a general law fit every case. The law takes the most common case, knowing that it won't always be right. This isn't the fault of the law or the lawmaker—it's because of the nature of human affairs. So, when the law speaks in general terms, but a specific case doesn't fit, fairness comes in to correct the mistake. Fairness allows us to make the decision that the lawmaker would have made if they were present and knew the situation.

Fairness is better than this kind of justice, though not better than justice in an absolute sense. It corrects errors that arise from the general nature of the law. This is why not everything can be decided by law—sometimes we need to make exceptions. Laws are like the flexible lead rulers used to make molds, which bend to fit the stone rather than staying rigid. In the same way, judgments are made to fit the facts.

It's clear now what fairness is and that it's a kind of justice, but better in certain ways. It's also clear who the fair person is—the one who chooses and acts fairly, not insisting on their rights to an extreme but often taking less than their share even when the law is on their side. This quality is fairness, which is a kind of justice, not a separate virtue.

Whether a person can treat themselves unjustly is clear from what we've said. One type of just actions is those based on virtue that are required by law. For example, the law doesn't allow suicide, and what it doesn't allow, it forbids. A person who harms another on purpose breaks the law and acts unjustly, knowing both the person they harm and the tool they use. So, if someone stabs themselves in anger, it goes against the right way to live, and the law doesn't permit it. They act unjustly, but toward whom? Surely toward the state, not themselves. They suffer willingly, but no one is treated unjustly willingly. This is why the state punishes suicide—because it's considered unjust to the state.

Also, in the sense of acting unjustly where a person acts unjustly but isn't completely bad, it's not possible to treat oneself unjustly. This is different from the first sense. The unjust person in this case is bad in a particular way, like a coward, not bad in every way. Their unjust action doesn't show full wickedness. In this case, it would mean that the same thing could be both added to and taken from the same person at the same time, which is impossible—justice and injustice always involve more than one person.

Additionally, unjust actions are voluntary and chosen. But if a person harms themselves, they are both the one suffering and the one causing the suffering at the same time. So, it's impossible to treat yourself unjustly. Besides, no one commits injustice without specific actions, and no one can commit adultery with their own spouse or steal from their own house.

The question of whether a person can treat themselves unjustly is solved in the same way as the question of whether a person can be treated unjustly willingly.

It's clear that both suffering injustice and acting unjustly are bad. One means getting less than the fair amount, and the other means getting more, similar to how health is the goal in medicine. But acting unjustly is worse, because it involves vice and deserves blame. Vice is either complete and absolute or close to it, though not every voluntary unjust action shows full injustice as a character trait. Being treated unjustly doesn't involve vice in oneself. In itself, being treated unjustly is less bad, but it can sometimes lead to a worse outcome. Theory doesn't care about that—it calls pleurisy a worse illness than a small injury, though the injury could become worse if it leads to being captured or killed.

Metaphorically, there is a kind of justice between a person and themselves, though not in the strict sense. It's like the justice between a master and servant or husband and wife. These relationships show how the rational part of the soul relates to the irrational part. People believe that a person can be unjust to themselves because these parts of the soul can conflict. This leads people to think there is a kind of justice between the parts of a person, like between ruler and ruled.

This is our account of justice and the other moral virtues.

Book 6

Since we have previously said that one should choose what is in the middle, not the extreme of too much or too little, and that this middle point is decided by the correct rule, let's discuss what these correct rules are. In all the states of character we have mentioned, as well as in other areas, there is a goal the person with the right rule aims for, and they either increase or decrease their actions to hit that goal. There is a standard that defines these middle points, which we call the balance between too much and too little, and this standard follows the right rule. But even though this statement is true, it's not very clear. It's like when we say in other areas of knowledge that we should not do too much or too little, but act in a balanced way as the right rule dictates. If someone only knew that, they wouldn't be much wiser, just as we wouldn't know what kind of medicine to use if someone only told us, "use what the medical art prescribes, as practiced by those who know it." That's why, when it comes to the soul, it's necessary not only to make the true statement but also to understand what the right rule is and what standard sets it.

We divided the virtues of the soul into two kinds: those related to character and those related to intellect. Now that we've talked in detail about moral virtues, let's talk about the others, starting with some comments about the soul. We said before that the soul has two parts: one part follows rules or reason, and the other part is irrational. Let's now make another distinction within the part that follows reason.

There are two parts here as well: one part thinks about things that don't change, and the other thinks about things that can change. Since the things they focus on are different, the parts of the soul that deal with them must also be different. The part that deals with what doesn't change can be called the scientific part, and the part that deals with what can change can be called the calculating part. This is because calculating and reasoning are the same thing, and we never calculate about things that don't change. So, the calculating part is a part of the soul that deals with rational principles.

Next, we need to understand what the best state of these two parts is, as that will be their virtue. The virtue of anything is related to its proper function. In the soul, three things control action and truth: sensation, reason, and desire.

Sensation doesn't start any actions. This is clear because animals can sense things but don't take actions the way humans do. In the same way that thinking can affirm or deny something, desire can lead to pursuit or avoidance. Since moral virtue is about choosing, and choice is thoughtful desire, both the reasoning must be correct and the desire must be right for the choice to be good. The desire should go after what the reasoning points to. This kind of thinking and truth is practical. For the thinking that is contemplative (not practical or productive), the good state is truth, and the bad state is falsehood. But in the part that is both practical and rational, the good state is when truth and right desire work together.

The source of action (not its goal) is choice, and choice comes from desire and reasoning toward a goal. This is why choice can't exist without reason and intellect or without a moral state. Good and bad actions need both intellect and character to happen. But intellect by itself doesn't cause anything to happen. Only the kind of intellect that has a goal and is practical leads to action. This kind of intellect even controls the intellect that produces things because anyone who makes something does it for a goal. The thing they make isn't the ultimate goal, but good action is. So, choice is either reason driven by desire or desire driven by reason, and this leads to action. This is why humans act. (It's important to note that nothing in the past can be chosen. No one chooses to have destroyed Troy, for example, because we don't deliberate about the past, only about the future, which can still change. As Agathon said:

"Even God cannot change what is done.")

The work of both intellectual parts is truth. Therefore, the best state for each part is the one that leads to truth, and that is their virtue.

Let's start from the beginning and talk about these states again. The ways the soul holds on to truth through affirmation or denial are five in number: art, scientific knowledge, practical wisdom, philosophical wisdom, and intuitive reason. We don't include judgment and opinion because they can be wrong.

Now, what exactly is scientific knowledge? If we are going to be precise and not just rely on similarities, we say that scientific knowledge is knowing something that cannot be otherwise. For things that could be different, we don't know whether they exist once they are out of our sight. Scientific knowledge deals with things that must be as they are, and therefore, it deals with things that are eternal. Things that are necessary are all eternal, and eternal things don't have a beginning or an end. Science is also thought to be teachable, and its object is something that can be learned. All teaching comes from what is already known, as we explain in Analytics. Teaching can happen either by induction or by syllogism. Induction starts from specifics and leads to a general understanding, and syllogism starts from general truths. The starting points of syllogisms are not proven by more syllogisms; they are learned through induction. So, scientific knowledge is a state where we can prove things, and it has the other characteristics that we explain in Analytics. Scientific knowledge occurs when a person believes something in the right way and knows the starting points of their argument. Otherwise, they only know things incidentally.

Let this be our explanation of scientific knowledge.

Both things that are made and things that are done are part of the variable. Making and acting are different. We can trust even the discussions outside of our own school on this. The capacity to act and the capacity to make are also different. Therefore, making isn't the same as acting, and acting isn't the same as making. Architecture, for example, is an art and is essentially the capacity to make something. Art is the ability to make, based on a correct understanding of how to do it. All art deals with creating something—figuring out how something can come into being that might or might not exist. The origin of this creation lies in the maker, not the thing being made. Art isn't about things that exist by necessity or nature, as those things originate from themselves. Since making and acting are different, art is about making, not acting.

In some way, both chance and art deal with the same objects. As Agathon said, "art loves chance, and chance loves art." Art, then, is the ability to make something by following correct reasoning, while lack of art is the opposite—it involves incorrect reasoning. Both art and chance deal with things that can vary.

Now let's talk about practical wisdom. We can understand what it is by considering who we think has it. A person with practical wisdom is able to think well about what is good and beneficial for themselves, not just in one specific area like health or strength, but in terms of living a good life overall. We also give credit to people who have practical wisdom in a specific area when they can figure out the best way to reach a good goal that is not the object of any art. So, in the general sense, a person who can deliberate well has practical wisdom. No one deliberates about things that don't change or about things they can't control. Since scientific knowledge involves proving things, and there's no proof of things that change (since they could be otherwise), practical wisdom can't be scientific knowledge or art. It's not science because the things we can do might be otherwise, and it's not art because making and acting are different. Practical wisdom must be the ability to act well concerning what is good or bad for humans. Making has an end beyond itself, but action is an end in itself.

That's why we say people like Pericles had practical wisdom—because they could see what was good for themselves and for others in general. We consider those who are good at managing households or states to have this wisdom. (This is also why we call temperance "sophrosune," which means it preserves practical wisdom. It helps preserve the kind of judgment we've described. Not all judgments are ruined by pleasure and pain—only those about what should be done. The starting point for actions lies in the goal they aim for. But someone who is corrupted by pleasure or pain can no longer see why they should choose certain actions. Vice destroys the cause of action.)

So, practical wisdom is the ability to act well concerning human goods. While there is excellence in art, there is no such thing as excellence in practical wisdom. In art, a person who makes mistakes on purpose is better than one who makes mistakes by accident, but in practical wisdom, the opposite is true, just as it is with the virtues. Practical wisdom is a virtue, not an art. There are two parts of the soul that can reason, and practical wisdom is the virtue of the part that forms opinions. Opinion is about things that can change, and so is practical wisdom. But practical wisdom isn't just reasoning. This is shown by the fact that reasoning can be forgotten, but practical wisdom cannot be.

Scientific knowledge is about things that are universal and necessary, and it deals with what can be proven. All scientific knowledge comes from first principles, but the first principles themselves cannot be the objects of science, art, or practical wisdom. Scientific knowledge deals with things that can be demonstrated, and art and practical wisdom deal with things that can change. First principles also can't be the objects of philosophical wisdom because philosophers need to prove things about them. So, if the mental states that give us truth are scientific knowledge, practical wisdom, philosophical wisdom, and intuitive reason, and first principles aren't objects of the first three, then it must be intuitive reason that grasps them.

Wisdom has two meanings. In the arts, we call people wise when they are highly skilled, like Phidias in sculpture or Polyclitus in making statues. Here, wisdom simply means excellence in art. But we also think some people are wise in general, not just in one specific area. As Homer says in Margites:

"The gods made him neither a digger nor a ploughman,
Nor wise in anything else."

So, wisdom must be the highest form of knowledge. The wise person must know not only what follows from first principles but also the first principles themselves. Wisdom must be intuitive reason combined with scientific knowledge of the highest things, which is as complete as it can get.

We're talking about the highest things because it would be strange to think that politics or practical wisdom is the best kind of knowledge since humans aren't the best things in the universe. If what is healthy or good is different for humans and fish, but what is white or straight is always the same, we can say that what is wise is the same for all but practical wisdom differs. It applies to those things that are concerned with themselves. That's why we say that some animals have practical wisdom when they can take care of their own lives. It's also clear that philosophical wisdom and politics are not the same. If philosophical wisdom were about a person's own interests, there would be many different kinds of philosophical wisdom, just as there are many different kinds of medicine, one for each kind of being.

But if someone argues that humans are the best of animals, this doesn't change the point. There are other things that are much more divine than humans, such as the heavenly bodies. So, philosophical wisdom is scientific knowledge combined with intuitive reason about the highest things in nature. That's why we say that people like Anaxagoras and Thales had philosophical wisdom, even though they were often ignorant of what was good for themselves. They knew remarkable, admirable, difficult, and divine things, but they were useless because they didn't focus on human goods.

Practical wisdom, on the other hand, is concerned with human things and things that can be deliberated about. We say that practical wisdom involves deliberating well, but no one deliberates about things that can't change or that don't have an end goal. The person who is good at deliberating is the one who can aim at the best outcome for humans, based on reason, from the things that can be done. Practical wisdom isn't just about general truths; it must also deal with specific details. Practice deals with specific things. That's why someone with experience may be more practical than someone with theoretical knowledge. For example, a person may know that light foods are easy to digest, but if they don't know what kinds of food are light, they can't create a healthy diet. However, someone who knows that chicken is light food will be better at creating a healthy diet.

Practical wisdom is about action, so we should have both general and specific knowledge, or at least specific knowledge. But even within practical wisdom and philosophical wisdom, there are different kinds of control.

Political wisdom and practical wisdom are the same kind of state of mind, but their essence is different. The practical wisdom involved in managing a city includes legislative wisdom, which is concerned with creating laws, while the political wisdom that deals with specific actions is known simply as 'political wisdom.' This kind of wisdom deals with actions and decisions since laws are meant to guide individual actions. This is why people involved in this art are said to 'participate in politics,' just as manual workers are said to 'do things.'

Practical wisdom is mostly identified with the type that deals with a person's own life, and this is generally called 'practical wisdom.' Other types include household management, legislation, and politics. Politics can be divided into two parts: deliberative and judicial. Knowing what is good for oneself is one kind of knowledge, but it is very different from other types. The person who knows and focuses on their own interests is considered to have practical wisdom, while politicians are often seen as meddling in other people's affairs. This is reflected in the words of Euripides:

"How could I be wise, when I could have had
An equal share among the soldiers,
Instead of aiming too high and doing too much?"

People who think this way believe that one should look out for their own good, and they think this is the right thing to do. This belief is where the idea that such people have practical wisdom comes from. But maybe one's own good can't exist without household management or some form of government. Additionally, knowing how to manage your own affairs isn't easy and requires investigation.

What has been said is supported by the fact that while young people can become experts in geometry, mathematics, and other similar subjects, it's believed that a young person cannot have practical wisdom. The reason is that practical wisdom deals not only with general ideas but also with specific situations, which come from experience. A young person doesn't have experience because experience comes with time. We might also wonder why a boy can become a mathematician but not a philosopher or a physicist. It's because the things studied in mathematics exist in theory, while the first principles of philosophy and physics come from experience. Young people don't have firm beliefs about these first principles; they only know the words. But the nature of mathematical objects is clear to them.

Additionally, mistakes in deliberation can be about either general principles or specific details. For example, someone might not know that all water that weighs heavy is harmful, or they might not realize that this specific water weighs heavy.

It's clear that practical wisdom is not the same as scientific knowledge. Practical wisdom, as we've said, is about specific facts because the things to be done are specific in nature. It is different from intuitive reason. Intuitive reason deals with general starting points, which can't be explained, while practical wisdom focuses on specific facts. These facts aren't known through scientific knowledge but through perception—a perception similar to how we recognize that a certain shape is a triangle. In this way, there is a limit, just as there is with general rules. But this kind of perception is closer to practical wisdom, though it's different from the perception that involves the senses.

There's a difference between inquiry and deliberation. Deliberation is a specific kind of inquiry. We need to understand what excellence in deliberation is and whether it's a form of scientific knowledge, opinion, skill in guessing, or something else. It isn't scientific knowledge because people don't inquire about things they already know. But good deliberation involves inquiring and thinking carefully. It also isn't a skill in guessing because guessing doesn't involve reasoning and happens quickly, while people take time to deliberate. We say that people should act quickly once they've finished deliberating but should deliberate slowly. Quick thinking is different from excellence in deliberation because it's more like guessing. Excellence in deliberation also isn't the same as opinion. But since someone who deliberates badly makes mistakes, while someone who deliberates well does so correctly, excellence in deliberation must involve correctness. This correctness is different from knowledge or opinion. There's no such thing as correct knowledge (since knowledge doesn't include error), and correctness of opinion is the same as truth. At the same time, everything that is a matter of opinion is already decided. Excellence in deliberation involves reasoning. The only option left is that it's the correctness of thinking. Opinion is not the same as inquiry because it has already reached a conclusion, while someone who is deliberating is still searching and calculating.

Excellence in deliberation means being correct in deliberation. So, we need to first understand what deliberation is and what it deals with. Since there are different kinds of correctness, it's clear that excellence in deliberation is not just any kind of correctness. For example, a person without self-control or a bad person, if they are clever, may achieve their goal through deliberation. But they will have ended up with something harmful. To deliberate well is considered a good thing because it means being correct in achieving good ends. However, (1) it's possible to reach something good through incorrect reasoning, by using false premises. This means that even if someone achieves the right result, they didn't reach it in the right way, so this isn't excellence in deliberation. (2) It's also possible to achieve a result after long deliberation, while someone else might reach it more quickly. In the first case, we don't yet have excellence in deliberation, which is about being correct in terms of the goal, the method, and the timing. (3) Additionally, it's possible to deliberate well either in a general sense or about a specific goal. Excellence in deliberation in the general sense is when someone achieves a goal that is good in general, while excellence in deliberation in a specific sense is when someone succeeds in reaching a particular goal. (4) If it's true that people with practical wisdom are good at deliberating, then excellence in deliberation will be about correctly determining what leads to the goals that practical wisdom recognizes.

Understanding and goodness of understanding, which make people known as having good judgment, are not exactly the same as opinion or scientific knowledge. If they were, everyone would have good understanding. Nor are they part of specific sciences like medicine or geometry. Understanding isn't about things that are always true and unchangeable, nor is it about everything that comes into existence. It deals with things that can be questioned and deliberated about. So, it deals with the same objects as practical wisdom. But understanding and practical wisdom aren't the same. Practical wisdom leads to decisions, as its goal is to determine what should or shouldn't be done. Understanding, on the other hand, only makes judgments. Understanding and good understanding are the same thing. Having understanding isn't the same as having or gaining practical wisdom. Just as learning is called understanding when it's the use of knowledge, understanding is about using opinion to judge what others say about matters related to practical wisdom—and doing so correctly. The term 'understanding' has come from the ability to grasp scientific truth, and we often use it to describe that ability.

Judgment, which makes people known as having good judgment or as sympathetic judges, is the ability to correctly recognize what is fair. This is shown by the fact that we say the fair person is also a person of good judgment. Fairness is closely related to good judgment in certain matters, and judgment is about correctly recognizing what is fair. Correct judgment is the ability to recognize what is true.

All the states we've discussed seem to come together. When we talk about judgment, understanding, practical wisdom, and intuitive reason, we give credit to the same people for having these qualities. We say that they have reached an age of wisdom and possess practical wisdom and understanding. All these qualities deal with specifics, or what we might call ultimate things. Being a person of understanding and good judgment means being able to make decisions about the matters that practical wisdom deals with. What is fair is something that all good people recognize in their dealings with others. Everything we need to do in life involves specifics or ultimate things. People with practical wisdom must know specific details, and understanding and judgment are also about things that need to be done. These are ultimate things. Intuitive reason deals with ultimate things in both directions. It deals with both the first principles and the last conclusions. The intuitive reason that we use in demonstrations grasps the first, unchangeable principles, while the intuitive reason we use in practical matters grasps the final, changeable fact, or the minor premise. These variable facts are the starting points for reaching a goal, and we understand universals by looking at specifics. So, we must have a perception of these facts, and this perception is intuitive reason.

This is why these qualities are thought to be natural abilities. No one is considered a natural philosopher, but people are thought to have natural judgment, understanding, and intuitive reason. We believe these qualities come with age, and a person's natural development brings with it judgment and intuitive reason. This suggests that these qualities come from nature. Intuitive reason is both the starting point and the end. Demonstrations are based on intuitive reason and are about intuitive reason.

This is why we should listen to the sayings and opinions of experienced and older people, as well as people with practical wisdom. Their experience has given them insight, and they see things clearly.

We've now explained what practical and philosophical wisdom are and what they deal with. We've also said that each is a virtue of a different part of the soul.

We might wonder about the usefulness of these mental qualities. (1) Philosophical wisdom doesn't seem to deal with anything that makes a person happy, since it isn't concerned with things that come into being. Practical wisdom, on the other hand, does deal with things that make a person happy. But why do we need it? Practical wisdom deals with things that are just, noble, and good for humans. These are the things a good person does, but knowing about them doesn't make us better at doing them. Just as knowing what is healthy doesn't make us better at creating health (since health comes from the state of the body, not from the art of medicine), knowing what is just doesn't necessarily help us act justly. (2) If we say that a person should have practical wisdom to help them become good, practical wisdom is still useless for people who are already good. It's also useless for people who don't have virtue because it doesn't matter whether they have practical wisdom or follow the advice of someone who does. In the same way, we want to be healthy, but we don't need to learn the art of medicine to become healthy. (3) It also seems strange that practical wisdom, which is inferior to philosophical wisdom, would be in charge of it. This seems to be implied by the fact that the art that produces something also controls and commands it.

These are the questions we need to consider. So far, we've only mentioned the difficulties.

(1) First, we should say that these mental states are worth choosing for their own sake, even if they don't produce anything, because they are the virtues of the two parts of the soul.

(2) Secondly, these states do produce something, but not in the same way that the art of medicine produces health. Philosophical wisdom produces happiness, not by making something, but by existing and being used. Since it's part of virtue as a whole, possessing and using philosophical wisdom makes a person happy.

(3) Additionally, a person can only achieve their purpose through both practical wisdom and moral virtue. Virtue helps us aim at the right goals, and practical wisdom helps us find the right way to achieve them. (The fourth part of the soul—the part that deals with nutrition—doesn't have a virtue like this because it doesn't have control over what it does.)

(4) As for the idea that practical wisdom doesn't help us do what is noble and just, let's start by discussing something else. We've said that some people do just actions without being truly just. This includes people who follow the laws but do so unwillingly, out of ignorance, or for reasons other than the actions themselves. Even though they do the right things, they don't do them because they are good. To be truly good, a person must be in the right state when they act—they must choose to do good and do it for its own sake. Virtue helps us make the right choices, but knowing what to do to carry out those choices belongs to another ability.

We need to pay attention to this and explain it more clearly. There is an ability called cleverness, which helps people achieve the goals they aim for. When the goal is good, cleverness is praiseworthy, but when the goal is bad, cleverness is just smartness. This is why we call people with practical wisdom clever or smart. Practical wisdom isn't the same as cleverness, but it can't exist without it. This insight into practical matters doesn't develop without the help of virtue. This is because the reasoning behind actions starts with an understanding of what is good, but only good people can fully understand this.

Wickedness leads us astray and makes us misunderstand the starting points for action.

It's clear that it's impossible to have practical wisdom without being good.

We must now consider virtue again. Virtue is related to cleverness in the same way that practical wisdom is related to cleverness. They aren't the same, but they are similar. Natural virtue is like cleverness, while virtue in the full sense is like practical wisdom. People believe that certain character traits are natural. From the moment we are born, we might naturally be just, self-controlled, or brave, or have other moral qualities. But we still look for something else—something better. Both children and animals have these natural traits, but without reason, these traits can be harmful. It's like a strong body that moves without sight—it can fall badly because it can't see. But once reason is added, everything changes. The person still has the same natural traits, but now they are true virtues in the full sense.

In the part of us that forms opinions, there are two kinds of qualities: cleverness and practical wisdom. Similarly, in the moral part of us, there are two types of virtues: natural virtue and true virtue, and true virtue involves practical wisdom. This is why some people say that all virtues are forms of practical wisdom. Socrates was partly right and partly wrong. He was wrong to think that all virtues were forms of practical wisdom, but he was right to say that virtues include practical wisdom. This is supported by the fact that when people define virtue, they say it's a state of character and then add that it follows the right rule. The right rule is the one that follows practical wisdom. So, people seem to sense that true virtue is the kind that follows practical wisdom.

But we need to go a little further. Virtue isn't just the state that follows the right rule—it's the state that involves the right rule. Practical wisdom is the right rule about these matters. Socrates thought that virtues were rules or principles because he believed they were all forms of knowledge. We, however, believe that virtues involve a rational principle.

It's clear from what has been said that it's not possible to truly be good without practical wisdom, and you can't have practical wisdom without moral virtue. This also disproves the argument that the virtues can exist separately from each other. Some might argue that a person is not naturally equipped for all virtues, so they might have one virtue but not yet have developed another. This can happen with natural virtues, but not with the kind of virtues that make a person fully good. When a person has practical wisdom, they will have all the virtues. Even if practical wisdom didn't have any practical use, we would still need it because it is the virtue of this part of ourselves. It's also clear that we can't make the right choices without practical wisdom any more than we can without virtue. One helps us determine the right goal, and the other helps us do the things that lead to that goal.

However, practical wisdom isn't higher than philosophical wisdom, which is the higher part of us. It's like how medicine isn't above health—it doesn't use health but helps bring it about. Practical wisdom gives instructions for the sake of philosophical wisdom, but it doesn't command it. Saying practical wisdom is higher than philosophical wisdom would be like saying that politics rules the gods just because it gives orders about the state's affairs.

Book 7

Let's start fresh and explain that there are three kinds of bad character traits to avoid: vice, lack of self-control, and being brutish. There are opposites to two of these traits. One is called virtue, and the other is self-control. As for being brutish, the opposite would be a kind of superhuman virtue, something heroic and almost divine. Homer shows this when Priam says about Hector that he was so good:

"For he didn't seem like the child of a mortal man but as if he was born from a god."

So, if people say that humans can become like gods by having an excess of virtue, then the state of being godlike must be the opposite of being brutish. This is because, just like a brute doesn't have vice or virtue, a god doesn't either. A god's state is higher than virtue, and a brute's state is different from vice.

Now, since it's rare to find a godlike person—using a term from the Spartans, who called someone 'godlike' when they admired them greatly—it's also rare to find a brutish person among humans. You mainly find them among barbarians, though some people develop brutish qualities because of disease or deformity. We also call people who are extremely wicked 'brutish.' We'll talk more about this type of character later. While we've already discussed vice, now we need to talk about lack of self-control and weakness (or softness), as well as self-control and endurance. We need to look at these as neither exactly the same as virtue or wickedness nor as a completely different category. As always, we should look at the facts and, after addressing the difficulties, try to prove that most of the common ideas about these traits are true—or at least the majority of them and the most trustworthy ones. If we can refute objections and leave the common beliefs untouched, we will have proven our case well enough.

Both self-control and endurance are seen as good and praiseworthy, while lack of self-control and softness are seen as bad and blameworthy. The same person can be considered either self-controlled and sticking to their decisions or lacking self-control and abandoning them. A person who lacks self-control knows what they're doing is wrong but gives in to passion, while a self-controlled person knows their desires are wrong but refuses to follow them because of their reasoning. Everyone calls a person with self-control and endurance 'temperate.' Some think that a person with self-control is always temperate, while others disagree. Some also use the terms 'self-indulgent' and 'lacking self-control' interchangeably, while others make a distinction between the two. Some say that a person with practical wisdom cannot lack self-control, while others claim that even some practically wise and clever people can lack self-control. People also say that someone can lack self-control not just with physical desires but also with anger, the desire for honor, and the desire for profit. These are the things people say.

Now we can ask how someone who makes the right judgment can still lack self-control. Some say it's impossible for someone to act this way when they have knowledge because, as Socrates thought, it would be strange if knowledge could be overpowered and controlled like a slave. Socrates completely disagreed with the idea of lack of self-control. He believed there was no such thing because he said that no one acts against what they believe is best—they only do wrong because of ignorance. But this view clearly goes against what we observe, so we must investigate what happens with such a person. If they act out of ignorance, how exactly are they ignorant? It's clear that the person who lacks self-control doesn't think, before they give in, that they should act this way. But some people agree with some of Socrates' points but not all of them. They accept that knowledge is stronger than anything else, but they don't think that someone acts against what they think is best. Instead, they say that the person who lacks self-control doesn't have knowledge when they're overpowered by their desires; they only have an opinion.

But if it's just an opinion and not true knowledge, if it's not a firm conviction but a weak one, like someone who hesitates, we can understand why they fail to stick to it against strong desires. However, we don't feel the same way about wickedness or other bad states. So, is it practical wisdom that's overpowered? That would be the strongest state of all, but that idea doesn't make sense. It would mean that the same person could be both practically wise and lack self-control, but no one would say that a practically wise person would willingly do the worst things. Besides, we've already shown that a practically wise person is someone who acts (because they're concerned with real-world situations) and has all the other virtues.

Furthermore, if self-control means having strong, bad desires, then a temperate person can't be self-controlled, and a self-controlled person can't be temperate. This is because a temperate person wouldn't have bad or excessive desires, but a self-controlled person must have them. If the desires are good, then the state of resisting them would be bad, so not all forms of self-control would be good. If the desires are weak and not bad, there's nothing impressive about resisting them, and if they're weak and bad, there's still nothing great about resisting them.

Additionally, if self-control means sticking to every opinion, then it would be a bad thing, especially if it means sticking to false opinions. And if lack of self-control means abandoning every opinion, then there could be a good form of lack of self-control, like in Sophocles' play "Philoctetes," where Neoptolemus is praised for not sticking to the plan Odysseus convinced him to follow because he was upset about telling a lie.

Moreover, there's a problem with certain clever arguments. These arguments are designed to create paradoxes in an opponent's viewpoint to make the person who proves the paradox seem clever. But these arguments can confuse us. For example, one argument might suggest that foolishness combined with lack of self-control could be a kind of virtue. The reasoning is that a person who lacks self-control acts against what they believe is right, but they wrongly believe that something good is bad and that they shouldn't do it. So, as a result, they end up doing the good thing and avoiding the bad one.

Further, a person who chooses to pursue what is pleasant through careful thought might seem better than someone who does it out of lack of self-control. The first person is easier to correct because they might be persuaded to change their mind. But with a person who lacks self-control, we might say, "When water chokes you, what do you wash it down with?" If they had been persuaded that what they were doing was right, they would have stopped when they were persuaded to change their mind. But now, they act even though they've been persuaded to do something different.

Finally, if lack of self-control and self-control apply to everything, then who exactly is lacking self-control in the general sense? No one seems to lack control in every way, yet we still call some people lacking self-control without qualification. These are the kinds of difficulties we face. Some of these points must be disproven, while others should be accepted, as solving these difficulties is the key to finding the truth.

We should first ask if people who lack self-control act knowingly or not, and in what way they act knowingly. Then, we should ask what kinds of things the self-controlled and the uncontrollable person are concerned with—whether they deal with all pleasures and pains or just certain ones. We should also ask if self-control and endurance are the same thing or different, and we should approach the other relevant questions similarly. Our starting point is whether a person is self-controlled or lacking self-control because of the specific things they desire or because of their attitude toward them, or perhaps because of both. The next question is whether lack of self-control and self-control apply to every type of thing or just some. A person who lacks self-control in the general sense doesn't apply this to every object. They are mostly concerned with the same things as a self-indulgent person, but they differ in how they approach them. One person is led by their choices, thinking they should always pursue immediate pleasure, while the other person doesn't think so but still pursues it.

As for the idea that it's opinion and not knowledge that people act against when they lack self-control, that doesn't make a difference. Some people have firm opinions and don't hesitate but feel as if they know for sure. If the idea is that people with opinion are more likely to act against their judgment because their convictions are weaker, we can respond that there's not much difference between knowledge and opinion in this respect. Some people are just as convinced of their opinions as others are of their knowledge. This is shown by the views of Heraclitus. But since we use the word 'know' in two ways—for a person who has knowledge but isn't using it and for a person who is using it—it makes a difference whether someone has knowledge but isn't exercising it or is exercising it when they act wrongly. The latter case seems strange, but not the former.

Also, since there are two kinds of premises, a person can have both premises but still act against their knowledge, provided they are only using the universal premise and not the particular one. This is because particular actions are what must be done. There are also two types of universal terms: one applies to the person acting, and the other applies to the object. For example, "dry food is good for everyone" and "I am a person," or "this food is dry." But whether the person knows "this food is such and such," the person who lacks self-control either doesn't have that knowledge or isn't using it. So there's a big difference between these types of knowledge, and knowing in one way but acting incontinently wouldn't seem strange, while knowing in the other way would be extraordinary.

There's also a way that people can have knowledge without using it, which is like when someone is asleep, mad, or drunk. This is similar to the state of people under the influence of their desires. It's obvious that anger, sexual desire, and other such passions can change our bodily condition and can even make some people act mad. So, we can say that people who lack self-control are like people who are asleep, mad, or drunk. The fact that they use language based on knowledge doesn't prove anything. Even people under these passions can recite scientific proofs or poetry by Empedocles. Those who have just started learning something can repeat the words but don't yet fully understand it. They haven't made the knowledge part of themselves, and that takes time. So we should think that when people in a state of lack of self-control use language, it's no different from an actor reciting lines on a stage.

We can also think about the cause by considering human nature. One opinion is universal, and the other is about particular facts. When both opinions are combined, the soul must accept the conclusion. In cases of practical decisions, the person must immediately act. For example, if "everything sweet should be tasted" and "this is sweet," the person who can act and isn't prevented must immediately act. When the universal opinion is present and tells the person not to taste, but the opinion that "everything sweet is pleasant" and "this is sweet" is active, and when appetite is also present, one opinion tells the person to avoid the sweet thing, but appetite leads them toward it. This is why a person acts against self-control, not because of a contrary opinion but because of appetite. This also explains why animals don't lack self-control—they don't have universal judgments but only imagination and memory of particular things.

The explanation for how ignorance is removed and the person who lacks self-control regains knowledge is the same as for someone who is drunk or asleep. This is something for natural scientists to explain. Since the last premise is about a particular object and it leads to action, the person in a state of passion either doesn't have this knowledge or has it in the sense that knowing doesn't mean fully understanding, like a drunken person reciting the lines of a poem. And because this final term is not universal and isn't an object of scientific knowledge like the universal term, it seems that Socrates was right in saying that true incontinence doesn't arise in the presence of proper knowledge. The problem lies in perceptual knowledge, not in true knowledge.

This is enough to answer the question of how people can act with or without knowledge and how it's possible to act incontinently even when they have knowledge.

We should now discuss whether some people are generally lacking in self-control or whether all of them are lacking in a particular sense, and if so, what kinds of things they are concerned with. It's clear that both people with self-control and people who lack it, as well as people with endurance and those who are soft, are concerned with pleasures and pains.

Some pleasures come from things that are necessary, while others are desirable for their own sake but can be excessive. The bodily pleasures are necessary, such as those related to food and sexual desire. These are the same physical pleasures we mentioned earlier when talking about temperance and self-indulgence. The other pleasures aren't necessary but are still desirable, like victory, honor, wealth, and other good and enjoyable things. So, people who go to excess with these latter pleasures, going against what they know is right, aren't called lacking self-control without qualification. Instead, we say they lack self-control "with respect to money, gain, honor, or anger," because they are different from those who lack self-control in general, and we call them this way because of their resemblance to those who do.

For example, Anthropos (Man) won a contest at the Olympic Games. While the general definition of 'man' didn't differ much from his specific case, it was still different. We can see this because incontinence in general or in relation to physical pleasure is blamed as both a fault and a vice, but no one blames the people who lack control in other respects like that.

As for those who lack self-control with respect to bodily pleasures, which are the same pleasures that temperance and self-indulgence are concerned with, the person who pursues too much pleasure and avoids pain—whether it's hunger, thirst, heat, cold, or other physical sensations—against their better judgment and without choice is called lacking self-control, not with a specific qualification like "with respect to anger," but simply lacking self-control. This is confirmed by the fact that we call people 'soft' with regard to these pleasures, but not with regard to any of the others. That's why we group together the person lacking self-control with the self-indulgent person, and the self-controlled person with the temperate one, but we don't do this with other types of people. This is because they are all concerned with the same pleasures and pains, though they don't respond to them in the same way. Some people make deliberate choices, while others don't.

This is why we should call someone self-indulgent if they seek too much pleasure without having much appetite, or avoid moderate pain, rather than someone who does this because of strong desires. What would the first person do if they also had strong desires and suffered greatly from missing the "necessary" things?

Now, some desires and pleasures are connected to things that are generally good and noble. Some pleasant things are naturally worth choosing, while others are the opposite, and some fall in between, like wealth, profit, victory, and honor. People aren't blamed for being drawn to these things, for desiring or loving them, but for wanting them in the wrong way—that is, for going to excess. This is why people who go against what's right and either are controlled by or pursue one of the naturally noble and good things, like honor or love for children and parents, aren't considered bad. These things are good, and people who focus on them are praised. But there can still be excess, like in the case of Niobe who fought against the gods, or someone as devoted to their father as Satyrus, nicknamed "the filial," who was considered silly for it. So, there's no wickedness connected to these things because they are naturally worth choosing for their own sake. But still, excess is harmful and should be avoided. Similarly, there's no incontinence with these things, because incontinence is not just something to avoid, it's also something blameworthy. But because the feeling is similar, people use the term "incontinence" and add what it refers to, just like we call someone a bad doctor or actor without saying they're completely bad. In the same way, we don't call it incontinence without a qualifier, because these conditions aren't entirely bad, but only like badness. So, it's clear that true incontinence and continence are connected with the same things as temperance and self-indulgence. We use the word incontinence with anger because of the similarity, and this is why we say "incontinent in respect of anger," just like we say "incontinent in respect of honor or gain."

Some things are naturally pleasant. Of these, some are pleasant without exception, while others are pleasant only to specific types of people or animals. There are other things that aren't naturally pleasant, but (1) some become pleasant because of damage to the body, (2) some because of habits, and (3) some because of bad natures. Given this, we can find similar traits in these types of people, like we do in the first type. These are the brutish traits, like in the case of the woman who, they say, rips open pregnant women and eats the babies, or the things that savage tribes near the Black Sea are said to enjoy—like raw meat or human flesh, or even lending their children to each other to eat. Or there's the story of Phalaris.

These traits are brutish, but others come from disease or sometimes madness, like the man who sacrificed and ate his mother, or the slave who ate the liver of his companion. Other cases are bad habits, like pulling out one's hair, biting nails, or even eating coal or dirt, and also pederasty. These can be caused by nature in some people, and in others, they develop as bad habits from childhood.

People whose nature causes them to act this way aren't considered incontinent, just like we don't call women incontinent because they take the passive role in sex. Nor do we call those who act this way because of bad habits incontinent. These habits go beyond vice, just like brutishness does. A man with these habits doesn't experience normal continence or incontinence, but something that's only similar. A man with this problem in regard to anger is called incontinent in anger, but not simply incontinent. All extreme states—whether of foolishness, cowardice, self-indulgence, or bad temper—are either brutish or caused by disease. A man who's naturally afraid of everything, even the squeak of a mouse, is brutish in his cowardice, while a man who feared a weasel did so because of illness. In the case of foolish people, those who are naturally thoughtless and live by their senses are brutish, like some remote barbarian tribes, while others are foolish because of disease (like epilepsy) or madness. Some of these traits only show up sometimes, and people aren't always controlled by them. For example, Phalaris might have resisted the urge to eat a child or avoided unnatural sexual urges. But it's also possible for people to be controlled by these feelings, not just to have them. Just like human wickedness is called wickedness, but not simply wickedness—it's called brutish or diseased. In the same way, some types of incontinence are brutish or diseased, but only the type connected to human self-indulgence is simply incontinence.

It's clear, then, that incontinence and continence are connected to the same things as self-indulgence and temperance. Incontinence related to other things is a different type of incontinence, called incontinence only by metaphor and not in the true sense. Also, incontinence related to anger is less shameful than incontinence related to desires, as we'll now explain. Anger seems to listen to reason in some way, but it mishears it, like hasty servants who run off before they've heard everything, and then mess up the instructions, or like dogs that bark just because they hear a knock, without checking to see if it's a friend. Anger, because it's hot and quick, hears but doesn't really understand an order, and it rushes to take revenge. Reason or imagination tells us that we've been insulted, and anger, reasoning that such things should be resisted, boils up immediately. On the other hand, desire jumps to enjoy something when reason or perception only says that it's pleasant. So, anger follows reason in a way, but desire doesn't. That's why incontinence connected to desires is more shameful, because someone who's incontinent in anger is in some way defeated by reason, while someone controlled by desire is defeated by appetite and not by reason.

Also, we forgive people more easily for following natural desires, because we forgive them more easily for following common desires that everyone has, as long as they aren't excessive. Anger and bad temper are more natural than desires for excessive, unnecessary things. For example, there's the man who defended hitting his father by saying, "Yes, but he hit his father, and he hit his, and" (pointing to his child) "this boy will hit me when he's grown up; it's a family tradition." Or the man who, when being dragged along by his son, asked him to stop at the doorway, because he himself had only dragged his father that far.

Also, those who plot against others are more blameworthy. An angry person doesn't usually plot, and neither does anger itself—it's open. But the nature of desire is like what the poets say about Aphrodite, the "cunning daughter of Cyprus," or Homer's description of her "embroidered girdle":

"And in it is the whisper of seduction,
which steals the wits of the wisest,
however sensible they are."

If this type of incontinence is worse than the type related to anger, then it's both incontinence in the strict sense and, in a way, vice.

Also, no one commits an act of violence because of anger without feeling pain, but everyone who acts violently because of anger feels pain, while someone who acts violently for pleasure does it with enjoyment. If acts done out of anger are the most justifiable, then incontinence driven by desire is worse because there's no justice in violent acts driven by desire.

It's clear, then, that incontinence connected to desire is more shameful than incontinence connected to anger, and continence and incontinence are tied to bodily desires and pleasures. But we need to understand the differences among these pleasures. As we said earlier, some are human and natural in both kind and amount, while others are brutish or result from illness and disease. Temperance and self-indulgence are only concerned with the first type of pleasure. That's why we don't call animals temperate or self-indulgent, except metaphorically, and only if one species of animal is more wanton, destructive, or greedy than another. Animals can't choose or plan; they're simply deviations from the norm, like how madmen deviate from normal humans. Brute behavior is less evil than vice, even though it's scarier, because there's no better part to corrupt in animals as there is in humans. Comparing a lifeless object to a living one in terms of badness is like comparing injustice itself to an unjust person. Both are bad, but a bad person will do far more evil than a brute.

When it comes to pleasures, pains, desires, and dislikes that arise from touch and taste, which temperance and self-indulgence are mostly concerned with, people can either be defeated by even the easiest of these, or they can resist the hardest ones. When it comes to pleasures, incontinence and continence are the relevant traits, while when it comes to pain, softness and endurance are the terms. Most people fall somewhere in the middle, though they often lean toward the worse traits.

Since some pleasures are necessary while others aren't, and since the necessary ones are only necessary to a point, but excesses of them aren't, the person who seeks out too many pleasures or pursues necessary things to an extreme, and does this by choice, for their own sake and not for some other result, is self-indulgent. This person is unlikely to regret their actions and is therefore incurable, because someone who can't regret their actions can't be fixed. The person who doesn't pursue them enough is the opposite of self-indulgent. The person who is in the middle is temperate. Similarly, there's a person who avoids physical pain, not because they're overwhelmed by it, but because they choose to. (Some people are drawn to certain acts because of the pleasure involved, others because they want to avoid the pain that comes from the desire for pleasure, so these types of people are different.) Now, we'd think worse of someone with no desire, or weak desires, if they did something disgraceful than we would if someone did it under the influence of strong desire. We'd also think worse of someone who hit someone else, not in anger, than if they did it out of anger. For what would they have done if they had been strongly affected? This is why the self-indulgent person is worse than the incontinent one. Of these states, softness is a kind of weakness, and self-indulgence is the opposite. The incontinent person is opposed by the continent one, while the soft person is opposed by the person of endurance. Endurance means resisting, while continence means conquering, and resisting and conquering are different, just like not being defeated is different from winning. This is why continence is better than endurance. A person who fails to resist things most people can handle is soft and effeminate. Effeminacy is also a type of softness. This kind of person drags their cloak to avoid the pain of lifting it, and pretends to be sick without thinking they're miserable, though the person they're imitating really is miserable.

The same goes for continence and incontinence. If someone is defeated by violent and overwhelming pleasures or pains, it's not surprising. We're even willing to forgive them if they tried to resist, like Theodectes' Philoctetes when bitten by a snake, or Carcinus' Cercyon in the Alope, or like people who try not to laugh but burst out in laughter anyway, like what happened to Xenophantus. But it's surprising when someone is defeated by, and can't resist, pleasures or pains that most people can handle, when it's not due to heredity or illness, like the softness that runs in the Scythian kings, or the softness that's more common in women than in men.

The person who loves amusement is thought to be self-indulgent, but is really soft. Amusement is a form of rest, since it's a break from work, and the person who loves amusement is one of those who go to excess with it.

There are two types of incontinence: impulsiveness and weakness. Some people, after deciding what's right, fail to stick to their decision because of their emotions. Others, because they don't deliberate at all, are led by their emotions. Some people, like those who first tickle others but don't get tickled themselves, if they've already seen what's coming and have stirred up their rational mind, aren't defeated by their emotions, whether the emotion is pleasant or painful. It's quick and excitable people who suffer the most from impulsive incontinence. Quick people, because they're so fast, and excitable people, because their passions are so strong, don't wait for reasoning to catch up, because they tend to follow their imagination.

The self-indulgent person, as we've said, is unlikely to regret their actions, because they stick to their choices. But the incontinent person is more likely to regret. This is why, contrary to how we initially framed the issue, the self-indulgent person is incurable, while the incontinent person can be cured. Wickedness is like a disease, like dropsy or tuberculosis, while incontinence is like epilepsy. Wickedness is a lasting problem, while incontinence comes and goes. In general, incontinence and vice are different in nature. Vice doesn't realize its own nature, but incontinence does. Of incontinent people, those who temporarily lose control are better than those who have reason but fail to follow it. The latter are defeated by weaker emotions and don't act without thinking first, unlike the former. The incontinent person is like someone who gets drunk easily and quickly on a small amount of wine, less than what most people would need.

It's clear, then, that incontinence isn't the same as vice (though in some cases it might be). Incontinence goes against choice, while vice aligns with choice. However, both lead to similar actions. As Demodocus said of the Milesians, "The Milesians aren't without sense, but they do senseless things." Similarly, incontinent people aren't criminals, but they do criminal acts.

Since the incontinent person tends to pursue excessive bodily pleasures against their better judgment, while the self-indulgent person pursues them because that's just who they are, it's easier to persuade the incontinent person to change, while it's harder to change the self-indulgent person. Virtue and vice either preserve or destroy the first principle, and in actions, the final cause is the first principle, just like in math the hypotheses are the first principles. In neither case does reasoning teach the first principles. Here, it's virtue, either natural or developed by habit, that teaches the right opinion about the first principle. A temperate person is like this. The opposite is the self-indulgent person.

But there's a person who is driven by passion and acts against the right rule. Their passion controls them so they don't follow the right rule, but it doesn't control them to the point where they believe they should pursue such pleasures without limit. This is the incontinent person, who is better than the self-indulgent person and not entirely bad, because the best part of them, the first principle, is still intact. Opposite to them is the person who sticks to their beliefs and isn't swayed by passion. From these points, it's clear that the latter state is good, and the former is bad.

Is someone continent if they stick to any rule or choice, or if they stick to the right rule? Is someone incontinent if they abandon any rule or choice, or if they abandon the right rule and the correct choice? We raised this question earlier. Or is it true that people only incidentally stick to any rule or choice, but in reality, they stick to the true rule and right choice, and abandon what is wrong? If someone chooses this for the sake of that, they're really choosing the latter, but only incidentally the former. When we speak without any qualification, we mean what is true in itself. Therefore, in a sense, the continent person sticks to any opinion, and the incontinent person abandons any opinion, but without qualification, the continent person sticks to the true opinion.

Some people are very stubborn and stick to their own opinions. We call these people "strong-headed." These people are hard to convince at first, and even after that, they don't easily change their minds. They are similar to people who have self-control, just like a person who wastes money is somewhat like a generous person, and a reckless person is a little like someone who is brave. But there are many differences between them. The strong-headed person doesn't give in to their feelings or desires, while someone with self-control might be convinced sometimes. The strong-headed person refuses to listen to reason. They still have desires, and many of them are led by their pleasures. These stubborn people are usually opinionated, ignorant, or rude, and their opinions are influenced by feelings of happiness or sadness. They feel proud if they don't change their minds, like they've won something, but they feel disappointed when their decisions are rejected, much like how sometimes a law can lose its power. In this way, they are more like people who can't control themselves than those who can.

However, some people don't stick to their decisions, not because they lack self-control, but for other reasons, like Neoptolemus in Sophocles' play Philoctetes. He changed his mind not because of shameful pleasure, but because of a good reason—he thought telling the truth was the right thing to do, even though Odysseus had convinced him to lie. So, not everyone who changes for pleasure is self-indulgent or bad; only those who do it for shameful reasons are.

There are also people who enjoy physical things less than they should and don't follow the proper path. A person who is somewhere between this kind of person and one who lacks self-control is a person with self-control. The person without self-control breaks the rules because they enjoy physical things too much, while the other breaks the rules by not enjoying them enough. The person with self-control, however, follows the rules and doesn't let either extreme affect them. Since self-control is good, both of these opposite states must be bad, as they usually seem to be. But because the other extreme is less common, we often think that self-control is only the opposite of self-indulgence, just as temperance is the opposite of self-indulgence.

Since many words are used similarly, we also use the word "self-control" to describe both a person with self-control and a temperate person. Both of these types of people don't do anything against the rules because of physical pleasures. The person with self-control still has bad desires but doesn't act on them, while the temperate person doesn't feel any pleasure that goes against the rules. The self-indulgent person and the person without self-control are similar, too. Both pursue physical pleasures, but the self-indulgent person believes they should, while the person without self-control does not.

A person cannot be wise and lack self-control at the same time. A person who has wisdom is also good in terms of character. A wise person not only knows what is right but can also act on it, while the person without self-control cannot. However, it's possible for a clever person to lack self-control. This is why some people mistakenly believe a clever person is wise, even if they lack self-control.

Cleverness and wisdom are similar in how they think, but they are different in their purpose. The person without self-control is not like someone who fully understands the truth but more like someone who is asleep or drunk. They act willingly in some way, knowing what they are doing and why, but they are not evil because their purpose is still good. In this way, they are only halfway to being bad. They are not criminals because they don't act out of malice. Of the two types of people without self-control, one type can't stick to their decisions after thinking things through, and the other doesn't think things through at all. So, a person without self-control is like a city that has good laws but doesn't follow them, like in Anaxandrides' joke, "The city made a law but doesn't care about laws." The wicked person is like a city that follows its laws, but those laws are bad.

Self-control and the lack of it deal with extremes compared to what is normal for most people. The person with self-control sticks to their decisions more than most people, and the person without self-control sticks to them less than most people can.

Among the types of people without self-control, those who act quickly are easier to fix than those who think things through but fail to follow their own decisions. People who lack self-control because of habit are easier to change than those who are naturally this way because it's easier to change a habit than to change one's nature. Even though habits are hard to break because they become like nature, as the poet Evenus says:

"I say that habit is just long practice, my friend, And it becomes people's nature in the end."

We have now explained what self-control, lack of self-control, endurance, and softness are, and how these states are connected to one another.

The study of pleasure and pain belongs to the political philosopher because it helps us understand what is good and bad in the purest sense. It's important to examine these things because we said that virtue and vice are tied to pleasures and pains. Most people also say that happiness includes pleasure, which is why we call happy people "blessed," using a word that suggests enjoyment.

Some people think that no pleasure is a good thing in itself, while others think that some pleasures are good, but most are bad. A third view is that even if all pleasures are good, the best thing in the world is not pleasure. The arguments for these views include: (1) Every pleasure is a process toward a natural state, and no process is the same as its result, like how building a house is not the same as the house itself. (2) A temperate person avoids pleasure. (3) A wise person seeks freedom from pain, not pleasure. (4) Pleasures get in the way of thinking, especially intense pleasures like sexual pleasure. (5) There is no art of pleasure, and all good things come from some kind of art. (6) Both children and animals seek pleasure.

The arguments for the idea that not all pleasures are good include: (1) Some pleasures are shameful, and (2) Some pleasures are harmful to health. Finally, the argument that the best thing isn't pleasure is based on the idea that pleasure is a process, not an end result.

These are the main points of these arguments. But these reasons don't necessarily prove that pleasure isn't a good thing, or even the best thing. First, good things can be good in different ways—some are simply good, while others are good for certain people. In the same way, natural states and the actions that come from them can be divided this way, too. Some things that seem bad might only be bad for some people or for a short time, but not bad in general. Others only seem like pleasures, but they actually involve pain and are just healing processes, like what happens to sick people.

Also, there are two types of good things: activities and states of being. The processes that restore us to our natural state are only pleasant by accident. The pleasure comes from the part of our nature that isn't damaged. Some pleasures, like those from contemplation, don't involve pain or desire at all. This shows that the other pleasures are only accidental because people don't enjoy the same things when they are healthy as when they are recovering. When they're recovering, they enjoy even things that are sharp or bitter, which aren't naturally pleasant.

It's also wrong to say that pleasure is always a process. Pleasures are more like activities that come from a natural state. Some people confuse pleasure with process because they think activities are processes, but they are not.

The argument that some pleasures are bad because they can harm your health is like saying that health is bad because some healthy things are bad for making money. Both are bad in certain ways, but not bad overall. Even thinking can sometimes harm your health.

Pleasures that come from the activity of practical wisdom don't get in the way, but foreign pleasures do. For example, the pleasures of learning and thinking help us do those activities better.

The fact that there is no art of pleasure is because there is no art for any other activity either—just for the ability to do them. But people think that the arts of cooking and perfume-making are arts of pleasure.

The arguments that temperate people avoid pleasure and that wise people seek a painless life, and that animals and children seek pleasure, are all answered in the same way. We've already pointed out in what way pleasures are good or not. Both animals and children seek the wrong kind of pleasures, the ones that involve desire and pain—bodily pleasures. Wise people seek calmness and freedom from these desires. That's why temperate people avoid bodily pleasures, though they still have pleasures of their own.

It's also widely agreed that pain is bad and something we should avoid. Some pain is bad without question, and other kinds of pain are bad because they get in the way of our lives. The opposite of something bad is good, so pleasure must also be good. Speusippus' argument that pleasure is opposed to both pain and good things, like how more is opposed to less and equal, doesn't work because he wouldn't say that pleasure is a kind of evil.

Even if some pleasures are bad, that doesn't mean the highest good can't be a pleasure. Just like how the highest good can be a kind of knowledge, even though some kinds of knowledge are bad. If happiness is the unimpeded activity of our natural state, and activities are pleasant, then the highest good might well be a pleasure. This is why all people think the happy life is also a pleasant one. No activity is perfect when it is blocked, and happiness is the most perfect state. That's why the happy person needs physical and external goods, not because happiness depends on them, but to avoid being hindered. People who say a person being tortured on the rack can still be happy because they are good are mistaken.

We need external things to be happy, which is why some people think good fortune is the same as happiness. But it isn't. Even good fortune, when it goes too far, can get in the way, and then it's no longer good fortune. Happiness has a limit when it comes to external things.

Finally, the fact that all animals and people pursue pleasure suggests that pleasure is somehow the highest good. Even though not everyone seeks the same pleasures, and not all pleasures are good, everyone still seeks pleasure because it is part of our nature. Bodily pleasures are common and shared by all, which is why people think they are the only pleasures.

It's also clear that if pleasure is not good, the happy person wouldn't need it. But if pleasure isn't a good, then pain can't be bad either, and the good person's life wouldn't be any more pleasant than anyone else's life. If their activities aren't more pleasant, why would they avoid pain?

Regarding bodily pleasures, some people think noble pleasures should be chosen but not bodily ones, like those the self-indulgent person pursues. But why, then, are the opposite of these pains considered bad? Necessary pleasures are good, even if not as good as noble ones, because their opposite, pain, is bad.

We also need to explain why bodily pleasures seem more desirable than they really are. First, it's because they relieve pain. People experience so much pain that they seek extreme bodily pleasure to get rid of it. Relief from pain makes these pleasures seem better than they are. Also, some pleasures come from a bad nature or bad habits, like those of animals or bad people. Others are meant to cure a problem, but being healthy is better than getting healthy. These pleasures only seem good because they are part of a healing process.

Second, some people pursue intense pleasures because they can't enjoy anything else. They create artificial desires, like thirst, just to satisfy them. When these desires aren't harmful, it's okay, but when they are harmful, it's bad. These people can't enjoy the more subtle pleasures because their nature is restless. Young people and those with a lot of energy are always in need of release. Their bodies are always uncomfortable because of their unique makeup, and they are driven by strong desires. This is why they seek intense pleasures and become self-indulgent. But pleasures that don't come with pain can't be excessive. These are the natural pleasures that are good on their own, not by accident.

When we talk about things that are pleasant by accident, we mean those that act as cures. We think these processes are pleasant because they help fix something that is wrong in our nature. Natural pleasures, on the other hand, are those that stimulate healthy parts of our nature.

There isn't one thing that is always pleasant because our nature isn't simple. We have another part to us since we are mortal creatures. So, if one part of us is doing something, it can feel unnatural to the other part of our nature. When both parts are balanced, what we do doesn't feel either painful or pleasant. If our nature were simple, the same action would always be the most enjoyable. This is why God experiences a single and simple pleasure all the time. There's not only an activity of movement but also an activity of stillness, and pleasure is found more in rest than in movement. But, as the poet says, "change in all things is sweet," and this is because of some kind of flaw. Just like how a flawed person is always changing, a nature that constantly needs change is flawed because it's not simple or good.

We've now talked about continence and incontinence, and about pleasure and pain—what each of these is and how some of them are good and others are bad. What's left is to discuss friendship.

Book 8

After everything we've discussed, it makes sense to now talk about friendship, because it is either a virtue or involves virtue, and it is essential for living well. No one would want to live without friends, even if they had all other good things in life. Even rich people and those with power are thought to need friends the most. What good is success without people to help and share it with, especially with friends, who deserve it the most? How can success be maintained without friends to protect it? The more success someone has, the more they are at risk of losing it. In times of poverty and misfortune, people feel that friends are their only source of comfort. Friendship helps young people avoid mistakes, and it supports older people by taking care of their needs and helping with the things they can't do because of weakness. Friendship also inspires people in their prime to do great things—"two people working together." With friends, people are better at both thinking and acting. Parents naturally feel friendship for their children, and children for their parents. This is true not just for humans but also for birds and most animals. People of the same race also feel friendship for each other, especially among humans, which is why we praise those who love humanity. We even notice this when we travel and see how every person seems to be connected to others. Friendship also seems to be what holds communities together, and lawmakers seem to value friendship even more than justice. Unity is something like friendship, and lawmakers strive for this, while removing division as their greatest enemy. When people are friends, they don't need justice, but when they are just, they still need friendship. The highest form of justice is thought to be something like friendship.

Friendship is not only necessary, but also noble. We praise those who love their friends, and it is considered a good thing to have many friends. We also believe that good people are the same people who make good friends.

There is much debate about friendship. Some say that friendship is based on similarity, and that similar people become friends. This is where sayings like "like attracts like" and "birds of a feather flock together" come from. Others, however, say, "two of a trade never agree." People have also asked deeper questions about this, like Euripides' saying that "dry land loves rain, and the sky filled with rain loves to fall to earth," or Heraclitus' idea that "what is opposite helps" and "the best harmony comes from different notes" and "all things are born from conflict." Empedocles, along with others, says the opposite: "like attracts like." These are physical questions that we can leave for now because they aren't part of this discussion. Let's focus on the human aspects, like whether friendship can form between any two people, or whether wicked people can be friends. Is there only one type of friendship, or are there different kinds? Those who believe there is only one kind of friendship say this because they think friendship can vary in degree. But even things that are different in kind can vary in degree. We've already discussed this point before.

The kinds of friendship may become clearer if we first understand what it is that people love. Not everything is loved—only what is lovable. The lovable is something that is good, pleasant, or useful. Something useful is what brings about some good or pleasure. So, the good and the useful are loved as ends. Do people love the good itself, or what is good for them? These things sometimes conflict. The same goes for what is pleasant. It's believed that each person loves what is good for themselves, and that what is good is lovable in general, but what is good for each person is lovable for them specifically. But each person doesn't love what is truly good for them, but what seems good to them. This difference doesn't matter much, though; we just have to say that "the lovable" is "what seems lovable."

There are three main reasons why people love something. We don't call the love of non-living things friendship, because it's not mutual love, and we don't wish good things for the non-living object itself. For example, it would be silly to say you wish wine well; if you wish anything for it, it's that it stays good so you can enjoy it. But for a friend, we should wish what is good for them for their sake. If someone wishes good for another person, but the feeling isn't returned, we call this goodwill, not friendship. Goodwill becomes friendship only when the feeling is returned and recognized. Many people feel goodwill toward those they've never met but believe to be good or useful. If this feeling is returned, they seem to have goodwill for each other, but we can't really call them friends if they don't know how the other person feels. To be friends, people must recognize that they both have goodwill and wish good for each other for one of the reasons mentioned.

These reasons are different from each other, and so are the types of love and friendship that come from them. There are three kinds of friendship, based on the three things that are lovable. For each of these, there is mutual and recognized love, and those who love each other wish each other well for the reason they love one another. People who love each other for their usefulness don't love each other for who they are, but for the good they get from each other. The same goes for those who love for pleasure—they don't love someone for their character but because they find them enjoyable. So, people who love for usefulness love for what is good for themselves, and those who love for pleasure love for what is pleasant to themselves. They don't love the person for who they are, but for how they are useful or enjoyable. These types of friendships are only based on circumstances. The loved person isn't loved for who they are, but for providing some good or pleasure. These friendships end easily if the person is no longer pleasant or useful.

What is useful doesn't last, and it always changes. When the reason for the friendship disappears, so does the friendship, because it only existed for a particular purpose. This kind of friendship is most common among older people, because at that age, people look for what is useful, not what is pleasant. Younger people, or those in their prime, seek friendships based on utility, too. These people don't spend much time together because they don't always enjoy each other's company. They only need each other when they are useful. They only find each other pleasant when they expect to get something good in the future. Friendships between host and guest also fall into this category.

Friendships between young people, on the other hand, seem to be based on pleasure. Young people live by their emotions and mostly chase what is pleasant to themselves at the moment. But as they grow older, their pleasures change. This is why young people become friends quickly and lose friendships just as fast. Their friendship changes with whatever they find enjoyable, and their pleasures change quickly. Young people also fall in love easily because most of their romantic friendships are based on emotions and the pursuit of pleasure. This is why they fall in love quickly and fall out of love just as fast, sometimes in a single day. But these people do want to spend their days and lives together, because this is how they fulfill the purpose of their friendship.

Perfect friendship is the friendship between good people who are alike in virtue. These friends wish well to each other because they are good, and they are good people themselves. People who wish well to their friends for their friends' sake are the truest friends. They do this because of who they are, not because of any outside factor. So, their friendship lasts as long as they are good—and goodness is something that lasts. These friends are good in general and good to each other, because good people are both good overall and useful to each other. They are also pleasant to each other because good people are pleasant in general and pleasant to each other. Each person finds their own activities and those of similar people enjoyable, and the actions of good people are either the same or similar. Such a friendship is permanent because it has all the qualities that friendship should have. All friendship is based on the desire for something good or pleasant— whether that good or pleasure is abstract or something the friend enjoys—and is based on a certain similarity. In the case of good people, all the qualities of friendship we've discussed belong to them because of who they are. For this kind of friendship, the other qualities are similar in both friends, and what is good without qualification is also pleasant without qualification. These are the most lovable qualities. Love and friendship, then, are found most often and in their best form between good people.

It is natural for such friendships to be rare because people like this are hard to find. Also, this kind of friendship takes time and familiarity to form. As the saying goes, people can't know each other until they've "eaten salt together." They can't become friends or be friends until each has been found lovable and trustworthy. Those who quickly show signs of friendship may want to be friends, but they aren't true friends until they both recognize the other as lovable and know this to be true. A desire for friendship can form quickly, but real friendship takes time.

This kind of friendship is perfect in both how long it lasts and in all other ways. In it, each friend gives and receives the same thing, or something similar to what they give. This is how things should be between friends. Friendships based on pleasure are similar to this kind of friendship, because good people also find each other pleasant. Friendships based on utility are also similar because good people are useful to each other, too. Friendships between lesser people tend to last longer when both friends get the same thing from each other, like pleasure, and also when they get this from the same source. This happens with witty people, for example, but not with lovers. Lovers do not enjoy the same things—the lover enjoys seeing their beloved, and the beloved enjoys receiving attention. When youth fades, the friendship often fades, too, because one no longer finds pleasure in seeing the other, and the other no longer receives attention. But many lovers stay together when they come to love each other's character through familiarity, especially if their characters are alike. Those who love each other for utility or pleasure are less likely to be true friends and less likely to stay friends for long. Those who are friends for utility part ways when they no longer benefit from each other, because they didn't love each other but loved the profit they gained.

When it comes to friendship for pleasure or utility, even bad people can be friends, or a good person can be friends with a bad person, or someone who is neither good nor bad can be friends with any kind of person. But when it comes to friendship for its own sake, only good people can truly be friends because bad people don't take pleasure in each other unless they get something from it.

Friendship between good people is the only type that cannot be harmed by slander. It's hard to believe bad things about someone you've known and trusted for a long time. Among good people, you find trust, the belief that "he would never wrong me," and all the other qualities that make true friendship. But in the other kinds of friendship, these problems can easily arise. People use the word "friend" even when their relationship is based on utility, like how alliances between states are made for mutual advantage. Friendships based on pleasure are like the friendships between children. So, we should probably call these people friends, too, and say that there are different kinds of friendship. The highest and truest form is the friendship between good people, but the other types are friendships by analogy. They are friends because of something good and something like what we find in true friendship, since even pleasure is good to those who love pleasure. These two kinds of friendship (pleasure and utility) are rarely combined, and people don't usually become friends for both pleasure and utility at the same time. Things that are only related by chance don't often come together.

Friendship is divided into these kinds. Bad people can be friends for the sake of pleasure or utility because they are alike in that way, but good people are friends for each other's sake because of their goodness. These are true friends, while the others are friends only by coincidence and because they resemble true friends.

Just as with virtue, some people are called good because of their character, while others are called good because of their actions. The same is true for friendship. Those who live together enjoy each other's company and help each other, but those who are apart or asleep aren't performing the activities of friendship, though they are ready to do so. Distance doesn't destroy friendship, but it stops the activity of it. However, if the distance lasts too long, people can forget their friendship. This is why people say, "out of sight, out of mind." Older people and sour people don't seem to make friends easily because they aren't very pleasant, and no one can spend time with someone who is unpleasant. Nature avoids what is painful and seeks what is pleasant. People who like each other but don't spend time together seem to have goodwill for each other rather than real friendship. There's nothing more characteristic of friends than living together. Even people who need something from others want their company, and those who are perfectly happy still want to spend their time with friends. Solitude is not good for these people. But people can't live together if they aren't pleasant and don't enjoy the same things, as friends who are companions do.

The truest friendship, as we've said many times, is the friendship of good people. What is good or pleasant without qualification is lovable and desirable, and for each person, what is good or pleasant to them is lovable. The good person is lovable and desirable to another good person for both reasons. It seems that love is a feeling, while friendship is more of a character trait. You can love non-living things, but friendship involves mutual choice, and choice comes from character. People wish good things for those they love, for their sake, not just because of a feeling but because of their character. When you love a friend, you love what is good for yourself, because a good person, in becoming a friend, also becomes a good thing for their friend. Each person loves what is good for themselves and returns this love equally with goodwill and pleasantness. Friendship is said to be based on equality, and this is most true in the friendship of good people.

Friendship doesn't easily form between sour or older people because they aren't as good-natured and don't enjoy company as much. These are considered the most important qualities for forming friendship. This is why younger people make friends more quickly than older people. It's because people don't become friends with those they don't find pleasant. The same goes for sour people—they don't make friends quickly. But these people may still have goodwill for each other because they wish each other well and help each other when needed. However, they aren't truly friends because they don't spend time together or enjoy each other's company. These two things are considered the most important parts of friendship.

You can't be a true friend to many people, just as you can't be in love with many people at once. Love is an intense feeling, and by nature, it can only be directed toward one person. It's also hard for many people to please the same person greatly, or to be considered good in the eyes of the same person. It also takes time to get to know someone and become familiar with them, and that's difficult to do with many people. However, when it comes to friendship based on utility or pleasure, it's possible to be friends with many people because many people can be useful or pleasant, and these kinds of relationships don't require as much time.

Of these two kinds of friendship, the one based on pleasure is more like true friendship, especially when both people get the same things from each other and enjoy each other's company, like in the friendships of young people. There is more generosity in these friendships. Friendships based on utility are more common among business-minded people. Those who are perfectly happy don't need friends for utility, but they do need friends for pleasure. They want to live with someone, and while they can endure what is painful for a short time, no one could put up with pain forever, not even if it came from something good. This is why they look for friends who are pleasant. Perhaps they should find friends who are both pleasant and good for them. That way, they will have all the qualities that friends should have.

People in positions of power tend to have friends who fall into two different groups: some are useful, and some are fun to be around. It's rare to find someone who is both useful and fun. They don't look for people whose fun side comes with virtue or whose usefulness is aimed at good things. Instead, they look for funny, witty people to entertain them, and other friends they choose are good at doing what they're told. These qualities rarely go together in one person.

We've already said that a good person is both fun and useful. However, a good person doesn't usually become friends with someone higher in status unless that person is also better in virtue. If they aren't, there's no equality in the friendship because one person isn't better in both ways. But finding someone who is better in both ways is not easy.

Still, the friendships we've talked about are about equality. Friends give and receive the same things from each other and want the same things for each other. Or, they might trade one thing for another, like fun for usefulness. However, we've already said that these types of friendships are less true and don't last as long.

People think these are friendships because they seem similar to friendships based on virtue. One involves fun, and the other involves usefulness. Both fun and usefulness are also part of virtuous friendships. However, these friendships don't last long and are not as strong against gossip and rumors as virtuous friendships are. So, they don't seem like true friendships because they are different from friendships based on virtue in many ways.

There's another type of friendship that involves inequality, like the friendship between a father and son, an older person and a younger person, or between a husband and wife. These friendships are also different from each other. The relationship between a parent and child isn't the same as the one between a ruler and a subject, and even a father's relationship with his son isn't the same as the son's relationship with his father. The same goes for husbands and wives. Each person has different roles and virtues, and they love each other for different reasons. This means the love and the friendship are different as well.

In these friendships, each person doesn't give or receive the same things from the other, and they shouldn't expect to. But when children give their parents what they owe them for bringing them into the world, and parents give their children what they need, these friendships will be lasting and excellent. In friendships where there is inequality, the love should also be unequal. The person who is better should be loved more than they love, and the more useful person should be loved more as well. When the love matches the merit of each person, a kind of equality is created, which is what we expect in friendship.

However, equality in friendship doesn't seem to work the same way as it does in justice. In justice, what's most important is proportional equality—each person gets what they deserve based on their merit. But in friendship, equal amounts of love and affection come first, and proportional merit comes second. This becomes clear when there's a big difference in virtue, wealth, or anything else between two people. They stop being friends because they no longer expect to be. This is especially clear with the gods, who are far greater than us in every way. It's also true for kings because people who are much lower in status don't expect to be friends with kings, just like ordinary people don't expect to be friends with the best or wisest people.

It's hard to say exactly how much difference two people can handle before they stop being friends. Friendship can still survive even if one person becomes a little different, but when one person becomes too different—like the difference between people and gods—friendship is no longer possible. This is why people wonder whether friends really want the greatest good for their friends, like becoming gods. If a friend becomes a god, they won't be friends anymore, and that wouldn't be a good thing for them. The answer is that a friend wants good things for their friend as long as they stay the same person they are now. So, they want the greatest good for their friend, but only as long as they stay human. But not every great thing; each person mostly wants the best things for themselves.

Most people seem to want to be loved more than they want to love. This is because of ambition, and it's why many people love flattery. The flatterer acts like a friend who is lower in status and pretends to love more than they are loved. Being loved is similar to being honored, which is something most people aim for. But people don't want honor for its own sake. Most people enjoy being honored by important people because they believe it will help them get what they want in the future. So, they like honor because it's a sign that good things will come. People who want honor from good people, or people who know them well, aim to confirm their own belief in their goodness. They enjoy honor because it makes them believe they are good based on what others think.

On the other hand, people enjoy being loved just for the sake of being loved. This makes it seem like being loved is better than being honored, and friendship seems to be desirable in itself. But it seems that loving is more important than being loved, as shown by how much mothers love their children. Some mothers give their children to others to raise, and as long as they know their children are okay, they love them even if they don't get love in return. They are happy just to see their children do well. Mothers still love their children even if the children don't know enough to return their love.

Since friendship depends more on loving, and people who love their friends are praised, it seems like loving is the main virtue of friendship. Only those who love in the right way can have lasting friendships, and only their friendships last over time.

This is also how unequal people can still be friends; their love can be made equal. Equality and similarity are what friendship is about, especially when it comes to people who are similar in virtue. Virtuous people are steady and loyal to each other. They don't ask for or offer bad favors, and they even stop each other from doing wrong. Good people try to keep themselves and their friends from doing anything bad.

Wicked people, however, are not steady. They don't even stay the same as themselves. They become friends for a short time because they enjoy each other's wickedness. Friendships based on usefulness or pleasure last longer because the friends continue to enjoy each other's company or benefit from each other. Friendships based on usefulness seem to happen most easily between opposites, like rich and poor, or ignorant and knowledgeable, because people want what they lack, and each gives something different in return. This can also be true in the case of lovers, where one is beautiful, and the other isn't.

Sometimes lovers seem ridiculous when they demand to be loved as much as they love, especially if they aren't equally lovable. Their demand might make sense if they were equally lovable, but if they aren't, it's silly. Still, opposites don't always seek each other out on purpose, but more by accident. What people really want is something in the middle, because that's what's best for them. For example, it's better for something dry not to become wet, but to reach a balanced, in-between state. The same goes for hot and cold and other opposites. We don't need to get too deep into this because it's not really the focus of our discussion.

Friendship and justice seem to focus on the same things and apply to the same people, as we said at the beginning. In every group, there seems to be some kind of justice and some kind of friendship. People call their fellow travelers and soldiers their friends, and the same goes for those they are connected to in other types of groups. The extent of their connection is the extent of their friendship, just as the extent of their connection determines how much justice exists between them. The saying "friends share everything" is true because friendship depends on sharing. Brothers and close friends share everything, but other friends share specific things—some more, some less. Friendships can be more or less true friendships, just like there are different levels of justice. The duties parents owe to their children aren't the same as those brothers owe each other, and the duties of close friends aren't the same as those of fellow citizens. The same is true for other kinds of friendship.

Because of this, there's also a difference in what it means to act unjustly toward each type of friend. It's worse to cheat a close friend than a fellow citizen, and worse not to help a brother than a stranger. It's also worse to hurt a father than anyone else. The demands of justice seem to grow stronger as the friendship becomes closer, which shows that friendship and justice apply to the same people and work in similar ways.

All kinds of groups are like smaller parts of a political community. People come together in groups for some specific advantage, to get something they need for their lives. This is also why political communities originally formed and why they still exist—people want what's best for the whole group. This is what lawmakers focus on when they create laws, and they call just what benefits everyone. Other groups aim for specific advantages, like sailors trying to make money on a voyage or soldiers trying to win a war. People in villages or religious groups act the same way. Some groups form for the sake of pleasure, like religious gatherings or social clubs. These groups exist for offering sacrifices and socializing.

But these groups are still part of the larger political community, which aims not just for short-term benefits but for what's good for life as a whole. They offer sacrifices, arrange gatherings, and assign honors to the gods, all while giving themselves some time to relax and enjoy life. These activities usually happen after the harvest when people have the most free time. So, all groups seem to be part of the larger political community, and the type of friendship depends on the type of group.

There are three main types of government, and each has a corrupted version of it. The good types are monarchy, aristocracy, and government based on property, which is often called "timocracy," although some people call it a "polity." Of these, monarchy is the best, and timocracy is the worst. The corrupted version of monarchy is tyranny. Both are types of one-man rule, but they are very different. A tyrant rules for his own benefit, while a king rules for the benefit of his people. A man is only a king if he doesn't need anything for himself and is better than his subjects in every way. A man like this doesn't have to worry about himself, so he focuses on what's good for his people. A king who doesn't act like this is just a king in name only.

Tyranny is the exact opposite of this. A tyrant only cares about himself. This is why tyranny is the worst form of government—it's the opposite of the best. Monarchy turns into tyranny when a bad king becomes a tyrant. Aristocracy turns into oligarchy when the rulers become corrupt. They divide the wealth of the city unfairly, keeping most of it for themselves and giving important jobs to the same small group of people. In this way, a few bad people end up in power instead of the best people. Timocracy turns into democracy because democracy is just timocracy taken a step further. Timocracy is government by the majority, and in democracy, everyone is considered equal if they meet the property requirement. Democracy is the least bad of the corrupted forms because it's only a small step away from timocracy.

These are the changes that governments are most likely to go through because they are the easiest and smallest transitions.

You can see examples of these types of governments even in households. The way a father deals with his children is like a monarchy because the father cares for them. This is why Homer calls Zeus "father." The ideal of monarchy is for it to be like a father's rule. However, in Persian families, the father's rule is more like a tyranny because they treat their sons like slaves. Tyranny is also like the way a master rules over his slaves because it's only for the master's benefit. This might seem like a proper form of government, but the Persian version is corrupt because different types of relationships should be governed in different ways.

The relationship between a man and his wife is like an aristocracy because the husband rules based on his worth. In matters where he should lead, he does, but in areas that suit his wife's abilities, he lets her handle them. If the husband tries to rule over everything, the relationship becomes more like an oligarchy because he's not ruling based on what's right. Sometimes, the wife rules because she's an heiress, and in that case, her rule is based on wealth and power rather than virtue, like in an oligarchy. The relationship between brothers is like timocracy because they are mostly equal, except for differences in age. If the age gap is too big, the friendship is no longer a brotherly one.

Democracy is seen in households where there's no clear leader, and everyone is treated equally. It's also found in households where the head of the family is weak, and everyone does as they please.

Each of these types of government involves friendship, just like they involve justice. The friendship between a king and his subjects depends on the king's ability to do good things for them. A good king takes care of his people like a shepherd cares for his sheep. This is why Homer called Agamemnon the "shepherd of the people." The friendship between a father and his children is even stronger because the father gives the greatest gifts: life, care, and upbringing.

Ancestors are respected for the same reasons. By nature, a father rules over his children, ancestors rule over their descendants, and a king rules over his people. These friendships are based on the superiority of one person over the other, which is why ancestors are honored. Justice in these relationships isn't the same for both sides. It's based on what each person deserves, just like the friendship is. The friendship between a man and his wife is like an aristocracy because the better person gets more of the good things, and each person gets what suits them. The same is true for justice in these relationships. The friendship between brothers is like the friendship between comrades because they are equal in age and similar in feelings and character. This is also similar to the friendship in timocratic governments, where the goal is for all citizens to be equal and fair. The leadership is shared equally, and the friendship fits this kind of equality.

In the corrupted forms of government, there is little friendship, just as there is little justice. The worst form of government, tyranny, has almost no friendship. Where there's nothing shared between the ruler and the ruled, there's no friendship because there's no justice. For example, there's no friendship between a craftsman and his tool, between the soul and the body, or between a master and a slave. The tool benefits its user, but there's no friendship or justice toward lifeless things. The same is true for horses or oxen, and even for slaves as slaves. There's nothing shared between a master and a slave. The slave is a living tool, and the tool is a lifeless slave. As a slave, a person can't be a friend, but as a human, they can be. There can be some justice between any two people who are part of a system of law or agreement, and so there can also be friendship between them as humans.

In tyrannies, there's almost no friendship or justice. But in democracies, there's more of both because the citizens are equal and have more in common.

Every type of friendship involves some kind of partnership, as we've said. But we can separate the friendships of family members and comrades from the rest. Friendships between fellow citizens, members of the same tribe, or people traveling together seem more like partnerships because they are based on agreements. We can also include the friendships between hosts and guests in this group. Family friendships seem to come in many forms, but they all depend on the parent-child relationship. Parents love their children because they are a part of themselves, and children love their parents because they come from them.

Parents know their children better than children know their parents, and the parent feels a stronger connection to the child than the child feels to the parent. The child comes from the parent, not the other way around. Also, parents start loving their children as soon as they are born, but children only start loving their parents later when they gain understanding. This explains why mothers love their children more than fathers do.

Parents love their children as they love themselves because children are like another version of them. Children love their parents because they were born from them, and brothers love each other because they share the same parents. This is why people talk about "the same blood" or "the same family." In a way, brothers are the same person in different bodies. Two things that help build friendship are being raised together and being close in age. "People of the same age stick together," and people who grow up together tend to be comrades. This is why the friendship between brothers is similar to that of comrades. Cousins and other relatives are connected because they come from brothers or the same ancestors. They are closer or more distant based on how close the original ancestor is to them.

The friendship between children and parents, and between humans and gods, is based on viewing them as something good and superior. Parents and gods give the greatest gifts—they are the reason for their existence, nourishment, and education from birth. This kind of friendship is more pleasant and useful than friendship with strangers because they live more closely together. The friendship between brothers is similar to that of comrades, especially when they are good people. In general, people who are alike become friends more easily because they share more with each other, and brothers naturally love each other from birth. Since they are born to the same parents, grow up together, and receive the same education, they tend to be more similar in character. The test of time strengthens and confirms their bond.

Friendship among other relatives is proportional to the closeness of the relationship. The friendship between a husband and wife seems to be natural because humans are naturally inclined to form couples, even more than to form cities. The household comes before the city, and reproduction is a common drive in both humans and animals. While animals unite only for reproduction, humans live together not just for this purpose but also for the various needs of life. From the start, their roles are divided, with men and women contributing different skills to the household. This cooperation makes their friendship both useful and pleasant. If the husband and wife are good people, their friendship can also be based on virtue, as each has their own virtues, and they take pleasure in them. Children seem to strengthen the bond between them, which is why childless couples tend to separate more easily. Children are a shared good, and what is shared tends to keep people together.

The way a husband and wife, or any friends, should treat each other is similar to how justice requires them to act. A person doesn't owe the same duties to a friend as they do to a stranger, a comrade, or a classmate.

There are three types of friendship, as we mentioned earlier: some friendships are between equals, while others are between those who are superior or inferior. Not only can equally good people become friends, but also a better person can be friends with someone worse off. In friendships based on pleasure or usefulness, the friends can be equal or unequal in the benefits they provide. When friends are equals, they should balance things equally in love and all other matters. When they are unequal, they should give and receive in proportion to their differences. Complaints and resentments arise mostly in friendships based on usefulness, which makes sense. Friends who care about virtue try to help each other, as this is a sign of both virtue and friendship. When people are competing to help each other, there are no complaints or quarrels. No one is upset with someone who loves them and treats them well. If a person is kind, they will repay kindness with kindness. A friend who excels at helping won't complain because they are achieving what they aim for, which is to do good. In friendships of pleasure, there aren't many complaints because both friends get what they want by enjoying each other's company. Even if one friend didn't bring enough pleasure, it would be silly to complain since they can simply stop spending time together.

Friendships of utility are full of complaints because each person uses the other for their own gain. They always want to get more than they give and feel like they are receiving less than they deserve. They often blame their partners for not meeting their expectations. Those who do favors for others can't always help as much as the other person wants.

It seems that, just as there are two kinds of justice—one unwritten and one legal—there are two kinds of friendship based on utility: moral and legal. Complaints arise when people don't end the friendship in the same way they started it. The legal kind is based on fixed terms. In purely business relationships, repayment happens immediately, while more generous relationships allow for delayed payment but still expect something in return. In these relationships, the debt is clear and not confusing, but the delay adds a friendly element. Some societies don't allow lawsuits over such agreements, believing that those who lend on credit should accept the risks. The moral kind of friendship isn't based on set terms. In this case, a person gives something to a friend without expecting immediate repayment, but they still expect to receive as much or more eventually. If they end up worse off after the friendship ends, they will complain. This happens because people often want to be noble but choose what benefits them. It's noble to help someone without expecting repayment, but receiving help is more beneficial. Therefore, if we can, we should repay what we received. We shouldn't force someone to be our friend against their will. We must acknowledge that we made a mistake by accepting a benefit from someone we shouldn't have and should settle the debt as if it were a business transaction.

There is some debate about whether we should measure a favor by how useful it was to the person who received it or by the kindness of the giver. The receivers often say they didn't get much because it was something small for the giver, or they could have gotten it from someone else, downplaying the favor. On the other hand, the givers say they gave the best they had and something that couldn't be easily obtained elsewhere, especially if it was given in a time of need. In friendships based on utility, it seems that the benefit to the receiver should be the measure. After all, the receiver asks for the favor, and the giver expects an equivalent return. The help given is equal to the advantage received, so the receiver should repay what they got or even more, as that would be nobler. In friendships based on virtue, complaints don't arise because the intention of the giver is the true measure. Intention is central to virtue and character.

Friendships between people of different status can also lead to disagreements because each expects to get more out of it. When this happens, the friendship falls apart. The superior friend thinks they should get more because they are better, while the more useful friend expects more because they believe a lesser person shouldn't receive the same benefits. They argue that, just like in business partnerships, those who invest more should receive more in return. But the friend in need argues the opposite, thinking that a good friend should help those in need. They ask, "What's the point of being friends with someone powerful or virtuous if it brings no benefits?"

Both sides seem justified in their expectations. Each should receive more from the friendship but in different ways. The superior friend should receive more honor, while the lesser friend should gain more material benefits. Honor is the reward for virtue and generosity, while material gain helps those in need.

This is also true in political arrangements. A person who doesn't contribute to the common good isn't honored. Public resources are given to those who benefit the public, and honor is one of these resources. It's impossible to receive both wealth and honor from the public at the same time because no one is willing to take the smaller share of everything. Therefore, the person who sacrifices wealth is given honor, while the person who wants to be paid receives wealth. This balance keeps the friendship intact, as we mentioned earlier. This is also how we should treat unequal friendships. The person who receives wealth or virtue should give honor in return, repaying what they can. Friendship asks a person to do what they are capable of, not necessarily what matches the merits of the situation. For example, no one can fully repay their debt to the gods or their parents. But a person who serves them to the best of their ability is considered good. This is why a person can't disown their father, although a father can disown his son. Since the son is always in debt, he should always try to repay it. However, just like creditors can forgive a debt, a father can forgive his son. At the same time, people think that a father wouldn't reject his son unless the son was extremely wicked. Besides the natural bond between father and son, it's human nature not to reject help from a child. But if the son is wicked, he will likely avoid helping his father or won't do so with much enthusiasm. Most people like to receive help but avoid giving it, seeing it as unprofitable. That covers these issues.

Book 9

In all friendships between people who are different, as we have said, it is balance that keeps things equal and preserves the friendship. For example, in political friendships, the shoemaker gets something back for his shoes that equals their value, and the weaver and all other workers do the same. Here, a common way to measure value is money, so everything is judged by this and compared to it. But in the friendship of lovers, sometimes the lover complains that their great love isn't returned (maybe because they aren't lovable), while the beloved might complain that the lover, who used to promise everything, now delivers nothing.

These problems happen when the lover loves the beloved for pleasure, while the beloved loves the lover for usefulness. They don't both have the qualities the other person expects. If these are the reasons for their friendship, it falls apart when they no longer get what they originally wanted. Each person didn't love the other for who they are but for certain qualities, and these qualities weren't lasting. That's why these friendships don't last. But the love between two good people, as we've said, lasts because it's based on their character.

Problems arise when what each person receives is different from what they wanted. It feels like you're getting nothing if you don't get what you were aiming for. There's a story of someone who promised rewards to a lyre-player, saying they would give more the better he played. But in the morning, when the player asked for his rewards, the person said they had given him pleasure for pleasure. Now, if both wanted the same thing, that would have been fine. But if one wanted enjoyment and the other wanted money, and only one person got what they wanted, then the friendship wasn't balanced. Each person focuses on what they want, and they give what they have in order to get that.

But who gets to decide the value of the service—the person making the sacrifice or the person who benefits from it? It seems like the second person leaves it up to the first. This is what Protagoras supposedly used to do; whenever he taught anything, he let the learner decide how much the teaching was worth and accepted whatever amount they set. But in situations like this, some people prefer the saying "let a man have his fixed reward." Those who get paid first and then don't do what they promised are naturally complained about, especially if their promises were exaggerated. This happens a lot with sophists because no one would pay for what they actually know. So, if these people don't do what they were paid to do, it's no surprise that others complain about them.

But where there is no official contract, people who give something up for the sake of someone else can't be complained about (as we said earlier). This is the nature of virtuous friendships. The return should be based on the intention behind the act because intention is what matters most in friendships and in virtue. This also applies to people who study philosophy together. The value of what they offer can't be measured in money, and no honor is enough to repay what they've done. Still, like with the gods or our parents, it may be enough to repay them by doing what we can.

If the gift wasn't like that but was given expecting something in return, then it's best to make sure the return is fair to both parties. If this can't be achieved, it seems fair and necessary that the person who got the service should set the value. If the person who gave the service gets back something equal to the benefit the other person received or what they would have paid for the pleasure, then they've gotten what's fair.

We see this happening with things that are sold. In some places, there are even laws that say no one can take legal action over voluntary agreements. This is because the law assumes that if you gave someone credit, you should settle with them based on the terms you originally agreed to. The law believes it's more fair for the person who received credit to set the terms than the one who gave it. Most people don't value things the same way when they have them as they did before they got them. They tend to think what they own is worth more than what others have. Still, the return is made based on what the receiver thinks it's worth. The receiver, though, should value the gift based on what they thought it was worth before they received it, not afterward.

There's another question: Should we always put our father first and obey him, or should we trust a doctor when we're sick? When choosing a general, should we pick someone with military skills? And, similarly, should we help a friend or a good person, or should we repay a benefactor or help a friend if we can't do both?

These kinds of questions are hard to answer clearly, aren't they? There are many variations depending on how important the help is and how noble it is. But it's clear that we shouldn't always put the same person first. Most of the time, we should repay benefits rather than do favors for friends, just like we should repay a loan before lending to someone else. But even this isn't always true. For example, if someone has been rescued from kidnappers, should they rescue the person who saved them, or should they save their father? It seems like they should save their father, even before saving themselves.

As we've said, the general rule is to repay what you owe, but if the gift is exceptionally noble or necessary, we should consider that first. Sometimes, it's not even fair to return an equal favor, like when one person does something good for someone they know is virtuous, but the other person repays someone they believe is bad. In such cases, it wouldn't be fair to repay the favor. Even if the person lent to you, expecting to be repaid, they might not expect the same if you believe they are bad. So, if the situation really is that way, the demand for repayment isn't fair. And if it only seems that way, people might still refuse to repay, thinking they aren't doing anything wrong.

As we've often said, discussions about emotions and actions can only be as precise as the topic allows.

It's clear that we shouldn't repay everyone in the same way, and we shouldn't always put our father first in everything, just like we don't sacrifice everything to Zeus. But we should give different things to our parents, brothers, friends, and benefactors. We should give each group what's appropriate and fitting. This seems to be what people actually do. They invite relatives to weddings because relatives are part of the family, and family events affect them. At funerals, relatives gather for the same reason. In matters of food, we should help our parents first because we owe our own nourishment to them. It's more honorable to provide for the people who gave us life, even before providing for ourselves. We should honor our parents like we honor the gods, but not with just any honor. We shouldn't give our parents the same honor we give a philosopher or a general. We should honor them as parents. We should also show respect to older people by standing when they enter and offering them seats. For friends and brothers, we should allow more freedom and sharing of everything. For other relatives, fellow citizens, and people from the same community, we should try to give each group what's appropriate, considering how close we are to them, their virtue, and their usefulness.

It's easier to compare people when they belong to the same group, but it's harder when they're from different groups. Still, we shouldn't avoid the task, but we should do our best to make a fair decision.

Another question is whether or not friendships should be ended when the other person changes. It seems natural to end a friendship based on usefulness or pleasure when the person no longer has those qualities. After all, we were only friends because of those qualities, and when they're gone, it's reasonable to stop loving them. But someone could complain if, while they loved us for our usefulness or pleasantness, we pretended to love them for their character. As we said earlier, most disagreements between friends come when they don't really understand the basis of their friendship. So, if someone believed they were being loved for their character when that wasn't the case, they should blame themselves. But if they were tricked by the other person pretending to love them for their character, then they have a right to complain. They could even argue that the deception was worse than counterfeiting money because the wrong was done to something more valuable.

If someone thought another person was good and that person turns out to be bad, should they still love them? It doesn't seem possible because not everything can be loved—only what is good. We can't and shouldn't love what is evil. It's not right to be a lover of bad things or to become like what's bad. We've said that people love what is similar to them. So, should we immediately end the friendship? Not always. This should only happen if the person's badness can't be fixed. If they can be reformed, it's better to help them improve their character or their situation. This is more in line with what friendship is about. But if someone breaks off a friendship with someone who can't be saved, they aren't doing anything wrong. After all, they didn't become friends with this bad person, and since their friend has changed and they can't help them, they give up on the friendship.

But what if one friend stays the same while the other gets better and becomes far more virtuous? Should the more virtuous person still treat the other as a friend? It seems they can't. When the gap between them becomes too large, it's obvious that the friendship can't continue. For example, in childhood friendships, if one friend remains childlike in their thinking while the other matures into an adult, how could they still be friends? They wouldn't enjoy or value the same things, and without that, they can't be friends because they can't share their lives together. We've already discussed these ideas.

Should the person who's changed treat their former friend as a complete stranger? Not exactly. They should still remember the old friendship, and just like we treat old friends better than strangers, we should also give some credit to people we used to be friends with, as long as the reason for ending the friendship wasn't too severe.

The way people treat their neighbors and the signs of friendship seem to come from how people relate to themselves. For example, we call someone a friend if they want and do what is good for their friend, or at least what seems good, for their friend's sake. Or we call someone a friend if they wish their friend to live and thrive, which is what mothers do for their children, and what friends do for each other even if they've fought. Others define a friend as someone who lives with you and has the same interests. Or they define a friend as someone who shares your joys and sorrows, which mothers do more than anyone. Friendship is defined by one or more of these traits.

Each of these traits applies to how a good person relates to themselves (and to everyone else in so far as they see themselves as good). Virtue and the good person, as we've said, seem to be the standard for everything. A good person's desires are consistent, and they want the same things with all their heart. So, they wish what's good for themselves and do what's good. It's part of being good to put good into action. They do this for their own sake because they do it for the part of them that thinks, which is considered to be the true self.

A good person wishes to live and be preserved, especially the part of them that thinks. Existence is good for a virtuous person, and everyone wishes good for themselves. No one would choose to possess everything if it meant becoming someone else. Even now, we believe God possesses the good. People only want good things if they can remain who they are while getting them. The part of us that thinks seems to be the real person, or at least more so than any other part.

A good person enjoys spending time with themselves. They find pleasure in remembering their past actions, and they have good hopes for the future, which makes them happy. Their mind is full of things to think about. They feel grief and joy with themselves more than anyone else because the same things are always painful or pleasant to them. Their feelings don't change from one moment to the next. It's like they never have anything to regret.

Since all these traits apply to how a good person relates to themselves, and they treat their friends the same way they treat themselves (because a friend is like another self), friendship is thought to be based on these traits. People who have these traits are friends.

Whether or not someone can be friends with themselves is a question we can put aside for now. But there does seem to be friendship within a person in so far as they are like two or more people. This can be seen from the traits of friendship we've mentioned and from the fact that the highest form of friendship is compared to a person's love for themselves.

Even though most people have these traits, even if they aren't great, should we say that when they are happy with themselves and think they are good, they share in these traits? Definitely, no one who is completely bad or irreligious has these traits or even seems to have them. These traits barely apply to less-than-great people either, because they are in conflict with themselves. They want one thing but logically know they should want something else. This happens to people who lack self-control; they choose things that feel good but are harmful instead of the things they know are better. Others, because they are afraid or lazy, avoid doing what they know is best for them. Those who have done many terrible things and are hated for their wickedness even avoid life and might hurt themselves. Wicked people often look for others to spend time with and avoid being alone with themselves. When they are by themselves, they remember all the awful things they've done and imagine doing more bad things, but when they're with others, they forget. Because they don't have anything lovable about them, they don't love themselves. This is also why they don't feel happy or sad with themselves. Their soul is split apart because of their wickedness. One part of them feels sad when they stop themselves from doing certain things, while the other part feels pleased. They feel pulled in different directions, almost like they are being torn apart. Even if a person can't feel happy and sad at the same time, they might soon feel sad because they were once happy, and they wish those things hadn't made them feel happy at all. Bad people are weighed down by regret.

Because of this, a bad person doesn't seem to even like themselves since there's nothing in them to love. If this is the height of misery, we should do everything we can to avoid wickedness and try to be good. Only then can someone be a friend to themselves or someone else.

Goodwill is a friendly feeling but is not the same as friendship. You can have goodwill toward someone you don't know and without them knowing it, but that's not true of friendship. This has been mentioned before. Goodwill isn't even the same as feeling friendly because it doesn't involve strong feelings or desire. Those feelings come with real friendship. Friendship means being close, but goodwill can happen suddenly, like when we feel it for competitors in a contest. We feel goodwill toward them and hope for the best for them, but we wouldn't necessarily do anything with them. As mentioned before, goodwill happens suddenly and is only a surface-level feeling of love.

So, goodwill seems to be the start of friendship, like how admiring someone's looks is the start of love. No one loves someone if they aren't first pleased by their appearance. But just liking someone's appearance doesn't mean you love them. Love only happens when you long for the person when they're not around and crave their presence. In the same way, people can't be friends unless they first feel goodwill for each other. But just because people feel goodwill doesn't mean they're friends. They only wish good things for each other, but they wouldn't go out of their way for each other or put in the effort. So you could say that goodwill is like friendship that hasn't been acted on yet. But when it grows stronger and leads to closeness, it can become friendship—not the kind based on usefulness or pleasure since goodwill doesn't start that way either. If someone has goodwill toward someone because they received help from them, that's just being fair. If someone wishes success for another person because they hope to get something from them in return, that's not really goodwill toward the other person but more like goodwill toward themselves. It's like how someone isn't truly a friend if they only care for someone because they can get something out of it. In general, goodwill comes from admiring something good in another person, like their beauty or bravery, as we pointed out earlier with competitors in contests.

Unanimity also seems to be a kind of friendly relationship. That's why it isn't just agreeing on the same opinion, because that could happen between people who don't even know each other. We don't say that people who agree about everything are unanimous, like people who agree on facts about the stars. Unanimity about things like that doesn't create a friendly bond. But we do say that a city is unified when everyone agrees on what's best for them and chooses to take the same actions together. Unanimity, then, is about actions, especially those that are important and where both or all parties can get what they want. For example, a city is unified when everyone agrees that government officials should be elected or that they should form an alliance with Sparta. Or, when they agree that Pittacus should be their ruler and he is willing to lead them. But when two people both want the same thing only for themselves, like the captains in the Phoenissae, they aren't unified; they are in conflict. Unanimity only happens when everyone agrees that the same person should have something. For example, both the common people and the upper class want the best people to lead. Only in this way can everyone get what they want. Unanimity, then, seems to be political friendship, and it is often said to be so. It deals with things that benefit everyone and that affect our lives.

True unanimity is only found among good people. They are unified with themselves and with others because they have one purpose. They want justice and what is beneficial, and these are the things they work toward together. But bad people can only be unified a little, just like they can't truly be friends. They try to take more than their fair share of benefits while avoiding their share of work and public service. Each person tries to get what they want for themselves and criticizes others for doing the same. They get in each other's way, and when people don't watch out for each other, things quickly fall apart. As a result, they end up in conflict, forcing others to do what's right while they refuse to do the same.

People often think that those who help others love the people they've helped more than the people who received the help love the person who helped them. This idea is often seen as strange. Most people think it's because the person who was helped feels like they owe something, while the person who helped is like a creditor. Just like in financial debts, the person who owes money wishes their creditor didn't exist, while the creditor wants the debtor to be safe so they can be repaid. So, people think that benefactors want those they've helped to be around so they can get gratitude, while the people who received help don't care much about returning the favor. Epicharmus might say that this way of thinking is negative, but it's natural for people to act this way. Most people are forgetful and would rather receive kindness than give it.

But the reason for this goes deeper. The comparison to financial debts doesn't even fit. Creditors don't necessarily feel friendship toward their debtors; they just want them to be safe so they can get their money back. But people who help others feel love and friendship toward the people they've helped, even if they never expect anything in return. This is similar to how a craftsman loves his work more than the work could ever love him if it came alive. Poets feel this way about their poems, loving them like their children. This is the same for benefactors. The people they help are like their creations, and that's why they love them more than the recipients of the help love them. The reason for this is that life itself is something everyone values and loves. We exist by living and doing things. When a person helps another, they are acting, and that action makes them feel alive. So, the person who helps loves the person they've helped because it is through their actions that they experience life.

At the same time, the benefactor sees something noble in their actions, so they feel pleasure in the person they helped. But the person who was helped doesn't necessarily see anything noble in the benefactor. At most, they see something useful, and that's less pleasant or lovable. What is pleasant is the act of doing something in the present, the hope of the future, and the memory of the past. But the most pleasant thing is the act itself, and that's also the most lovable. For the person who did the act, the memory of the good thing they did stays with them because what is noble lasts. But for the person who was helped, the benefit fades away. Memories of noble things bring joy, but memories of useful things are not as pleasant, though the opposite is true when we think about the future.

Also, loving is like doing something, while being loved is like being on the receiving end. Loving someone is more active, while being loved is more passive.

Everyone loves what they've worked hard for more than what they've gotten without effort. For example, people who earned their money love it more than those who inherited it. Being treated well doesn't require effort, but treating others well does. This is why mothers often love their children more than fathers do. They went through more pain to bring their children into the world, and they know for sure that the children are theirs. The same applies to benefactors.

There's also the question of whether people should love themselves the most or someone else. People criticize those who love themselves most, calling them selfish, and they use the term in a negative way. A bad person seems to do everything for themselves, and the worse they are, the more they do it. People criticize them for not acting on their own accord. But a good person acts for the sake of honor, and the better they are, the more they act for the sake of their friends, even sacrificing their own interests.

But this idea doesn't quite match the facts, which isn't surprising. People say that we should love our best friend the most. And our best friend is someone who wishes well for us for our own sake, even if no one else knows about it. These traits are found most of all in how a person relates to themselves. The other traits that define a friend are also true of how a person treats themselves. As we said, the way we treat ourselves is the model for how we treat our friends. The old sayings agree with this, like "a single soul," "what friends have is shared," "friendship is equality," and "charity begins at home." All these sayings apply most to how a person relates to themselves. We are our own best friend, so it makes sense to love ourselves the most. This makes it a reasonable question: which of the two views should we follow? Both seem reasonable.

We need to separate these arguments and figure out where and in what way each view is correct. If we understand how each group uses the term "self-love," the truth becomes clear. People use the term "self-love" as an insult when they talk about people who give themselves more wealth, honors, and physical pleasures than anyone else. These are the things most people want and compete for because they think they are the best things. So, people who are selfish in this way satisfy their desires and emotions, especially the irrational part of their soul. Most people act like this, which is why the term "self-love" has a negative meaning—it reflects this common but bad form of self-love. It's only fair, then, that people who are selfish in this way are criticized. It's clear that most people call someone selfish when they give themselves more of these things.

However, if someone was always concerned with acting justly, with self-control, or with other virtues, and always tried to do what is right, no one would call that person selfish or criticize them.

But that kind of person is actually more of a "self-lover" than the others because they are giving themselves the best and noblest things. They satisfy the most important part of themselves and always listen to it. Just like a city or any organized system is identified with its leading part, a person is most identified with their reasoning mind. So, the person who loves and follows this part of themselves is the true "self-lover." Besides, people are said to have self-control if their reason is in control because that part is considered to be the true self. The things we do based on rational thought are considered our most real and voluntary actions. It's clear that this is the true self, or at least more so than any other part. It's also clear that the good person loves this part of themselves the most. So, it follows that they are the truest "self-lover," but in a very different way from those who are criticized for being selfish. The difference is like the difference between living according to reason and living according to emotion, or between wanting what is noble and wanting what seems useful. People admire and praise those who focus on noble actions. If everyone aimed for what is noble and worked hard to do the best deeds, everything would be better for everyone. Each person would also get the greatest good for themselves, which is virtue, the highest good.

Therefore, a good person should love themselves because they will benefit from doing good deeds, and they will help others too. But a bad person shouldn't love themselves because they will harm themselves and those around them by following their bad desires. A bad person does things that go against what they should do, but a good person does what they ought to do. Reason always chooses what is best for itself, and a good person follows their reason. It's also true that a good person does many things for their friends and country, even giving up their life if necessary. They will give up wealth, honors, and other things people usually compete for in order to gain something greater—nobility. They prefer a short time of intense pleasure over a long period of mild enjoyment, a year of noble life over many years of dull living, and one great and noble action over many small ones. People who die for others achieve this kind of greatness. So, they are really choosing something wonderful for themselves.

They will also give up wealth if it means their friends will gain more because while their friend gains money, they achieve nobility. They are actually giving themselves the better good. The same goes for honor and power. They will give these things up for their friend because doing so is noble and praiseworthy. This is why they are rightly considered good because they always choose what is noble over everything else. Sometimes, they will even let their friend take action instead of them because it might be nobler to help their friend act than to act themselves. In all the ways people are praised for their actions, a good person takes the larger share of what is noble for themselves. In this way, as we said before, a person should love themselves, but not in the way most people do.

There is also a debate about whether a happy person needs friends. Some say that those who are perfectly happy and self-sufficient don't need friends because they already have everything good. If they are self-sufficient, they don't need anything else. A friend, who is like another self, provides something a person can't give themselves, which is why people say, "When fortune is kind, what need is there for friends?" But it seems strange to say that a happy person has everything good but not friends, who are considered the greatest of external goods. Also, if it's more characteristic of a friend to do good for someone else than to be helped themselves, and if doing good is the mark of a virtuous person, and it's nobler to help friends than strangers, then a good person needs people to help.

This is why people ask whether we need friends more in good times or bad. It's assumed that people need friends in bad times to help them, but those who are doing well also need friends to do good for. It would be strange to think of the happiest person as being all alone. No one would choose to have the whole world if it meant being alone. Humans are social beings who naturally live with others. Therefore, even a happy person needs to live with others because they have all the good things in life. It's clearly better to spend your time with friends and good people rather than with strangers or random people. So, the happy person needs friends.

What exactly is the first group saying, and in what way are they right? Do they mean that most people think of friends as useful? If so, then a truly happy person wouldn't need these kinds of friends because they already have everything they need. They also wouldn't need friends just for enjoyment, or they'd need them very little because their life is already pleasant without outside pleasures. And since they don't need these types of friends, people think they don't need friends at all.

But this isn't true. We said before that happiness is about activity, and activity happens over time, not all at once like owning something. If (1) happiness comes from living and being active, and a good person's actions are virtuous and naturally pleasant, as we mentioned earlier, and (2) doing something yourself makes it more enjoyable, and (3) we can observe other people's actions more easily than our own, and (4) the actions of virtuous friends are pleasant to good people— then, if this is all true, a truly happy person will need friends like these. Their goal is to think about worthy actions, especially their own, and a good friend's actions are both good and pleasant.

Moreover, people believe that a happy person should live a pleasant life. If they were alone, life would be difficult because it's not easy to stay active all the time by yourself. But with others, it's easier to stay active. With friends, their activity will be more constant, and it's naturally pleasant, as it should be for a truly happy person. A good person enjoys virtuous actions and is bothered by bad ones, much like a musician enjoys good music and dislikes bad music. Spending time with good people also helps train us in virtue, as Theognis said before.

If we think more deeply about it, it seems that a virtuous friend is naturally something a good person would want. That which is naturally good is good and pleasant for a virtuous person. Life for animals is defined by their ability to sense things, and for humans, it's defined by their ability to sense or think. Abilities are defined by the activities they lead to, and life is essentially about perceiving or thinking. Life itself is one of the things that are good and pleasant because it is definite, and definite things are naturally good. That which is naturally good is also good for a virtuous person. This is why life seems pleasant to everyone. But we shouldn't apply this to a wicked or painful life, since such a life is undefined, as are its qualities. The nature of pain will become clearer later. But if life is good and pleasant—and it seems to be, since everyone desires it, especially those who are good and truly happy—and if someone who sees knows they are seeing, and someone who hears knows they are hearing, and someone who walks knows they are walking, and this applies to all other activities too—if we know that we are being active, and if knowing we are active is also knowing we are alive (since being alive is defined as perceiving or thinking), and if knowing we are alive is itself pleasant (since life is naturally good, and it's pleasant to be aware of good things in ourselves), and if life is desirable, especially for good people because for them existence is good and pleasant (since they are happy to be aware of the good within them)—and if a good person feels about their friend the same way they feel about themselves (because their friend is like another self)—then, if all this is true, just as each person's own existence is desirable, so is the existence of their friend. A person's existence is desirable because they are aware of their own goodness, and this awareness is pleasant in itself. Therefore, a person needs to be aware of their friend's existence, which happens through living together and sharing thoughts and conversations. This is what "living together" means for humans, unlike animals who just share a space for feeding.

If being alive is naturally good and pleasant for a truly happy person, and their friend's life is much the same, then a friend is something they will desire. Since they desire this, they must have it, or they will be missing something important. Therefore, a truly happy person will need virtuous friends.

Should we then try to have as many friends as possible? Or, like with hosting guests, should we aim for something in between—not too many but not none at all? Should this apply to friendship as well?

When it comes to friendships based on usefulness, this idea makes sense. Doing favors for many people can be exhausting, and life isn't long enough to help everyone. So, having more friends than necessary is pointless and can get in the way of living a good life. We don't need too many of these friends. The same goes for friendships based on pleasure. Just a few are enough, like a little seasoning is enough in food.

But when it comes to good friends, should we have as many as possible, or is there a limit, like there is with the size of a city? You can't have a city with only ten people, but if there are 100,000, it's not really a city anymore. So, there's probably no single perfect number of friends, but there is a range. The largest number of friends we can have is probably the most we can live with, since living together is a key part of friendship. And it's clear that we can't live closely with too many people or divide ourselves among them. Also, these friends should all be friends with each other if they're going to spend time together. It's hard for this to happen with a large group. It's also difficult to share happiness and sadness deeply with many people because you might have to rejoice with one friend while mourning with another. So, it's best not to aim for as many friends as possible, but just enough to live well with. It's actually impossible to be a great friend to many people. This is why we can't truly love many people at once. Love is an intense form of friendship, and that can only be felt for one person. Great friendships, too, are only possible with a few people. We see this in real life—famous deep friendships are always between two people. Those who have many friends and are close with all of them are often thought to not really be close to anyone. These people are more like fellow citizens than true friends, and they may be seen as overly eager to please. In the case of fellow citizens, you can be friends with many without being seen as insincere, but you can't have deep, virtuous friendships with many people. We should be satisfied if we find even a few true friends.

Do we need friends more in good times or bad? We need them in both. In bad times, people need help, and in good times, they need people to share their lives with and to be generous toward. People want to do good for others. Friendship is more necessary in bad times because useful friends are needed, but it's more noble in good times because we seek good friends to help and share our lives with. The very presence of friends is comforting in both good and bad times because sorrow is lessened when friends share in it. Some might ask if they help carry the burden of our grief, or if their presence alone, and knowing they feel sad for us, makes our pain lighter. Whether it's this or something else that lightens grief doesn't matter. What we've said seems to be true.

Their presence seems to have a mix of effects. Simply seeing our friends is comforting, especially in tough times. They help us cope with grief, both by being there and by offering comforting words if they know us well. A friend knows what pleases and pains us, and seeing them upset by our problems can also be painful because no one wants to make their friends sad. That's why strong-willed people try not to burden their friends with their troubles. They avoid sharing grief because they don't want to cause their friends pain. They also don't like to grieve themselves, so they avoid having others mourn with them. On the other hand, people who are more sensitive enjoy sharing their sorrow with friends and see them as companions in their grief. But in all things, we should aim to imitate the better type of person.

In contrast, having friends around in good times makes life more enjoyable. It's pleasant to see friends happy for our success. This is why we should eagerly invite our friends to share in our good fortune. A generous spirit is a noble one. But we should hesitate to bring them into our bad times because we want to burden them as little as possible with our troubles. Hence the saying, "Enough with my misfortune." We should only ask for help when our friends can do something important for us with little effort.

On the other hand, it's right to go to a friend's aid without being asked and to do so quickly, especially when they're in need. This is a key part of friendship, and it's nobler to help without being asked. It's also more pleasant for both people. But when friends are doing well, we should join them in their activities, but we shouldn't be quick to take advantage of their kindness. It's not noble to be eager to receive help. Still, we should avoid seeming ungrateful or rude by turning down their kindness, as that can sometimes happen.

So, it seems that having friends around is desirable in all circumstances.

Doesn't it follow, then, that just like lovers want to see their beloved most of all, friends most desire to live together? Friendship is a partnership, and as a person feels about themselves, they feel about their friend. Just as we enjoy being aware of our own existence, we also enjoy being aware of our friend's existence. This happens when we live together, so it's natural that friends aim for this. Whatever life means to each person, whatever they value most, they want to share that with their friends. Some people drink together, others play games or sports, go hunting, or study philosophy. Each person spends time with their friends doing what they love most in life. This is how they experience living together. The friendship of bad people leads to bad things because they unite in harmful activities and become worse by being like each other. On the other hand, the friendship of good people is good because they improve each other through their companionship. They become better through their activities together and by influencing each other's virtues. That's why it's said that "noble deeds come from noble people." So much for friendship. Our next topic will be pleasure.

Book 10

Next, we should probably talk about pleasure. It seems to be deeply connected to human nature, which is why when we teach children, we guide them with pleasure and pain. It is also believed that knowing how to enjoy the right things and hate the wrong things is very important for developing good character. These feelings affect our whole lives and play a significant role in both virtue and happiness because people tend to choose what feels good and avoid what feels bad. For this reason, we shouldn't skip over discussing pleasure, especially since it's a topic of much debate. Some people say pleasure is the ultimate good, while others say it's entirely bad. Some believe this because they think it's true, while others say it's better to claim pleasure is bad, even if it's not, to help people avoid it. They think that since most people are naturally drawn to pleasure, they should push them in the opposite direction to reach a balanced middle ground. But this way of thinking isn't right.

Arguments about feelings and actions are less trustworthy than facts. When they go against what people actually experience, they are often dismissed, which hurts the truth. For example, if someone argues against pleasure but is then seen seeking it, people might assume that all pleasure is worth pursuing because they aren't good at making distinctions. So, truthful arguments are the most useful, not just for gaining knowledge, but for living well. Since truthful arguments match the facts, they are more believable and motivate people to live by them. That's enough on that topic; let's move on to reviewing the opinions people have had about pleasure.

Eudoxus believed pleasure was the ultimate good because he saw that both rational and irrational beings aim for it. In everything, what is most sought after is considered the best, and the fact that all living things seek pleasure suggests it is the greatest good for all. He argued that just as every being finds its own good, like how each species finds the right food, the good is what all living things aim for. His argument was taken seriously, not just because of what he said, but because of his reputation for self-control. People believed he wasn't just defending pleasure because he liked it, but because it really was the truth. He also believed that this was obvious when you consider the opposite of pleasure: pain. Since all living things avoid pain, its opposite, pleasure, must be something they choose. He also argued that the things we choose for their own sake are the most desirable, and pleasure fits this description because no one asks why they are pleased—they just are. Finally, he said that when pleasure is added to any good, such as a just or temperate action, it makes it even more desirable. This shows that pleasure is one of the goods and that it can increase the value of other good things.

This argument suggests that pleasure is a good but not necessarily the highest good, because every good thing is more desirable when paired with another good. This is how Plato argued that pleasure is not the highest good. He said that a life with both pleasure and wisdom is more desirable than one with only pleasure. If the combination of pleasure and wisdom is better than just pleasure, then pleasure can't be the highest good because the highest good wouldn't become better by adding something else. This idea shows that if any good thing becomes more desirable when combined with another good, then it's not the ultimate good. So, what exactly meets this standard and is something we can experience? That's what we're trying to figure out.

Some people argue that just because all living things aim for something doesn't mean it's good. But that idea seems wrong. We believe that what everyone seeks must be good, and anyone who challenges this belief probably doesn't have a better argument. If only unintelligent creatures sought after pleasure, maybe there would be something to this objection. But since intelligent beings also seek pleasure, this argument doesn't make sense. Even among lower animals, there seems to be a natural drive toward their own good.

The argument about pleasure's opposite also doesn't seem right. Some say that just because pain is bad doesn't mean pleasure is good because good and bad are opposites, and both are also opposed to neutral things. While this is true in some cases, it doesn't apply here. If both pleasure and pain were bad, we should avoid both. If they were both neutral, we shouldn't avoid or seek either one. But clearly, people avoid pain as something bad and seek pleasure as something good. This shows that they are opposed in nature, not both bad or both neutral.

They also argue that because pleasure isn't a quality, it can't be a good. But activities connected with virtue aren't qualities either, nor is happiness. Some say that the good is fixed and unchanging, while pleasure is changeable because it comes in different degrees. But if they're judging pleasure based on how it feels, then the same could be said about justice and other virtues. We often say people are more or less just or brave and that their actions can also be more or less virtuous. Just like people can act more or less justly, they can experience different degrees of pleasure. If they're judging based on the variety of pleasures, they aren't identifying the real cause, especially since some pleasures are pure and others are mixed. Just like health can come in degrees without being uncertain, why couldn't the same be true for pleasure? The same amount of health isn't always present, and its intensity can vary. The same could be true for pleasure.

They also say that the good is complete, while movement and change are incomplete. They try to show that pleasure is a type of movement or change. But this doesn't seem right either. Movements, like walking, are described as having speed or slowness, and if a movement doesn't have its own speed, it still has it in relation to something else. But pleasure doesn't work like that. While you can quickly become pleased or angry, you can't be pleased quickly in the same way you can walk or grow quickly. You can shift into a state of pleasure quickly, but you can't experience pleasure as a fast process. So, pleasure isn't a type of movement.

How can pleasure be something that comes into being? We don't think just anything can come from anything else. Something can only come from what it's made of, so if pain is the destruction of something, pleasure must be the creation of the same thing. They say that pain comes from lacking what's natural, and pleasure comes from being restored. But these are bodily experiences. If pleasure is the restoration of what's natural, then the body would be the one feeling pleasure. But that's not what people think. Therefore, restoration itself isn't pleasure, although being restored can cause pleasure, just like an operation can cause pain.

This idea seems to come from the pain and pleasure connected with hunger. When people are hungry, they feel pain, and when they eat, they feel pleasure from being filled. But this doesn't apply to all pleasures. Learning, and even some physical pleasures like smells, sounds, sights, memories, and hopes, don't come from a lack of something. So, what are these pleasures restoring?

To answer those who bring up shameful pleasures, we can say that these pleasures aren't truly pleasant. If things are pleasant to people with bad character, that doesn't mean they are pleasant for everyone else. Just like we don't trust the tastes of sick people when it comes to food, we shouldn't trust the judgments of people with poor character. Or we could say that while pleasure is desirable, not all sources of pleasure are. For example, wealth is desirable, but not if it comes from betrayal, and health is desirable, but not if it comes from eating anything and everything. It's also possible that pleasures differ in kind. The pleasure that comes from good things is different from the pleasure that comes from bad things. You can't experience the pleasure of a just person without being just, or the pleasure of a musician without being musical, and so on.

The fact that a true friend is different from a flatterer also shows that pleasure isn't the highest good or that pleasures differ in kind. A friend is thought to be with us for our good, while a flatterer is there for our pleasure. The friend is praised, and the flatterer is criticized because their intentions are different. No one would choose to have the mind of a child for their whole life, even if they could enjoy the things children enjoy. Nor would they want to gain pleasure from doing something disgraceful, even if they never had to feel pain afterward. There are many things we would pursue even if they brought no pleasure, like seeing, remembering, knowing, and having virtues. If pleasure does come with these things, that's fine, but we would still choose them even if they didn't bring pleasure. So, it seems clear that pleasure isn't the highest good, nor is all pleasure desirable. Some pleasures are good in themselves and differ from others in kind or in their sources.

What exactly pleasure is, or what kind of thing it is, will become clearer if we start again from the beginning. Seeing, for example, seems complete at any moment because it doesn't need anything else to finish it. Pleasure also seems to be like this. It's complete in itself, and you can't find a pleasure that needs to last longer to be complete. This is also why pleasure isn't a movement. All movements, like building, take time and are aimed at a goal. They are only complete when the goal is reached. During the process, each step is incomplete and different from the whole movement. For example, placing stones is different from shaping the columns, and both are different from finishing the temple. The temple is complete because it reaches its goal, but the parts are incomplete. Each part of the process is different, and the complete movement only happens when the entire project is finished. The same is true for walking and other types of movement. Moving from one place to another has many forms—walking, flying, jumping, and so on. Even within walking, there are differences depending on where you are going. But pleasure doesn't work this way. Pleasure is complete at every moment. So, clearly, pleasure is not a movement. It is whole and complete, unlike movement.

This shows that the thinkers who say pleasure is a movement or a process of becoming are wrong. These concepts only apply to things that are divisible and not complete. Seeing, a point, or a unit don't "come into being," and neither does pleasure, because it's already whole.

Since each sense is active in relation to its object, and a sense that's in good condition works perfectly when it encounters the best possible object, the best activity of any sense is when it's at its best and focused on the best object. This activity is the most complete and pleasant. While pleasure can come from any sense, as well as from thinking and contemplating, the most complete pleasure comes from the best-conditioned sense interacting with the best object. The pleasure completes the activity, not in the same way as the sense or object itself, but as something that adds to it, like the bloom of youth adds to a person's appearance. As long as the sense and the object are as they should be, pleasure will be part of the activity because the sense and the object naturally produce this result when they work together.

Why, then, can't anyone feel pleasure all the time? Is it because we get tired? That's likely, because no human can stay active all the time. Therefore, pleasure isn't continuous because it comes with activity. Some things delight us when they're new, but less so over time for the same reason. At first, our mind is highly engaged, but eventually, our activity slows down, and so does the pleasure.

One might think that everyone desires pleasure because they all seek life. Life is an activity, and each person is active in the things and with the abilities they love most. For example, the musician uses his hearing to listen to music, the student uses his mind to think about theories, and so on. Pleasure completes these activities and therefore completes life, which people desire. So, it makes sense that they also desire pleasure, since it completes life. But whether we choose life for the sake of pleasure or pleasure for the sake of life is a question we can set aside for now. It seems they are connected and can't be separated, because without activity, there's no pleasure, and every activity is completed by the pleasure that comes with it.

Because of this, pleasures seem to be different depending on the activity. For different things are completed by different things, as we see in nature and in man-made objects. For example, animals, trees, paintings, sculptures, houses, and tools are all completed by different processes. In the same way, activities are completed by different pleasures. The activities of thinking are different from those of the senses, and both are different from each other. So, the pleasures that complete these activities are also different.

This is clear because each pleasure is connected to the activity it completes. An activity is improved by its proper pleasure because when people enjoy an activity, they do it better. For example, those who enjoy geometry become better at it and understand its principles more easily. Similarly, people who enjoy music or building improve in those activities by finding pleasure in them. So, pleasure enhances activities, and what improves an activity is unique to it. But things that are different in kind have different pleasures.

This is even clearer when we see how activities are disrupted by pleasures from other sources. For example, people who love playing the flute can't focus on a conversation if they hear someone playing the flute because they enjoy flute-playing more than the conversation. So, the pleasure from flute-playing disrupts their ability to pay attention to the conversation. This happens in all cases where a person is doing two things at once; the more enjoyable activity takes over, and if it's much more enjoyable, it will cause them to stop the other activity. This is why when we enjoy something a lot, we don't do anything else, and when we don't enjoy something, we tend to do something else instead, like eating sweets during a boring play.

Since activities are made better by their proper pleasures and hindered by unrelated pleasures, it's clear that different kinds of pleasure are very distinct. Unrelated pleasures act similarly to pain because activities are harmed by their proper pains. For example, if someone finds writing or doing math unpleasant, they won't write or do math because the activity causes them pain. So, activities are affected in opposite ways by their own pleasures and pains. Unrelated pleasures can have the same effect as pain, but usually to a lesser degree.

Since activities differ in how good or bad they are—some are worth choosing, some are worth avoiding, and some are neutral—the same is true of pleasures. Each activity has its own proper pleasure. The pleasure that comes from a good activity is good, and the pleasure that comes from a bad activity is bad, just like desires for good things are praised, and desires for bad things are criticized. But the pleasures that come with activities are more closely tied to them than desires because desires are separate in time and nature, while pleasures are closely connected to the activities themselves. In fact, it can be hard to tell the difference between the activity and the pleasure, which leads some people to think they are the same thing. (Though it would be strange to think that pleasure is the same as thinking or perception, it can seem that way because they always happen together.) As activities differ, so do their corresponding pleasures. For example, sight is more refined than touch, and hearing and smell are superior to taste. The pleasures that come with these activities are also superior, and the pleasures of thinking are even greater. Within each category, some pleasures are also better than others.

Each type of animal seems to have its own specific pleasure, just as it has its own specific function. This corresponds to its unique activity. If we look at different species, this becomes clear. For example, horses, dogs, and humans enjoy different things. As Heraclitus said, "Donkeys would prefer trash to gold," because donkeys find food more enjoyable than gold. So, animals of different kinds experience different pleasures. It's reasonable to think that the pleasures of one species don't differ too much, but in humans, they vary quite a lot. The same things delight some people but cause pain to others, and what one person finds pleasant, another may find unpleasant. The same thing happens with food; what tastes sweet to a healthy person may not taste sweet to someone who is sick. The same is true for other experiences. But in all these cases, we trust what the good person finds pleasant. If this is correct—and it seems to be—then virtue and the good person are the standard by which we measure pleasure. The things that seem pleasant to a good person are truly pleasant. If someone enjoys things that a good person finds boring, it's no surprise, because people can be damaged and corrupted in many ways. In these cases, the things aren't truly pleasant but are only pleasant to those who are in this specific condition.

Clearly, shameful pleasures shouldn't be called true pleasures, except to those with a distorted sense of enjoyment. But of the pleasures that are considered good, what kind should be seen as the proper pleasure for humans? This can be understood by looking at the activities involved. Pleasures come from these activities. Whether a truly happy person has one or several activities, the pleasures that complete these activities will be considered the true pleasures for humans. The other pleasures will be secondary, just as the activities that bring them are secondary.

Now that we have discussed virtues, friendships, and the types of pleasures, we can outline the nature of happiness, which we say is the ultimate goal of human life. Our discussion will be shorter if we first summarize what we've already said. We've said that happiness is not a state of being because if it were, a person who slept through their life or someone who suffered terrible misfortunes could be considered happy. Since these implications are unacceptable, we must see happiness as an activity, as we've said before. If some activities are necessary and are chosen for the sake of something else, while others are desirable for their own sake, it's clear that happiness must be among those that are desirable for their own sake, not for the sake of something else. Happiness is self-sufficient and lacks nothing. The activities that are desirable for their own sake are those that don't aim for anything beyond the activity itself.

Virtuous actions are considered desirable for their own sake because doing good and noble deeds is valuable on its own. Fun activities are also thought to be like this because we don't choose them for the sake of something else. In fact, we might neglect our bodies and possessions for the sake of fun, which can actually harm us. But many people who are thought to be happy focus on these kinds of activities, which is why quick-witted entertainers are highly valued at the courts of tyrants. They make themselves enjoyable companions in the tyrants' favorite activities, which makes them desirable. But just because people in power enjoy these activities doesn't mean they represent true happiness. People in power don't prove anything about what true happiness is because virtue and wisdom, which lead to good activities, don't depend on having power. Just because these powerful people, who have never experienced pure and meaningful pleasure, choose physical pleasures doesn't mean those pleasures are more valuable. Even children think the things they value most are the best things. It's natural that just as different things seem valuable to children and adults, different things seem valuable to bad people and good people. As we've often said, the things that are valuable and pleasant are those that seem so to a good person. To each person, the activity that matches their character is most desirable, and for a good person, the activity that matches virtue is most desirable.

Therefore, happiness is not found in amusement. It would be strange if the goal of life were amusement and we went through all the struggles of life just to have fun. Almost everything we choose, we choose for the sake of something else—except happiness, which is the ultimate goal. Working hard just to have fun would seem childish. But having fun so that we can work hard, as Anacharsis said, seems right. Fun is a kind of relaxation, and we need relaxation because we can't work all the time. But relaxation isn't the goal of life; it's something we do so we can get back to activity.

A happy life is thought to be a life of virtue. A virtuous life requires effort and isn't focused on fun. Serious things are better than trivial, amusing things. The activity of the better part of ourselves—

or the better person—is the more serious activity. And the activity of what's better is automatically superior and more like happiness. Even a slave can enjoy physical pleasures just as much as the best person, but no one would say a slave shares in happiness unless they also think the slave shares in human life. Happiness isn't found in these kinds of activities but, as we've said before, in virtuous activities.

If happiness is activity according to virtue, it makes sense that it would come from the highest virtue, which is the best part of us. Whether this is reason or something else that is our natural guide and helps us think about noble and divine things, the activity that comes from this part of us will be perfect happiness. We've already said that this activity is contemplation.

This seems to fit with what we said before and with the truth. First, this activity is the best because reason is the best part of us, and the things reason thinks about are the best things to know. Second, it's the most continuous because we can think about the truth for longer periods than we can do anything else. Happiness is thought to include pleasure, and the activity of philosophical wisdom is considered the most pleasant of all virtuous activities. The pursuit of wisdom offers pleasures that are pure and lasting, and those who know the truth are expected to enjoy life more than those who are still searching for it. The self-sufficiency that we talk about must also belong most to the contemplative life. While a philosopher needs the necessities of life just like a just person or someone with any other virtue, once they have those things, the just person needs other people to act justly toward. The temperate person, the brave person, and everyone else needs other people to live out their virtues. But the philosopher, even when alone, can contemplate the truth, and the wiser they are, the better they can do this. They may do it better with companions, but they are the most self-sufficient. This activity is loved for its own sake because nothing comes from it except the act of contemplation itself. In contrast, practical actions give us something beyond the action itself. Happiness is thought to depend on leisure because we work so that we can have leisure, and we make war so that we can live in peace.

The practical virtues are shown in political and military actions, but these activities seem to be the opposite of leisure. Warlike actions are completely unleisurely because no one chooses to go to war for the sake of being at war. A person who starts fights just to fight would be considered murderous. Political actions are also unleisurely because they aim at something beyond themselves, like power, honor, or happiness for oneself and others.

So, even though political and military actions are considered noble and important, they are not leisurely and aim at something beyond themselves. But the activity of reason, which is contemplation, seems to be superior in value and doesn't aim for anything beyond itself. It also brings its own pleasure, which enhances the activity. The self-sufficiency, leisure, lack of exhaustion (as much as possible for a human), and all the other attributes of the truly happy person are connected to this activity. Therefore, this is the complete happiness of a person, if they are allowed to live a full life, because none of the qualities of happiness are incomplete.

However, such a life might seem too lofty for a human. A person doesn't live this way because they are human, but because there is something divine within them. The activity of this divine part is far greater than the activity of the other kind of virtue, just as this part of us is greater than our human nature. If reason is divine compared to a human being, then living according to reason is divine compared to living a human life. We shouldn't listen to those who say that since we are humans, we should focus only on human things, or that since we are mortal, we should think about mortal things. Instead, we should do our best to live according to the highest part of ourselves. Even if this part is small in size, it far surpasses everything else in power and worth. This part of ourselves seems to be our true self because it is the most authoritative and valuable part of us. It would be strange to choose to live according to something else instead of this.

What we said earlier applies here as well: what is natural to each thing is the best and most enjoyable for that thing. So, for humans, the life according to reason is the best and most pleasant, because reason is the most human part of us. Therefore, this life is also the happiest.

But in a secondary sense, a life lived according to the other kind of virtue is also happy. The activities that come from this virtue are suited to our human nature. Acts of justice, bravery, and other virtues are things we do in relation to each other. We fulfill our duties when it comes to contracts, services, and various actions, and we deal with emotions. All of these things seem to be distinctly human. Some of them seem to come from the body, and the virtues of character are closely tied to emotions. Practical wisdom is also connected to virtue of character, and virtue of character is linked to practical wisdom, since the principles of practical wisdom align with moral virtue, and moral virtue is guided by practical wisdom. Since moral virtues are connected to emotions, they belong to our human nature. Therefore, the life and happiness that come from these virtues are also human. The excellence of reason is something separate from this. We don't need to go into too much detail here because that would go beyond the scope of our discussion. However, it seems that this kind of life needs fewer external things than a life of moral virtue. Both need the basics, of course, but the work of a statesman is more concerned with the body and material things. For this reason, there is little difference between the two. But there is a big difference in what each life needs to carry out its activities. A generous person will need money to do generous things, and a just person will need money to repay others because intentions are hard to see, and even people who are unjust can pretend to act justly. A brave person will need power to carry out acts of bravery, and a temperate person will need the right circumstances to show their temperance. Otherwise, how can anyone recognize them?

People also debate whether virtue is more about intention or action, and virtue is assumed to involve both. It's clear that virtue is complete when both are present. But to carry out virtuous actions, many things are needed, and the greater and nobler the action, the more things are required. But someone who is focused on contemplating the truth doesn't need any of these things, at least not for the sake of their activity. In fact, these things can even be obstacles to contemplation. However, since they are human and live in society, they will choose to do virtuous acts, so they will need these aids to live a human life.

We can see that perfect happiness is a contemplative activity from this thought: we believe the gods are the most blessed and happy of all beings. But what kind of actions can we attribute to them? Do they perform acts of justice, like making contracts or returning deposits? Wouldn't it seem silly for gods to do such things? How about brave acts, where they face dangers because it's noble? Or generous acts? Who would they give to? It would be strange if gods had money or needed anything like that. What about self-control? Praising them for not having bad desires seems pointless. If we consider all kinds of human action, none of them seem to fit gods—they seem trivial and unworthy of divine beings. But everyone assumes gods are alive and active; we don't think they just sleep like the myth of Endymion. If we take away action and productivity from a living being, what is left except contemplation? So, the activity of God, which is superior in blessedness, must be contemplative. And of all human activities, the one most like this is contemplation, which makes it closest to true happiness.

We see this in the fact that other animals don't share in happiness because they are completely deprived of this kind of activity. The whole life of the gods is blessed, and humans can share in this blessedness when they engage in similar activity. But animals aren't happy because they can't contemplate. So, happiness extends as far as contemplation does, and those who contemplate more deeply are more truly happy—not as a side effect, but because contemplation itself is valuable. Therefore, happiness must be some form of contemplation.

However, being human means we also need external things for happiness. We aren't self-sufficient for contemplation—we need a healthy body, food, and other necessities. Still, we shouldn't think that a happy person needs a lot of material things. Just because we need some external goods doesn't mean we need an excess of them. We don't need to rule the earth and sea to do noble deeds. Even with modest means, people can live virtuously. This is clear enough because private individuals are seen to do virtuous acts as much as rulers—perhaps even more. So, having enough of the basics is sufficient for a happy life lived according to virtue. Solon may have been right when he described a happy person as having modest possessions but having performed noble acts and lived a temperate life. Anaxagoras also seemed to think the happy person didn't need wealth or power, saying that to most people, the happy person would seem strange because they judge happiness by external things. The opinions of wise people seem to support these ideas.

But even though such ideas are convincing, we must look at the facts of life because they are the final test. If what we've said matches the facts, we should accept it. If not, we should see it as just a theory. A person who uses reason and develops it is likely to be in the best state of mind and closest to the gods. If the gods care about human affairs, it makes sense that they would value what is best and closest to them—reason—and reward those who value and honor it most. Those who care for what the gods care about and act rightly and nobly will be most dear to the gods. It's clear that this best describes the philosopher, so the philosopher must be most dear to the gods. And because of this, the philosopher will also be the happiest.

If we've covered the topics of virtue, friendship, and pleasure well enough, are we done? Not quite. As the saying goes, when there are things to be done, the goal isn't just to recognize them but to do them. So, with virtue, it's not enough to know about it—we must try to have it and use it. We must find any way we can to become good. If arguments alone were enough to make people good, they would deserve great rewards, as Theognis said. Such rewards should be given, but in reality, while arguments can inspire and encourage young people with noble hearts, they can't make most people good. Most people don't naturally respond to shame but only to fear. They don't avoid bad actions because they are bad, but because they fear punishment. They live by their desires, chasing after their pleasures and avoiding pain, without understanding what is truly noble and pleasant because they've never experienced it. What argument could change such people? It's hard, if not impossible, to remove bad traits through argument alone, especially when those traits have become deeply rooted. We should be satisfied if, with all the available methods for developing virtue, we can get people to develop even a little bit of it.

Some think we are made good by nature, others by habit, and others by teaching. The role of nature is clearly beyond our control and comes from divine causes in the truly fortunate. Argument and teaching, on the other hand, don't work for everyone. A person's soul must already have been shaped by good habits to enjoy noble things and hate what is bad, like soil prepared to nourish seeds. Someone who follows their desires won't listen to arguments against their behavior, and even if they do, they won't understand them. How can we convince someone like that to change? Passion doesn't usually yield to reason but to force. So, people's character must already have a natural tendency toward virtue, where they love what is noble and hate what is base.

It's hard to train people in virtue from a young age if they aren't raised under good laws. Living a temperate and disciplined life isn't pleasant for most people, especially when they're young. That's why their upbringing and activities should be regulated by law. When something becomes a habit, it stops feeling painful. But it's not enough to raise children well—they must continue practicing good habits as adults. We'll need laws for this too, covering the whole of life, because most people obey necessity rather than reason, and punishments rather than what is noble.

This is why some believe that lawmakers should encourage people toward virtue by appealing to what is noble, assuming that those who are well-raised will respond to such influences. They think punishments and penalties should be used for those who disobey or have worse natures, while those who are incurably bad should be banished completely. Good people, who live with their minds focused on what is noble, will follow reason, while bad people, who seek pleasure, can be corrected by pain, like a beast of burden. This is why punishments should be opposite to the pleasures that bad people love.

If a person is to become good, they must be well trained and continue to practice good habits. They must spend their time on worthy activities and avoid doing bad things, either by choice or by necessity. This can only happen if people live according to reason and order, enforced by laws. The command of one person, even a parent, doesn't have the same power as the law, unless that person is a king or something similar. The law has force because it's based on reason and practical wisdom. While people often dislike those who oppose their desires, they don't find the law as burdensome when it directs them toward what is good.

In Sparta, the lawmaker seems to have focused on upbringing and activities, but in most states, these things are neglected, and people live as they please, like the Cyclops, making their own laws for their family. It's best when the state takes care of these matters publicly, but if the state neglects this, individuals should help their children and friends toward virtue. They should at least have the will to do this if not the power.

From what we've said, it seems a person can do this better if they become capable of making laws. Public life is governed by laws, and good governance requires good laws. It doesn't matter whether these laws are written or unwritten, or whether they guide individuals or groups—just as in music or athletics. In cities, laws and the character of the people hold power. In households, it's the father's guidance and habits that hold power, and these are even stronger because of the natural bond between parent and child. Children are naturally affectionate and obedient. Private education has an advantage over public education, just like private medical treatment. While rest and fasting are generally good for someone with a fever, they might not be good for a specific person. A boxing coach doesn't train all his students the same way. So, personal education can be more precise because it's tailored to the individual.

However, it's best if a doctor, coach, or teacher has general knowledge of what's good for everyone or people of a certain type. After all, sciences are concerned with what is universal. But an experienced, non-expert person can sometimes take good care of themselves because they've studied their own case carefully. Some people seem to be their own best doctors, even though they couldn't help anyone else. Still, if someone wants to master an art or science, they should study what is universal and understand it as well as possible. Sciences deal with general principles.

So, anyone who wants to make people better—whether a few or many—must learn how to make laws if we become good through laws. It's not just anyone who can guide people toward the right condition. If anyone can do it, it's the person with knowledge, just like in medicine or any other skill that requires care and wisdom.

We must now ask where or how someone can learn to make laws. Is it, like in other fields, from experts? It used to be considered part of being a statesman. Or is there a difference between statesmanship and other sciences and arts? In other fields, the same people who practice the art also teach it, like doctors or painters. But while sophists claim to teach politics, they don't actually practice it. Politicians seem to do their work through skill and experience, not theory. Politicians don't write or talk much about politics, even though it would be more valuable than writing speeches for courts or assemblies. They also don't train their own children or friends to become statesmen. If they could, it's reasonable to think they would have done so, because there's no greater skill they could have passed on to their cities or kept for themselves and their loved ones. Experience clearly plays a role. Otherwise, how could they have become politicians by practicing politics? So, those who want to understand the art of politics need both knowledge and experience.

But the sophists who claim to teach politics seem far from actually teaching it. They don't even know what kind of thing it is or what subjects it deals with. If they did, they wouldn't confuse it with rhetoric or think it's less important. They wouldn't believe that you can legislate well just by collecting laws that seem good. They think it's possible to choose the best laws as if doing so didn't require intelligence. But good judgment is the most important thing, as it is in music. People who are experienced in a field can judge whether something is well-made and understand how it was achieved and what works well together. But those without experience can only see whether a work is good or bad, like people judging a painting. Laws are like the 'works' of politics. How can someone learn to be a lawmaker from them or judge which laws are best? Even doctors aren't trained just by reading books. Some medical books include not only treatments but also how to treat specific types of people and their conditions. These books are helpful to experienced people but useless to beginners. So, while collections of laws and constitutions might be helpful to people who can study and judge them, those without experience won't be able to make good judgments unless they have some natural gift. Still, they might become more knowledgeable.

Our predecessors didn't fully study the subject of lawmaking, so we should take it up ourselves. We should study the constitution to complete our understanding of human nature. First, let's review what earlier thinkers said on the topic. Then, using the constitutions we've collected, we should study what helps or harms states and what influences preserve or destroy different types of constitutions. We should also consider why some states are well-governed while others are poorly run. Once we've studied these things, we'll be in a better position to understand which constitution is best, how it should be organized, and what laws and customs it should use to be at its best. Let's begin our discussion.

Rhetoric

Aristotle

Book 1

Rhetoric is the counterpart of Dialectic. Both of these arts deal with topics that are familiar to everyone and don't belong to any specific science. As a result, most people use both rhetoric and dialectic to some degree because, at some level, everyone tries to discuss and defend their ideas, as well as attack the ideas of others. Ordinary people do this either randomly or based on practice and habit. Since people succeed either by practice or naturally, it is clear that we can analyze why some succeed through training while others do so naturally. Everyone would agree that figuring this out is part of the skill involved.

The writers of current rhetoric treatises, however, have only dealt with a small part of this art. The true heart of rhetoric lies in the methods of persuasion, and everything else is just secondary. But these writers often neglect enthymemes (a core element of persuasion) and instead focus on unimportant details. Stirring emotions like pity, anger, or prejudice does not focus on the core facts but simply appeals to the personal feelings of the judge. In places where rules for trials are stricter—like in well-governed states—this kind of rhetoric would have no place. For instance, in the court of the Areopagus, they avoid such irrelevant talk. This is a wise legal practice. Just as you wouldn't bend a carpenter's ruler before using it, you shouldn't manipulate the judge's feelings to influence the case. A litigant should only focus on showing whether something is true or false and whether it happened or didn't. Questions about the importance or fairness of the case should be left to the judge, not to the disputants.

It's important for laws to be written in a way that clearly defines as many details as possible, leaving only a few matters to the discretion of judges. There are several reasons for this. First, it's easier to find a few people who are sensible and capable of making and applying laws than it is to find a large number of people who are just as wise. Second, laws are created after careful consideration, while court decisions are often made quickly, which makes it harder for judges to ensure justice and fairness. Most importantly, lawmakers make general, long-term decisions, while members of the assembly or juries are tasked with ruling on specific cases. These people can be swayed by personal feelings like friendship, hatred, or self-interest, which clouds their judgment. So, in general, we should limit the number of decisions left to judges. However, questions about whether something happened or will happen, or whether it is true or not, must be left to the judge, since these can't be predicted by lawmakers.

Given this, it's clear that those who write about things like how to construct an introduction or narration in a speech are focusing on unimportant matters as if they were essential to the art of rhetoric. What these writers care about is how to influence the judge's feelings, but they say little about the real methods of persuasion, particularly enthymemes.

This explains why, although the same principles apply to both political and legal speeches, most writers have focused on legal rhetoric. Political rhetoric deals with more important matters and is more suited to citizens, but it tends to involve fewer irrelevant tactics. In political speeches, the audience is more likely to focus on the facts, as they are making decisions that directly affect their own interests. In court, it's not enough to prove the facts—you must also win over the listener's favor. In courts, judges are making decisions about other people's affairs, so they may listen with bias and focus on their own satisfaction, allowing the speakers to influence them instead of focusing on the truth. This is why some places, as mentioned earlier, have strict rules that forbid irrelevant arguments in court, whereas in public assemblies, the audience is better equipped to protect themselves from such distractions.

It's clear, then, that the true focus of rhetorical study is the methods of persuasion. Persuasion is a form of demonstration, as we are most convinced when we believe something has been proven. The main tool of persuasion for a speaker is the enthymeme, which is a kind of syllogism. And the study of all syllogisms falls under the field of dialectic. So, the person who best understands how syllogisms work will also be best at understanding enthymemes, once they've learned the differences between the two. The same faculty understands both truth and what seems close to truth, and people generally have a natural instinct for recognizing truth. This is why someone who is good at guessing the truth is also likely good at guessing what seems probable.

We've now seen that most writers on rhetoric focus on non-essential topics and have explained why they lean more toward legal rhetoric.

Rhetoric is useful for several reasons. (1) Things that are true and just naturally tend to prevail over their opposites, so if a judge's decision isn't right, it's likely the fault of the speaker, who should be blamed. (2) Some audiences can't be convinced by even the most accurate knowledge, because convincing someone through facts requires teaching, and not everyone can be taught. In such cases, we need to use ideas that are familiar to everyone to persuade them, as mentioned in the Topics, which deals with how to address general audiences. (3) We should also be able to argue both sides of an issue, not because we should use this skill unethically, but so that we can better understand the truth and defend against unfair arguments. Only dialectic and rhetoric allow us to argue both sides of a case, though the truth is usually easier to defend. (4) It's strange to think it's acceptable for someone to be unable to defend themselves with words and reason, even though using speech is what makes us human. If someone argues that the ability to speak can be misused, they should remember that the same can be said about most good things, such as strength, health, wealth, or leadership. All of these can be used for great good or great harm.

It's clear, then, that rhetoric isn't limited to any specific subject but is as universal as dialectic. It's also clearly useful. And its purpose isn't just to persuade, but to discover the best way to persuade in any given situation. In this way, rhetoric is like other arts. For example, the purpose of medicine isn't always to make someone completely healthy, but to help them become as healthy as possible. In the same way, rhetoric seeks to come as close as possible to persuading the audience, given the circumstances. Just as dialectic can distinguish between real and fake syllogisms, rhetoric helps distinguish between real and fake persuasion. Whether someone uses rhetoric ethically or not depends on their moral intentions, not their skill in the art.

Let's now begin discussing the systematic principles of rhetoric, focusing on the right methods and techniques for achieving success. We need to take a fresh look and define exactly what rhetoric is.

Rhetoric can be defined as the ability to find the ways to persuade someone in any situation. This is not something any other art or science does. Each other art teaches or persuades people about its specific subject, like medicine about health, geometry about shapes, or arithmetic about numbers. But rhetoric is about finding ways to persuade on almost any topic, which is why we say it isn't focused on just one specific area.

Some methods of persuasion are a part of rhetoric, while others are not. The ones that aren't are things like witnesses, evidence from torture, or written contracts—things the speaker doesn't create but are already there. The ones that are a part of rhetoric are the methods the speaker creates by using the rules of rhetoric. The first kind of persuasion just needs to be used, while the second kind needs to be invented.

There are three types of persuasion that come from speaking. The first type depends on the speaker's character; the second depends on putting the audience in a certain mood; the third comes from the proof or argument given in the speech. Persuasion happens through the speaker's character when the speech is given in a way that makes the speaker seem trustworthy. We believe good people more easily than others, especially when the facts aren't completely certain, and people disagree. This kind of persuasion should come from what the speaker says, not from what people already think about the speaker's character before the speech starts. It's not true, as some writers say, that a speaker's good character doesn't help them persuade others. In fact, a speaker's character is one of the most powerful ways to persuade.

Second, persuasion happens when the speaker stirs the audience's emotions. Our opinions change when we are happy or friendly compared to when we are upset or angry. This is the focus of most modern writers on rhetoric, and we will talk more about emotions later. Third, persuasion happens through the speech itself when the speaker proves something is true or seems true by using arguments that fit the case.

So, there are three ways to persuade. To master them, a person must be able to: (1) reason logically, (2) understand human character and what makes someone good, and (3) understand emotions—what they are, what causes them, and how they are stirred. It seems that rhetoric is related to both dialectic and ethics. We can even call ethics a part of political science. This is why rhetoric is often seen as political science, and those who teach it are seen as political experts— sometimes because they lack real knowledge, sometimes because they want to show off, and sometimes for other reasons. In reality, rhetoric is a branch of dialectic and similar to it, as we said earlier. Neither rhetoric nor dialectic studies any one specific subject; they are both about creating arguments. This should be enough to explain their scope and how they are related.

When it comes to persuasion through proof, or what seems like proof, rhetoric is like dialectic. In dialectic, there is induction and syllogism, or apparent syllogism, and the same is true in rhetoric. In rhetoric, an example is like induction, and an enthymeme is like a syllogism. I call the enthymeme a rhetorical syllogism and the example a rhetorical induction. Anyone who persuades through proof uses either enthymemes or examples; there is no other way. And since anyone who proves something has to use either syllogisms or inductions, as we know from the Analytics, enthymemes are syllogisms, and examples are inductions. The difference between an example and an enthymeme is explained in the Topics, where induction and syllogism are discussed. When we base a proof on several similar cases, this is induction in dialectic and an example in rhetoric. When we show that because certain things are true, another separate thing must also be true, whether always or usually, this is called a syllogism in dialectic and an enthymeme in rhetoric.

Both styles of oratory have their advantages. In some types of speeches, examples are more important, while in others, enthymemes are more effective. Similarly, some speakers are better at using examples, while others are better at using enthymemes. Speeches that rely on examples can be persuasive, but speeches that rely on enthymemes usually get more applause. We will talk about where examples and enthymemes come from and how to use them properly later. Next, we need to define these processes more clearly.

A statement is persuasive and believable either because it is obvious on its own or because it seems to be proven by other statements that are obvious. In both cases, it persuades because someone is convinced by it. But none of the arts deals with individual cases. For example, medicine doesn't focus on how to cure Socrates or Callias, but on how to cure anyone with a certain type of illness. It focuses on the general class of patients. Individual cases are too different from each other for any art to fully explain them. In the same way, the theory of rhetoric doesn't focus on what seems likely to a specific person like Socrates or Hippias, but on what seems likely to people in general. This is also true of dialectic. Dialectic doesn't make arguments based on random ideas or the thoughts of crazy people; it uses ideas that are worth discussing. Rhetoric also deals with common subjects that are debated. Rhetoric focuses on topics we talk about when we don't have an exact science or system to guide us, and when we are speaking to people who can't easily follow long, complicated arguments. We discuss things that seem to offer us choices. No one wastes time discussing things that are or will always be the same, because we can't change them.

We can form syllogisms and conclusions from previous syllogisms or from premises that haven't been proven and aren't accepted by everyone. The first type of argument is hard to follow because of its length, especially for an audience of untrained thinkers. The second type won't convince people because it's based on ideas they don't already accept.

Enthymemes and examples deal with what usually happens. The example is an induction, and the enthymeme is a syllogism about things that are not certain but likely. Enthymemes use fewer steps than normal syllogisms because if one of the steps is something well known, there's no need to mention it. The listener can add it themselves. For example, to prove that Dorieus won a contest where the prize was a crown, you just need to say, "He won at the Olympic games," because everyone knows the prize for the Olympics is a crown, so you don't need to mention that.

There are not many necessary facts that can be used in rhetorical syllogisms. Most of the things we make decisions about are not certain but give us options. We deliberate about our actions, and our actions are rarely controlled by necessity. Also, conclusions about things that usually happen must come from premises that also deal with what usually happens, just like necessary conclusions come from necessary premises. We know this from the Analytics. So, the statements used in enthymemes are usually about what happens most of the time, though some may be necessary truths. The materials for enthymemes are probabilities and signs. Probabilities are things that usually happen, but only if they are part of something that could happen differently. A probability is like a general truth, while the thing it applies to is like a specific case. Signs are of two kinds: one is like a specific case leading to a general conclusion, and the other is like a general truth leading to a specific case. The infallible kind is a "complete proof," or tekmerion, while the fallible kind doesn't have a specific name. Infallible signs are those that can be used to form proper syllogisms, which is why they are called "complete proofs." When people think their argument can't be refuted, they call it a complete proof, meaning it has been demonstrated and finished.

The first kind of sign can be illustrated by saying, "The fact that Socrates was wise and just is a sign that all wise people are just." This is a sign, but even if the statement is true, the argument can still be refuted because it isn't a syllogism. The second kind of sign can be shown by saying, "The fact that he has a fever is a sign that he is sick," or, "The fact that she is producing milk is a sign that she recently had a child." These are examples of infallible signs that form complete proofs, because if the particular statement is true, it cannot be refuted. The other kind of sign, where the general truth leads to a specific case, would be something like, "The fact that he is breathing fast is a sign that he has a fever." This argument can be refuted, even if the fast breathing is true, because someone could breathe fast without having a fever.

So, we have now explained what a probability is, what a sign is, what a complete proof is, and how they differ. The Analytics explains why some arguments can be formed into syllogisms and others can't.

An example is one type of induction, and we have already explained how it is different from other kinds of arguments. An example compares two things that are alike. When two statements are about similar things, but one is more familiar, the more familiar one is called an example. For instance, we might argue that Dionysius, by asking for a bodyguard, is trying to become a dictator. We can support this by giving examples from the past: Peisistratus asked for a bodyguard in order to take power and did become a dictator, and so did Theagenes in Megara. These examples are used to show that Dionysius has the same goal because he is asking for the same thing. This is an example of the general principle that anyone who asks for a bodyguard is trying to become a dictator. We have now explained the sources of these types of persuasion, which are often seen as proofs.

There is an important difference between two types of enthymemes that almost everyone overlooks. This is the same difference we find between types of syllogisms in dialectic. One kind of enthymeme belongs to rhetoric, just as one kind of syllogism belongs to dialectic. The other kind actually belongs to other skills or areas of knowledge, whether we already use them or haven't learned them yet. When people miss this difference, they fail to notice that the more they focus on the details of their specific topic, the more they move away from pure rhetoric or dialectic. This will make more sense with further explanation.

The proper subjects of rhetorical and dialectical syllogisms are the things we say the general or universal arguments deal with. These are arguments that apply equally to questions about ethics, science, politics, and other topics that are unrelated to each other. For example, an argument about "more or less" can be used in a syllogism or enthymeme about ethics, science, or anything else. But there are also special types of arguments based on specific ideas that apply only to certain subjects. For example, some ideas about science cannot be used to create an enthymeme or syllogism about ethics, and vice versa. This rule applies across the board. The general arguments don't focus on one specific subject, so they don't help us understand any one topic better. On the other hand, when we choose ideas that fit a specific argument better, we might accidentally create a new science that is separate from rhetoric and dialectic. We may explain the right principles, but then we're no longer talking about rhetoric or dialectic. Instead, we've moved into the field of knowledge that those principles belong to. Most enthymemes are actually based on these specific arguments, while fewer are based on the general ones. So, just like in other areas, we need to distinguish between the specific and general arguments when dealing with enthymemes. By specific arguments, I mean those that are unique to each subject. By general ones, I mean those that apply to all subjects equally.

Now let's classify the different types of rhetoric. Once we have these categories, we can look at each one individually and figure out what elements they are made of and what ideas they must use.

Rhetoric is divided into three parts, based on the three types of audiences that listen to speeches. In a speech, there are three things to consider: the speaker, the topic, and the audience. The audience is the one that determines the goal of the speech. The audience may be a judge, deciding on things that happened in the past or will happen in the future, or they may just be observers. A person in an assembly decides about future events, a juror decides about things that happened in the past, while an observer only judges the skill of the speaker. From this, we can see that there are three types of rhetoric: (1) political, (2) legal, and (3) ceremonial or display speeches.

Political speeches encourage people to do or not do something. This is true for both private counselors and people who speak to public assemblies. Legal speeches either accuse or defend someone. These are the only two options in any legal case. Ceremonial or display speeches either praise or criticize someone. These three kinds of rhetoric are focused on different times. The political speaker is focused on the future. They give advice about things that will happen. A legal speaker is focused on the past. One person accuses, and the other defends, based on things that have already happened. The ceremonial speaker is mainly focused on the present because praise or criticism is usually about current events. But they also sometimes refer to the past or make predictions about the future.

Rhetoric has three goals, one for each type of speech. The political speaker wants to show that a proposed action is either helpful or harmful. If they argue for it, they say it will do good. If they argue against it, they say it will cause harm. Other points, like whether the action is fair or honorable, are only brought up if they support the main point. Legal speakers want to prove that an action was either just or unjust, and they treat all other points as secondary to this. Ceremonial speakers want to prove that someone is worthy of honor or the opposite, and they treat everything else as secondary to that goal.

We can tell that each type of rhetoric focuses on these specific goals because speakers often ignore everything else. For example, in court, someone might admit that they did harm but still argue they weren't acting unjustly. Otherwise, there wouldn't be a trial. Similarly, political speakers may avoid admitting that they're recommending something harmful. They don't always worry about whether it's fair for a city to conquer innocent neighbors. Ceremonial speakers often praise someone for doing something noble, even if it wasn't in their best interest. For example, Achilles is praised for defending his friend Patroclus, even though he knew it would lead to his own death. While dying may not have been the smart choice, it was the more honorable one.

From this, we can see that these three types of rhetoric are the most important topics for a speaker to understand. Rhetorical arguments use complete proofs, probabilities, and signs. Every kind of syllogism is made of these ideas, and an enthymeme is a special type of syllogism made from these parts.

Since only possible actions, not impossible ones, can have been done in the past or will be done in the future, it's important for political, legal, and ceremonial speakers to know how to argue about what is possible or impossible, what has or hasn't happened, and what will or won't happen. Also, people try to show that good or bad, honor or disgrace, justice or injustice can be large or small, either absolutely or relatively. So speakers must also be able to argue about the size or importance of these things. They must be able to say which is the greater good, which is the greater act of justice, and so on.

These are the main topics that speakers need to understand. Now we can look at each type of rhetoric: political, ceremonial, and legal.

First, let's look at the things that political speakers advise people about. Political speakers don't deal with every subject, but only with things that might or might not happen. There is no advice to give about things that must happen or can never happen. Also, not all uncertain things are worth discussing, since some good things happen naturally, and some happen by accident, and it's useless to give advice about those. We only give advice about things we can control, things that depend on our own actions. We think about these things until we figure out whether we can do them or not.

To make a detailed list of the usual topics of political speeches and to define them all clearly would take too long here. That belongs to another, more detailed art. Rhetoric has already been given a much wider range of subjects than it really needs. As we've said before, rhetoric is a mix of logic and the ethical side of politics. It's a little like dialectic and a little like sophistical reasoning. But the more we try to turn rhetoric or dialectic into sciences, the more we lose their true nature. They are practical skills, not sciences. If we try to make them something else, we stop dealing with words and arguments and start getting into the details of specific subjects. Still, we can mention some important points that are practical to know, even though they belong more to political science.

There are five main topics that all political speakers discuss: (1) ways and means, (2) war and peace, (3) national defense, (4) imports and exports, and (5) laws.

On the topic of Ways and Means, the speaker needs to know how much revenue the country has and where it comes from. This way, if any source of revenue is being ignored, it can be added, or if any is weak, it can be increased. The speaker should also know about the country's spending so that wasteful spending can be cut, or large expenses reduced. People become wealthier by both increasing income and cutting expenses. To give good advice on this, a speaker must also know about how other countries handle these things.

On the topic of Peace and War, the speaker needs to know the country's military strength, both what it has and what it could have, and the type of strength it is. The speaker also needs to know the country's history of wars and how they were fought. This knowledge is important for both the speaker's own country and neighboring ones, especially those that could be enemies. The speaker should know whether another country's military is similar or different from their own because this can affect their relative strength. They should also study the wars of other countries and how they ended because similar causes tend to lead to similar outcomes.

On the topic of National Defense, the speaker needs to understand the current defense system, including the strength of the forces and the locations of the fortifications. This requires knowledge of the country's geography. With this information, they can suggest increasing garrisons where they are too small, removing them where they aren't needed, and guarding key points with extra care.

On the topic of the Food Supply, the speaker needs to know how much money is needed to feed the country, what kinds of food are produced domestically, and what needs to be imported. They also need to know what products the country exports. This helps them make trade agreements and treaties with other nations. There are two types of countries to be careful with: those stronger than your own, and those that are important trading partners.

Finally, and most importantly, the speaker must understand laws. The well-being of a country depends on its laws. The speaker needs to know how many types of constitutions there are and what conditions help each one succeed or fail. I am talking about how constitutions can be destroyed either by not being fully developed or by going too far. For example, democracy can turn into oligarchy if it's not developed enough or if it goes too far. In the same way, a nose that's too flat or too curved eventually stops looking like a nose at all. It's important to study the history of your own country's laws to understand which type of government is best for it now. It's also helpful to know the laws of other nations to learn which type of government suits different types of people. From this, we can see that travel books can be helpful for making laws since they teach us about the customs of different countries. History books are also useful. But all of this belongs to political science, not rhetoric.

These are the most important types of information that political speakers need. Let's now look at the arguments they use to support or reject proposals on these and other topics.

We can say that every person, and people in general, aim for a specific goal that guides what they choose and what they avoid. This goal, in short, is happiness and everything that makes it up. So, let's try to figure out what happiness is and what parts make it up. All advice about what to do or not do is focused on happiness and the things that either help or harm it. Whatever brings or increases happiness, or even part of it, should be done. Whatever destroys or stops happiness, or causes its opposite, should not be done.

We can define happiness as success combined with virtue, or as living an independent life, or as safely enjoying as much pleasure as possible. It can also be described as having good health, wealth, and property, along with the ability to protect and use them. Almost everyone agrees that happiness is one or more of these things.

From this, we can say that the parts of happiness include: good family, many friends, good friends, wealth, good children, many children, a happy old age, and physical qualities like health, beauty, strength, height, and athletic ability. It also includes fame, honor, good luck, and virtue. A person who has these inner and outer goods can't help but be independent, because there's really nothing else left to want. (Inner goods are those of the mind and body. Outer goods are things like family, friends, money, and honor.) We also think that a person needs resources and luck to live a truly secure life. Now that we've looked at what happiness is in general, let's break down its parts.

Good family in a community or country means that its people have been there for generations, that their first leaders were great people, and that many others have been born into this group who are admired for their qualities.

For an individual, good family—whether from the father's or mother's side—means both parents are free citizens. It also means that, like with a community, the family's ancestors were known for things like virtue, wealth, or some other quality people value. It's important that many members of the family, both men and women, young and old, have been admired for these qualities.

When we talk about having good children or many children, it's pretty clear what that means. For a community, it means having many young people who are strong, tall, beautiful, and athletic. It also means having young people who show virtues like self-control and courage. For an individual, it means having many children with these same qualities. Both sons and daughters are included here. For daughters, the virtues are beauty, height, self-control, and hard work that isn't considered degrading. Both communities and individuals should make sure that both men and women have these qualities. When women in a community, like in Sparta, are not treated well, half of human life is negatively affected.

Wealth is made up of having plenty of money and land, owning many large and beautiful properties, and having a lot of useful and fine tools, animals, and slaves. These possessions should be secure, respectable, and helpful. Useful property is what brings in income, while respectable property is what brings enjoyment. By "useful," I mean things that give us financial gain. By "enjoyable," I mean things we don't get much from other than pleasure. Property is secure if we can use it freely, and it's ours if we have the power to keep it or give it away, including selling it. Wealth is really about using things rather than just owning them. It's the activity of using property that truly makes someone wealthy.

Fame is being respected by everyone or having a quality that is admired by most people, or by the good and wise.

Honor is when someone is recognized for doing good. It's mainly given to those who have already done good but can also be given to someone who can do good in the future. Doing good involves helping others either by preserving life, providing resources, or giving access to things that are hard to get. Many people gain honor for things that might seem small, but the time and place often make them more important. Honor can come in many forms: sacrifices, recognition in writing, special privileges, land grants, front-row seats at public events, state-funded funerals, statues, and public support. Among foreigners, honor might be shown by bowing, giving someone priority, or giving gifts that are seen as symbols of respect. Gifts can be more than just property—they're also symbols of honor. This explains why people who love honor and people who love wealth both like receiving gifts. Gifts bring both groups what they want: property for the wealthy and honor for the respected.

Physical excellence is having good health, which means being free from illness and able to use your body without restrictions. Some people, like the historical figure Herodicus, are "healthy" but can't do anything because they must avoid most activities. That's not really something to admire. Beauty depends on age. In a young person, beauty is having a body that's fit for running and physical challenges, and being pleasant to look at. That's why well-rounded athletes are considered the most beautiful—they are naturally suited for both strength and speed. For someone in their prime, beauty is being fit for war and looking strong yet pleasant. For an older person, beauty is being strong enough for basic tasks and avoiding the deformities that often come with age and bother others.

Strength is the ability to move someone else when you want to, either by pulling, pushing, lifting, pinning, or holding them down. To be strong, you must be able to do these things in at least some ways, if not all. Physical size is about being taller, thicker, and wider than the average person, but not so much that it slows you down. Athletic excellence is made up of size, strength, and speed. Speed depends on strength. A fast runner is someone who can move their legs quickly and powerfully. A good wrestler is someone who can hold their opponent down. A strong boxer is someone who can hit hard and knock their opponent back. A great athlete can do all of these things.

Happiness in old age means aging slowly and without pain. A person is not happy if they age quickly or if they age slowly but with pain. Happiness in old age depends on good physical health and luck. If a person isn't healthy or strong, they will suffer. And even if they are strong, they can't live a long, painless life without luck. Some people live long lives without being physically strong, but that's a different issue and not something we need to focus on here.

The meaning of "having many friends" and "having good friends" is easy to understand. We define a friend as someone who always tries to do what they think is good for you. A person who has many people willing to do this has many friends. If these friends are good people, then they have good friends.

Good luck means getting or having all, or most, or the most important things that come from luck. Some things that seem to come from luck may actually be due to skill, but many things are beyond our control and happen by chance. For example, health can sometimes be controlled through effort, but beauty and height are natural. People envy things that come from good luck. Luck also explains things that happen unexpectedly, like if all your siblings are unattractive, but you are handsome, or if you find a treasure no one else noticed, or if a weapon hits the person next to you but misses you. Or if you skip going to a place where you usually go, and the others go there for the first time and get hurt. All of these are examples of good luck.

As for virtue, it's closely connected to praise, so we'll wait to define it when we talk about that topic.

It's now clear what we should aim for in supporting a proposal and what to avoid when arguing against it. The goals of political or deliberative speakers are based on what is useful. The purpose of deliberation is not to decide on the ultimate goals, but to figure out the best way to achieve them, meaning what is most useful. Since usefulness is a good thing, we need to understand what is generally considered "good" and "useful."

We can define something good as something that should be chosen for its own sake, or as something that we choose to achieve something else. It could also be what all living things seek, or what things with the ability to think or feel will seek once they gain that ability. Another definition could be what should be recommended to someone by reason or by their own personal judgment of what is good for them. Goodness could also be what brings something to a satisfying or self-sufficient state, or simply self-sufficiency itself. Something can also be called good if it creates, maintains, or leads to these characteristics while stopping or getting rid of their opposites. One thing can lead to another in two ways: either at the same time, or afterward. For example, learning leads to knowledge over time, while health leads to life at the same time. Things can produce other things in three ways: first, by directly causing them, like how being healthy produces health; second, by helping produce them, like how food produces health; and third, by usually leading to them, like how exercise generally helps maintain health.

Given all this, it's clear that getting good things and removing bad things are both good. Getting rid of bad things frees us from them right away, while getting good things gives us their benefits over time. It's also good to trade a smaller good for a greater one, or to reduce a greater evil in exchange for a lesser one. Virtue must also be good because it puts us in a good condition and leads to good actions. Virtues should be named and explained elsewhere. Pleasure is also good, since all animals aim for it. This means that things that are pleasant or beautiful are good too, because pleasant things bring pleasure, and beautiful things are either pleasant or desirable for their own sake.

Here is a more detailed list of things that are good. Happiness is one, because it is desirable for itself, is self-sufficient, and is the reason we choose many other things. Justice, courage, self-control, greatness of spirit, and generosity are all good too, because they are virtues of the soul. Physical qualities like health, beauty, and strength are also good, since they lead to other good things. For example, health brings both pleasure and life, which is why people often see it as the greatest good, because pleasure and life are two of the things people value most. Wealth is good because it's useful and leads to many other good things. Friends and friendship are good because a friend is valuable on their own and also brings other benefits. Honor and reputation are good too because they are both pleasant and often lead to other good things. Also, having honor usually means you already possess the qualities that bring it. The ability to speak and act is good because these qualities can lead to good outcomes. Good memory, quick learning, intuition, and similar abilities are good because they help us achieve good things. The same is true for the sciences and arts. Life itself is also good because it's desirable, even if no other benefits come from it. Justice is good because it helps the whole community.

These are the things most people agree are good. For things that people disagree about, we can argue like this: if the opposite of something is bad, then that thing must be good. Something is also good if its opposite benefits our enemies. For example, if it helps our enemies for us to be cowards, then clearly courage is valuable to us. In general, the opposite of what our enemies want or celebrate must be good. This idea is shown in lines like:

"Surely Priam would rejoice."

This rule holds true most of the time, but not always. Sometimes what benefits us may also benefit our enemies. That's why it's said that "troubles bring people together," meaning that the same thing can harm both sides.

Also, something that's not excessive is good, while something that's too much is bad. Something is also considered good if we've spent a lot of time, effort, or money on it. The mere fact that we've invested in it makes it seem valuable, and things that are seen as an end goal after a long journey are considered good. This is reflected in lines like:

"And for Priam (and Troy-town's folk) should they leave behind them a boast," and

"Oh, it were shame to have tarried so long and return empty-handed as erst we came,"

as well as the proverb about "breaking the pitcher at the door."

Anything that many people strive for or compete over is also seen as good, because, as we said before, what many people want is considered valuable. If something is praised, it must be good, since people don't usually praise what isn't good. This also applies to things praised by our enemies or even people we don't like, because if even they think something is good, it seems like everyone must agree.

Another way to argue something is good is if a wise or virtuous person has approved of it. For example, Athena helped Odysseus, Theseus helped Helen, the goddesses favored Paris, and Homer praised Achilles. Generally, anything people choose to do willingly is seen as good. This includes the things already mentioned and anything that might hurt our enemies or help our friends. A thing is "possible" in two ways: either it can be done, or it can be done easily. Things that are easy to do are those that don't cause pain or can be done quickly. The "difficulty" of something depends on how painful or time-consuming it is.

Something is good if it's what people want. People want to avoid evil, or at least to have more good than evil in their lives. This happens when any punishment is either small or barely noticeable. Good things are also things that are unique to us, something no one else has, because this increases their value. Things that fit a person's background, abilities, or needs are also good, as are things they feel they should have but currently lack. Even if these things seem small, people still pursue them. Anything that is easy to achieve is good, especially if most people, people like us, or people we look up to have succeeded in getting it.

Good things are also those that make our friends happy or our enemies upset. Things chosen by people we admire are also good.

Things that we are naturally or experientially suited for are good because we think we'll succeed more easily in them. Things that no unworthy person can achieve are considered better because they bring more praise. Finally, something is good if it's something we really desire, because what we desire is seen as both pleasant and better.

People tend to go after things that fit their character. People who love winning pursue victory. People who love honor pursue honor. Those who love money go after wealth, and so on. These are the sources we should use when we argue about what is good and useful.

Since people often agree that two things are useful but don't agree on which one is more useful, the next step is to talk about relative goodness and usefulness.

When something is better than another thing, it can be seen as the other thing but with something extra. The thing that is not as good is included in what makes up the better thing. When we say something is "greater" or "more," we're comparing it to something that is "smaller" or "less." Words like "great" and "small," or "many" and "few," are used to compare something to the normal amount. "Great" means something that is more than normal, and "small" means something that is less than normal. The same goes for "many" and "few."

When we call something "good," we mean that it is desirable for its own sake, not because of something else. It's something that everything aims for, something that everything would choose if they had wisdom and understanding. It's also something that tends to create or maintain these good things or always comes with them. The reason why things are done is to achieve an end, and the end is the good that everything aims for. For each person, what is good is whatever fulfills these conditions for them. So, a larger number of good things is better than a smaller number if that smaller number is included in the larger. In this way, the larger group is better because it surpasses the smaller one.

Also, if the largest member of one group is better than the largest member of another, then that whole group is better than the other group. If one group is better than another, the best member of that group is also better than the best member of the other group. For example, if the tallest man is taller than the tallest woman, then men as a group are taller than women. Similarly, if men are generally taller than women, the tallest man will be taller than the tallest woman. The superiority of one group over another is based on the superiority of their best members.

Another way to compare is when one good thing always comes with another, but the second thing doesn't always come with the first. The first thing is greater because its use includes the second thing. There are three ways one thing can come with another: at the same time, afterward, or as a possibility. Life comes with health at the same time (but health doesn't always come with life). Learning comes with knowledge afterward. Cheating can come with sacrilege as a possibility because someone who commits sacrilege could always cheat.

When two things are better than a third thing, the one that is better by a larger amount is greater than the other. A thing that produces a greater good than another thing is itself a greater good. We've already discussed how producing a greater good implies being a greater good. Similarly, something that comes from a greater good is itself a greater good. For example, if what is healthy is more desirable than what is pleasurable, then health is a greater good than pleasure.

Also, something that is desirable on its own is a greater good than something that isn't desirable on its own. For example, bodily strength is a greater good than being healthy because we don't want health just for its own sake, but we do want strength for its own sake. This is how we define what is good.

If one of two things is an end and the other is not, the end is the greater good because it's chosen for itself and not for something else.

For example, exercise is done for physical well-being, not for the sake of exercise itself. Of two things, the one that needs less help from other things is the greater good because it is more self-sufficient. Needing less help means it either needs fewer things or easier things. So if one thing cannot exist without another, but the second thing can exist without the first, the second thing is better. The thing that doesn't need help is more self-sufficient and therefore a greater good.

Also, something that causes other things is a greater good than something that doesn't, for the same reason: without a cause, nothing can exist or come into existence. If two sets of consequences come from two different causes, the consequences of the more important cause are themselves more important. In the same way, the cause that leads to more important consequences is the greater cause.

We can show that one thing is more important than another from two opposite perspectives. Something can seem more important either because it is a cause or because it isn't. A cause might be more important because it starts something, but an end might be more important because it is the goal. For example, Leodamas, when accusing Callistratus, said that the person who planned the crime was more guilty than the one who did it because it wouldn't have happened without the plan. But when accusing Chabrias, he said that the doer was worse than the planner because nothing would have happened without someone to carry out the plan.

Rare things are considered better than plentiful things. For example, gold is better than iron even though iron is more useful because gold is harder to get, which makes it more valuable. However, you could also argue that plentiful things are better because they are more useful. What we use more often is better than what we use less often, which is why there's a saying: "The best thing is water."

In general, hard things are better than easy things because they are rarer. But on the other hand, easy things are better because they are more in line with what we want.

Something is a greater good if its opposite is a greater evil or if losing it affects us more. Positive good and bad are more important than just the absence of them because positive good and bad are the actual goals, while simply not having good or bad is not.

The more noble or lowly the function of something is, the more good or bad that thing is. Similarly, the better or worse a thing is, the better or worse its function will be. The nature of a cause matches the nature of its effect, and the nature of the effect matches the nature of its cause.

Things are greater goods if being better at them is more desirable or honorable. For example, sharp vision is more desirable than sharp smell because sight is generally more valuable than smell. In the same way, loving friends more is more honorable than loving money more, so normal love for friends is more honorable than normal love for money.

One thing is also more honorable or better than another if it is more honorable or better to want it. The importance of what we want is linked to the importance of the desire itself. For this reason, if one thing is more honorable or better than another, it is also more honorable or better to desire it.

If one science is more valuable than another, the activity it deals with is also more valuable. The more valuable the subject of the science, the more valuable the science itself becomes.

Lastly, something is better if all or most people agree it is or if experts say so. People of understanding or the majority of people usually get it right, or at least as far as they use their understanding to make their decision. This general rule applies to all judgments, whether about goodness, size, or any other quality. Something is what it is because knowledge and understanding declare it to be so.

A thing is better if it belongs to better people, either because they are better or because the thing is better itself. For example, courage is better than strength. A greater good is something that a better person would choose, like choosing to suffer wrong instead of doing wrong, because that's what a just person would do.

The more pleasant of two things is better because everything seeks pleasure. People desire pleasurable experiences for their own sake, and pleasure is one of the characteristics of "the good" and "the end." One pleasure is greater than another if it has less pain or lasts longer.

Something that is more noble is better than something less noble because the noble is either pleasant or desirable for its own sake. Greater goods are things people desire more eagerly for themselves or their friends. On the other hand, greater evils are things people least want to happen.

More lasting things are better than things that fade quickly, and more secure things are better than less secure things. Lasting things give us longer enjoyment, and secure things are more convenient because they are always available.

Also, related words follow the same rule: if one is better, the others are too. For example, if a "brave" action is more honorable than a "temperate" action, then "bravery" is more desirable than "temperance," and "being brave" is better than "being temperate."

Something that everyone chooses is better than something that not everyone chooses. What is desired by more people is better because, as we've said, what everyone desires is good.

Something is better if it is chosen by competitors, enemies, authorized judges, or their representatives. In the first two cases, the choice is almost universal. In the last two cases, it's the decision of experts.

Sometimes, what is shared by everyone is better because it's shameful not to have it. Other times, what is rare is better because it is harder to get.

Things that are more praiseworthy are nobler and better. The same goes for things that earn more honors, as honor measures value. Things that have more severe penalties for not having them are also better, as are things that are better than others known or believed to be good.

Things look better when divided into parts because they seem to be better than more things this way. That's why Homer described the horrors of war in detail, showing how cities are destroyed, men are killed, and children and women are taken as slaves.

This same effect can be created by piling up examples or making a climax, like the comedian Epicharmus used to do. The reason this works is partly because division makes something look superior, and partly because the original thing seems to be the cause of important results.

A thing is better if it's harder or rarer than others, and its superiority can depend on the season, age, place, time, or the abilities of the person. When someone does something beyond their natural ability, age, or what others like them can do, their action is more noble, good, or just.

That's why there's an old saying about an Olympic winner: "I once carried loads of fish from Argos to Tegea, with a wooden yoke on my shoulders."

Similarly, Iphicrates used to boast about how far he had risen from humble beginnings.

What is natural is better than what is learned because it's harder to come by. Homer reflects this when he writes, "I have learned from no one but myself."

The best part of a good thing is especially good. Pericles once said in a funeral speech that losing the country's young men in battle was like losing the spring from the year.

Things that are useful when needed are also better, like things that help in old age or sickness. Of two things, the one that leads more directly to the goal is better. What benefits both people in general and individuals is also better.

Something that can be achieved is better than something that can't because what can be achieved is good in that situation, while the other isn't.

Something that comes at the end of life is better because it's closer to the ultimate goal.

What aims for reality is better than what aims for appearance. If a person wouldn't choose something if no one knew about it, it's aiming for appearance, not reality. This would suggest that receiving benefits is more desirable than giving them, since people will still want to receive them even if no one knows about it. But people wouldn't necessarily choose to give benefits if no one knew about it.

What people want to be is better than what they want to seem, because wanting to be something means aiming for reality. This is why people say justice isn't as valuable—because it's more desirable to seem just than to actually be just. This isn't true for health.

Something is better if it's more useful for many purposes. That's why wealth and health are considered very valuable—they provide many benefits, like helping people live, live well, feel pleasure, and act nobly.

Something is better if it brings both pleasure and less pain, because it gives multiple benefits. That way, you get the good of feeling pleasure and the good of not feeling pain.

Of two good things, the better one is the one that, when added to a third thing, makes a better whole. Also, things we can be seen to have are better than those that are hidden because they seem more real. Wealth may be considered a greater good if people know you have it.

Things that are highly valued are better than things that are not. For example, a one-eyed man suffers more from being blinded than a man with two eyes suffers from losing some sight because the one-eyed man has lost what he valued most.

These are the reasons we must use when speaking for or against a proposal.

The most important and effective skill for persuading people and speaking well in public affairs is understanding the different forms of government and recognizing their customs, rules, and interests. This is because people are always persuaded by what benefits them, and their benefit is tied to keeping things the way they are. Additionally, the final authority to make decisions depends on who holds the most power, and this varies depending on the type of government. There are as many types of supreme authorities as there are types of governments. The main forms of government are four: democracy, oligarchy, aristocracy, and monarchy. So, the ultimate power to judge and make decisions will always lie with either part or all of one of these types of government.

In a democracy, the people choose who will run the state by drawing lots. In an oligarchy, only those with a certain amount of wealth can hold office, while in an aristocracy, it's those with a specific education. By education, I mean the kind of education that is established by law, because it's the people who follow the country's traditions and laws who hold office in an aristocracy. These people are considered "the best," and that's where this form of government gets its name (which means "the rule of the best"). Monarchy, as the name suggests, is a system where one person has power over everyone else. There are two types of monarchy: kingship, which has certain limits, and tyranny, which has no limits at all.

We also need to pay attention to the goals that each type of government aims for because people choose actions that help them achieve their goals. The goal of democracy is freedom. The goal of oligarchy is wealth. In aristocracy, the goal is to protect education and national traditions, while tyranny's goal is to protect the tyrant. So, we need to identify the specific customs, rules, and interests that help each government achieve its ideal, because people choose their methods based on their goals.

Persuasion through rhetoric doesn't only happen through logical arguments but also through moral character. A speaker is more convincing if people believe that he is good, has goodwill towards them, or both. In the same way, we need to understand the moral qualities of each form of government, because the specific values of each will give us the best way to persuade them. We can learn the qualities of governments in the same way we learn about individuals—by looking at the choices they make. These choices are based on the goals that drive them.

We have now talked about the goals we should aim for, whether in the short term or the long term, when promoting any proposal. We've also discussed the reasons we should use to support the usefulness of that proposal. Finally, we've briefly touched on how to learn about the moral values and institutions of the different types of government—but only as much as is necessary for now. A more detailed discussion of this topic can be found in Politics.

Book 2

We have now discussed the materials needed to support or oppose a political measure, to give praise or blame, and to make a case in court for either prosecution or defense. We have also looked at the common opinions that we can use to best build our arguments in order to persuade our audience. These opinions are the ones our enthymemes are based on and developed from in each of the three kinds of oratory, depending on the specific needs of each type.

But since rhetoric's purpose is to influence decisions—whether it's the audience deciding between political speakers or a legal decision being made—the speaker must not only make their argument logical and believable. The speaker must also make sure their own character seems trustworthy, and they must help the audience, who will be making the decision, feel the right way. This is especially true in political speeches, but also applies in legal cases. It's very helpful if the speaker's character seems trustworthy and if they seem to have the right attitude toward the audience. Similarly, the audience must be in the right frame of mind. A speaker's character is most important in political speaking, while the audience's mood is more important in legal cases. When people feel friendly and calm, they think one way. When they feel angry or hostile, they think differently, or at least with different intensity. For example, when they feel friendly towards the person being judged, they think the person has done little or no wrong. But when they feel hostile, they take the opposite view. Also, if they're excited about something and hope it will be good for them, they believe it's likely to happen and will be good for them. But if they're feeling indifferent or annoyed, they don't think so.

There are three things that make people trust the speaker's character—these are the qualities that make us believe someone even without proof: good sense, good moral character, and goodwill. False statements and bad advice usually come from one or more of these three failures. Someone might form a false opinion because they lack good sense. Or they might know the truth, but because of bad moral character, they don't say what they really believe. Finally, they may be sensible and good, but because they don't have goodwill towards their audience, they fail to recommend the best course of action. These are the only possible reasons for bad advice. Therefore, someone who is believed to have all three of these good qualities will inspire trust in their audience. The way to make yourself seem sensible and morally good is the same as the way you would show others to have these qualities. Goodwill and friendliness will be part of our discussion on emotions, which we will now move to.

Emotions are feelings that change how people make decisions and that are also connected with either pain or pleasure. These include feelings like anger, pity, fear, and their opposites. We need to explain each of these emotions in three ways. For example, take anger. First, we must figure out what state of mind makes people angry. Second, we need to know who they usually get angry with. Third, we need to understand what reasons make them angry at those people. It's not enough to know just one or two of these things. If we don't know all three, we won't be able to make anyone feel anger. This applies to all the emotions. So, just as we previously listed useful points for the speaker to use in their arguments, let's now move on to analyze this topic in the same way.

Anger can be defined as a feeling, mixed with pain, that drives someone to seek revenge for an insult or wrong done to them or their friends without reason. If this definition is correct, anger is always directed at a specific person, like Cleon, rather than at people in general. It happens because someone has done or intended to do something harmful to you or one of your friends. Anger is always followed by a certain pleasure—the pleasure of expecting revenge. Since no one aims at something they think they can't achieve, the angry person is aiming at something they believe they can get. The belief that they will succeed is pleasurable. That's why it's been said that anger is "sweeter than honey," and that it "spreads through people's hearts."

There's also pleasure in anger because people think about taking revenge, and the images that come to mind are enjoyable, just like images that come in dreams.

Now, to slight someone means to think that they, or something about them, is clearly not important. We believe that both good and bad things are important and that things that lead to these are important too. But things that don't seem to matter much, or that don't lead to anything important, are considered unimportant. There are three types of slighting: contempt, spite, and insolence.

1. Contempt: This is feeling like something is unimportant. You slight what you think doesn't matter.

2. Spite: This is when you stop someone else from getting what they want, not because you want it, but just to prevent them from getting it. This kind of slighting happens because you don't care about getting anything yourself. You don't think the person can hurt you— otherwise, you'd be afraid of them, not slighting them. And you don't think they can help you, or you'd want to be friends with them.

3. Insolence: This involves doing or saying things that cause someone else shame, not because you want anything to happen for yourself, but simply for the pleasure of it. (Getting back at someone isn't insolence—it's revenge.) The person enjoying the pleasure of insolence thinks they are much better than the other person, which is why young people and wealthy people often act insolently. They think they're better than others when they act this way. One type of insolence is taking away someone's honor. You certainly slight them this way, because no one honors things that don't matter, for good or bad. That's why Achilles says, in anger, "He has taken my prize and dishonored me," and "Like a stranger, honored by no one," meaning this is why he is angry.

A person expects to be respected by those who are beneath them in birth, talent, goodness, or any area where they feel superior. For example, a rich man expects respect from a poor man, a skilled speaker expects respect from someone who can't speak well, a ruler expects respect from those they rule, and someone who believes they should be ruling expects respect from the person they think they should rule. That's why it's said, "Great is the anger of kings, sons of Zeus," and "Their anger lasts long after," because their great anger comes from their great sense of superiority.

A person also expects respect from those who they believe owe them something, whether because they have treated them well, are treating them well, or plan to treat them well—either directly or through their friends or at their request.

From what has been said so far, we can now understand (1) the mindset people are in when they get angry, (2) the types of people they get angry with, and (3) the reasons why they get angry.

1. The mindset: Anger comes from feeling some kind of pain. A person in pain is always trying to achieve something. So, if someone stands in their way, whether by stopping them from drinking when they're thirsty or in some other way, it feels the same to them. Whether someone opposes them or simply doesn't help them, or

annoys them while they're in this state, they'll feel angry in all of these situations. That's why people who are suffering from sickness, poverty, love, thirst, or any other unsatisfied desire are more prone to anger. They are easily angered, especially by those who ignore their suffering. A sick person gets angry if their illness is ignored, a poor person gets angry if their poverty is ignored, a soldier at war gets angry if the war is ignored, and a lover gets angry if their love is ignored. Any other kind of slight can cause anger when a person is already suffering. Everyone has their own source of anger based on their current feelings. People are also more likely to get angry when they expected the opposite to happen. An unexpected bad event is especially painful, just as an unexpected good event is especially pleasant. So, we can see what times, seasons, and situations lead people to be easily angered, and the more someone is in these conditions, the more easily they are angered.

2.   The people we get angry with: We get angry with people who laugh, mock, or make fun of us because this behavior is insolent. We also get angry with those who hurt us in ways that show insolence— when the harm is neither payback nor something that benefits the other person, it feels like pure insolence. We also get angry with people who speak badly of us or show disrespect for the things we care most about. For example, people who care about being known as philosophers get angry when their philosophy is disrespected. People who are proud of their looks get angry when their appearance is criticized, and so on in other cases. We get particularly angry if we suspect that we lack the very quality we're being criticized for or if we think others believe we lack it. If we're confident that we're good at the thing we're being mocked for, we can ignore the insult. We also tend to get angrier with friends than with strangers because we expect our friends to treat us well, not badly. We get angry with people who used to treat us with honor or respect but no longer do, because we believe they now think little of us. We also get angry with those who don't return our kindness or don't return it enough, and with those who challenge us when they are below us in some way. All these

people seem to be showing contempt for us—those who oppose us seem to think they're better than us, and those who don't return our kindness seem to think we were acting from a lower position.

We are especially angry when we are insulted by people we see as insignificant. Since the slight is felt to be unjust, and people who are beneath us have no right to slight us, we feel particularly angry.

We also get angry when friends don't speak well of us or treat us well, and even more when they do the opposite. We get angry when they don't notice our needs, like Plexippus in Antiphon's play, because this shows they're slighting us. We always notice the needs of people we care about.

We also get angry with people who seem happy about our problems or who stay cheerful when we're suffering, because this shows they either hate us or don't care about us.

We also get angry with those who don't care about the pain they cause us. This is why we get angry at people who bring bad news.

We also get angry with people who listen to negative stories about us or keep pointing out our weaknesses, because this seems like either they're slighting us or they hate us. People who love us share in our troubles, and it should bother anyone to constantly focus on their own weaknesses.

We also get angry with people who insult us in front of five specific groups: (1) our rivals, (2) those we admire, (3) those we want to admire us, (4) those we respect, and (5) those who respect us. If someone insults us in front of these people, we feel especially angry.

We also get angry with those who insult or neglect people we are bound to protect, like our parents, children, spouses, or subjects. We also get angry with people who don't return a favor because this kind of slight seems especially unjust.

We get angry with people who respond with jokes or sarcasm when we're speaking seriously because this shows disrespect.

We also get angry when we're treated worse than everyone else, which is another way people show disrespect by implying we don't deserve what others do. Forgetfulness also causes anger, such as when someone forgets our name, even though this seems like a small thing. Forgetting shows neglect, and neglect feels like disrespect.

Now that we've explained the people we get angry with, the mindset we're in when we feel anger, and the reasons behind our anger, it's clear that the speaker will need to talk in a way that puts the audience in a state of mind that makes them prone to anger. The speaker will also need to show the other side in a way that makes them seem like the kind of people who deserve the audience's anger.

Since calming down is the opposite of getting angry, and calmness is the opposite of anger, we need to understand what makes people feel calm, who they feel calm towards, and how they are calmed down. Calming down can be defined as settling down or quieting anger. We usually get angry with people who disrespect us, and since disrespect is done on purpose, it's clear that we feel calm towards those who don't act this way or who seem to do it accidentally. We also feel calm towards those who meant to do the opposite of what they actually did. We also feel calm towards those who treat themselves the way they treated us, because no one is believed to intentionally disrespect themselves. We feel calm towards those who admit their mistake and are sorry, because we take their regret as enough, and stop being angry. This is shown in how we punish servants: those who argue and deny their wrongdoing get punished more, but we stop being angry with those who admit they deserved their punishment. The reason for this is that it's shameless to deny something obvious, and when people act shamelessly, they disrespect and look down on us. In any case, we don't feel shame in front of people we totally look down on.

We also feel calm towards those who lower themselves in front of us and don't argue with us. We feel that this shows they admit they are beneath us, and people who are beneath us feel fear. No one can disrespect someone they are afraid of. The fact that our anger fades when people lower themselves in front of us can even be seen in dogs, which don't bite people when they sit down. We also feel calm towards people who are serious when we are serious, because then we feel like they are treating us seriously and not looking down on us. We also feel calm towards those who have done us more favors than we have done for them. We also feel calm towards those who pray to us and ask for mercy, because they lower themselves by doing so. We also feel calm towards people who don't insult, mock, or disrespect anyone, or at least not anyone worthy of respect or anyone like us.

In general, we can figure out what makes us calm by looking at the opposite of what makes us angry. We don't get angry with people we fear or respect, as long as we feel fear or respect. You can't fear someone and be angry with them at the same time. Also, we don't feel much anger towards people who did something because they were angry. We don't feel like they did it to look down on us because no one insults others when they are angry—insulting others is painless, while anger is painful. We also don't get angry with people who respect us.

As for the mindset that makes people calm, it is clearly the opposite of what makes people angry. People are calm when they are having fun, laughing, or enjoying a feast. They are calm when they feel successful, satisfied, or happy. Basically, they are calm when they feel no pain or when they're enjoying harmless pleasures or hopeful about something. Also, as time passes, anger fades because time ends anger. Taking revenge on one person also reduces even greater anger towards someone else. For example, when Philocrates was asked by someone why he wasn't defending himself when the public was angry with him, he answered, "It's not the right time yet." When they asked, "When is the right time?" he replied, "When I see someone else getting blamed." This was because people become calm once they've let out their anger on someone else. This also happened in the case of Ergophilus: although the people were angrier with him than with Callisthenes, they let him go free because they had sentenced Callisthenes to death the day before.

Also, people calm down when the person they are angry at has already been punished or if they have already suffered more than the punishment they would have been given in anger. This makes people feel like they've already gotten their revenge. People also calm down if they feel they were the ones in the wrong and deserved to suffer because people don't get angry at what is fair. Since anger means feeling like you've been treated unfairly, if you realize your suffering is justified, the anger goes away. This is why it's a good idea to punish people with words before giving a real punishment—if you do this, even slaves are less upset about the actual punishment.

We also calm down if we believe the person being punished won't realize that they are being punished because of how they treated us. Anger is personal, after all. This is clear from the definition of anger. This idea is also shown by the poet, who wrote: "Say that it was Odysseus, destroyer of cities." This means that Odysseus wouldn't have felt avenged unless the Cyclops knew both who had blinded him and why. Because of this, we don't get angry with people who can't be aware of our anger, and especially not with people who have died. Once someone is dead, we feel like the worst has already happened to them and that they can't feel pain or anything else, which is what we aim to make them feel when we're angry. This is why the poet wisely made Apollo say, to stop Achilles from being angry at the dead Hector, "For look, in his fury, he dishonors the lifeless body."

It is now clear that when you want to calm others, you must use these points in your arguments. You must help your audience feel calm, and show them that the people they are angry with are dangerous, deserving of respect, have helped them, acted unintentionally, or feel very sorry for what they did.

Now, let's look at friendship and enmity, and ask who we feel these emotions towards and why. We'll start by defining friendship. We can describe friendship as wishing good things for someone else, not because it benefits you, but because you want good things for them, and being willing to help make those things happen. A friend is someone who feels this way and causes you to feel the same way in return. When people feel this way toward each other, they think of themselves as friends.

With this understanding, it follows that a friend is someone who shares your happiness in good things and shares your pain in bad things, simply because they care about you. Their happiness and sadness reflect their good wishes for you, since we all feel happy when we get what we want and sad when we don't. So, friends are people who see the same things as good and bad, and who are friendly or unfriendly to the same people. This means they must share the same wishes, and by wanting for each other what they want for themselves, they show themselves to be true friends.

We feel friendly towards people who have treated us well or treated people we care about well—whether they helped us in a big way, willingly, or during a critical moment—as long as they did it for our sake. We also feel friendly towards people who we think want to treat us well. This includes the friends of our friends, and people who like or are liked by those we like. We also feel friendly towards people who are enemies of our enemies, and people who dislike those we dislike. These people seem to share our view of what is good, which makes us think they want good things for us, and this, as we've seen, is what friends do.

We feel friendly towards people who are willing to help us with our money or our personal safety. This is why we value generous, brave, and just people. We consider just people to be those who don't take advantage of others—these are people who earn their living, especially farmers and manual workers. We also like self-controlled people because they don't treat others unfairly, and for the same reason, we like those who mind their own business.

We also feel friendly towards people we want as friends, if it's clear they want to be our friends too. These are morally good people and those respected by everyone, by the best people, or by those we admire or who admire us.

We also feel friendly towards people who are fun to live with and spend time with, like those who are good-natured, who don't point out our mistakes too often, and who aren't argumentative or quarrelsome—people like this always want to fight, and we feel that those who want to fight us want the opposite of what we want. We like people who know how to joke and take a joke. Both sides enjoy the exchange when they can handle being teased and can tease back in a good-natured way.

We feel friendly towards people who praise the good qualities we have, especially if they praise qualities we're unsure of. We also feel friendly towards people who are clean in their appearance, their dress, and in how they live. We like people who don't remind us of things we've done wrong or of the help they've given us, because both actions feel like criticism. We like people who don't hold grudges or stay angry but are quick to make up because we assume they'll treat us like they treat everyone else.

We also feel friendly towards people who don't speak badly about others and who only notice the good qualities in us and others, as a good person would. We feel friendly towards people who don't try to oppose us when we are angry or serious, because opposing us would feel like they are trying to fight us.

We like people who admire us, believe in our goodness, or enjoy our company, especially if they admire us for the qualities we most want to be admired, respected, or liked for.

We feel friendly towards people who are like us in character or occupation, as long as they don't compete with us or earn their living in the same way we do. Otherwise, it's like the saying, "Potter against potter and builder against builder begrudge each other's success."

We also like people who want the same things we want, if it's possible for both of us to have those things. Otherwise, competition causes trouble here too.

We feel friendly towards people with whom we have a relationship where we respect their opinions but don't feel embarrassed around them when we do something that might not be seen as proper. We also feel friendly towards people in front of whom we would be ashamed to do something truly wrong.

We feel friendly towards our rivals and those who we want to envy us—though without any bad feelings. Either we like these people, or we want them to like us.

We feel friendly towards people we help to achieve something good for themselves, as long as helping them doesn't harm us. We also feel friendly towards those who treat us well even when we're not around, which is why everyone feels friendly towards those who stay loyal to their friends after they've died.

In general, we like people who are truly devoted to their friends and don't abandon them when times get tough. Of all good people, we feel friendliest towards those who show their goodness as friends.

We also like people who are honest with us, including those who admit their own weaknesses. As mentioned earlier, we aren't embarrassed to do something improper around our friends, and if we are embarrassed, it means we don't truly love them. So, if we aren't embarrassed, it seems that we do love them.

We also feel friendly towards people who don't make us feel scared or uncomfortable. No one can like someone they're afraid of.

Friendship has different forms—companionship, closeness, family relationships, and so on.

Things that create friendship are: doing kind things, doing them without being asked, and not bragging about them afterward. This shows that the kindness was done for our sake, not for some other reason.

Enmity and hatred can be understood by looking at the opposites of what creates friendship. Enmity can come from anger, spite, or slander. Anger comes from personal offenses, while enmity can happen without a personal offense. We might hate people simply because we think they have a bad character.

Anger is always directed at specific individuals, like Callias or Socrates, while hatred can be directed at whole groups: for example, we all hate thieves and informers. Anger can fade over time, but hatred doesn't. Anger aims to make someone feel pain, while hatred aims to harm them. Angry people want their victims to feel their anger, but haters don't care whether their victims feel anything at all. All painful things are felt, but the greatest evils—like injustice and foolishness—aren't always felt, since they don't cause physical pain.

Anger is always accompanied by pain, but hatred is not. An angry person feels pain, but a hater doesn't. Many things can make an angry person pity the one who offended them, but a hater never wants to feel pity for someone they hate. The angry person wants the offender to suffer for what they've done, while the hater wants them to cease to exist.

From all this, it's clear that we can prove whether people are friends or enemies. If they aren't, we can make them seem like they are. If they claim to be friends, we can disprove their claim. If there's a question of whether an action was motivated by anger or hatred, we can argue for whichever we choose.

Let's now talk about fear. The following will explain the things and people that make us feel afraid, and the situations in which we feel fear. Fear can be defined as a feeling of pain or disturbance caused by imagining something bad or harmful happening in the future. It's about harmful or painful things only, because there are some bad things, like wickedness or stupidity, that don't scare us. What I mean is things that cause serious pain or loss. And we only fear these things if they seem close, not far away. For example, we all know we're going to die, but we're not scared of it because death isn't near us yet. Based on this definition, fear is caused by whatever we think has the power to destroy or hurt us in a way that leads to great pain. This is why even the signs of such things scare us, making us feel like the bad thing is near. The idea of a bad thing coming close is what we call "danger."

Signs of danger include people who are angry at us and have the power to harm us. It's clear they want to do something to us, and they are ready to act. Also, when someone who has power is unjust, we fear them because unjust people want to do harm. Virtuous people who have been wronged and now have power are also scary because they want to retaliate. We also fear powerful people who are afraid because they're likely to strike first. Since most people are bad, greedy, and cowardly in danger, it's usually scary to be at someone else's mercy. So, if we've done something bad, we're scared those who know might betray or abandon us. People who can harm us are also scary if we're vulnerable. Usually, people harm others when they have the power to do so. We fear people we've wronged because they're looking for a chance to get back at us.

We also fear people who are feared by those stronger than us, because if they can hurt stronger people, they can definitely hurt us. The same goes for those who are already hurting weaker people. These people either are already strong or will be when they get stronger. Among those we've wronged or those who are our enemies, it's not the loud and emotional ones we should fear, but the quiet, sneaky, and dishonest ones. We never know when they'll strike, so we can't feel safe. All dangerous things are scarier if they don't give us a chance to fix our mistakes. And the worst things are the ones we can't stop or have little control over. In general, anything that causes us to feel pity when it happens to others will also cause us to feel fear when it threatens us.

These are the main things that cause fear. Now, let's look at the conditions in which we feel fear. If fear is connected to the belief that something bad will happen to us, then clearly, no one will feel afraid if they believe nothing bad can happen to them. We won't fear things we don't believe can happen to us, or people we think can't hurt us. And we won't fear things at times when we think we're safe from them. So, fear is felt by those who think something bad is likely to happen to them, at the hands of certain people, in a certain way, and at a certain time. People don't believe this when they're in the middle of great success and become arrogant, careless, or reckless—the kind of attitude that wealth, physical strength, lots of friends, and power can bring. Nor do they feel fear when they've already experienced every kind of horror and have become numb to what's coming, like people being beaten who are already close to death. If someone is going to feel the pain of uncertainty, they need to have some faint hope of escaping. This is because fear makes us think about what can be done, and no one does this when they feel completely hopeless. So, when an audience needs to be frightened, the speaker must make them feel they are truly in danger by pointing out that it has happened to others who were stronger than they are. The speaker should also show that it's happening now or has happened to people like them, at the hands of unexpected people, in unexpected ways, and at unexpected times.

Now that we understand the nature of fear, the things that cause it, and the different states of mind that lead to fear, we can also understand what confidence is. Confidence is the opposite of fear, and the things that cause confidence are the opposite of what causes fear. Confidence is the belief that what keeps us safe is near, and that what's harmful is either far away or absent. Confidence may come from the presence of things that make us feel safe or from the absence of things that scare us. We feel confident if we think we can do many or important things to fix or prevent trouble. We also feel confident if we haven't wronged others or been wronged by them, if we have no rivals or our rivals are weak, or if our strong rivals are our friends or have treated us well. We also feel confident if the people whose interests align with ours are more numerous or stronger than those against us.

We feel confident in ourselves if we believe we've succeeded many times and never faced defeat, or if we've often faced danger and come out safely. There are two main reasons people face danger calmly:

either they have no experience of it or they have ways to deal with it. For example, when people are in danger at sea, they feel confident either because they've never experienced a storm or because their experience has given them the skills to handle it. We also feel confident when nothing seems to scare people like us, people weaker than us, or people we believe we're stronger than. We believe this when we've defeated them or others as strong or stronger than they are.

We also feel confident if we think we have more and better resources than our rivals—things like wealth, physical strength, supporters, land, and weapons. We feel confident if we haven't wronged many people, or at least not the people we fear. And generally, we feel confident if we think our relationship with the gods is good, as shown by signs and oracles. Anger also makes us feel confident because it comes from the belief that we've been wronged, not that we are the ones doing wrong, and that divine powers support the wronged. We also feel confident when we start something new and believe we will not fail or that we will succeed completely.

Now, let's turn to shame and shamelessness. The following will explain the things that cause these feelings, the people in front of whom we feel them, and the situations in which they occur. Shame can be defined as a feeling of pain or disturbance about bad things, whether they're happening now, happened in the past, or are likely to happen in the future. These bad things seem like they will bring disgrace to us, while shamelessness is when we don't care about or look down on these same bad things. If this definition is true, it follows that we feel shame about things that we believe are disgraceful to ourselves or to those we care about.

These bad things are, first of all, caused by moral weakness. Examples are throwing away your shield or running away in battle because of cowardice. Also, refusing to return money or cheating others because of injustice. Engaging in sexual activities with forbidden people, at wrong times, or in wrong places shows a lack of self-control. Making money in petty or disgraceful ways, like taking advantage of the poor or the dead, also reflects greed and meanness. When it comes to money, we feel ashamed if we don't help others as much as we can, or if we take help from those worse off than ourselves. Similarly, borrowing when it looks like begging, or begging when it looks like asking for a favor to be returned, or asking for such a favor when it feels like begging—all of these actions show a lack of dignity. Praising someone just to get something out of them or being overly sympathetic to someone's sadness when you're with them also reveals a flatterer's mindset.

Refusing to endure hardships that are endured by people who are older, higher-ranking, or less capable than we are shows weakness. Accepting many favors from someone and then insulting them for giving those favors shows a low, ungrateful character. Talking too much about yourself, bragging loudly, or taking credit for others' achievements shows boastfulness. These, and similar actions, are disgraceful and show a lack of shame.

Another cause of shame is failing to have something honorable that everyone else, or nearly everyone like us, has. By "people like us," I mean people of the same race, country, age, family, or those on our level. Once we are on the same level as others, it's shameful to have less education or fewer advantages than they do. And it's even worse if it's our own fault. Whenever we are to blame for our past, present, or future situation, it's because of our own moral weakness. We also feel ashamed if we've had, or are about to have, something dishonorable done to us, like giving ourselves up to vile actions. Acts that involve giving in to others' desires are shameful, whether we do so willingly or unwillingly (being forced is an example of unwillingness), because surrendering without resistance shows weakness or cowardice.

These, and other similar things, cause us to feel shame. Since shame is a feeling connected to disgrace, and we want to avoid disgrace itself (not just its consequences), we care about the opinions of certain people. These are the people in front of whom we feel shame—the ones whose opinion matters to us. These people include those who admire us, those we admire, those whose admiration we seek, those with whom we compete, and those whose opinions we respect.

We admire people who have qualities we value, or those who can give us something we really want—just like a lover desires the approval of their beloved. We compete with those on our level. We respect the opinions of wise people, like our elders and those who are well-educated. We feel more shame if our actions are done publicly and everyone can see. This is why the saying goes, "Shame is in the eyes." For this reason, we feel the most shame in front of people who are always around us and notice what we do because they're always watching. We also feel ashamed in front of people who don't have the same faults as us, since it's clear their opinions are different from ours.

We feel ashamed in front of people who are harsh toward those they think are wrong. People usually don't mind their neighbors doing things they do themselves, but they get upset when their neighbors do things they don't do. We also feel ashamed in front of people who might tell others about what we've done. Not telling others is as good as not believing we've done something wrong. People are likely to spread news about us if we've wronged them because they're looking for ways to hurt us, or if they gossip about everyone, because those who attack innocent people will be even more eager to attack the guilty.

We also feel shame in front of people whose job is to criticize others, like satirists and comedy writers. These people are basically gossips and tale-bearers. We feel shame in front of people who don't yet know anything bad about us, because so far, they've admired us. That's why we feel embarrassed to refuse favors to those who ask us for something the first time—we haven't lost their good opinion yet. These people include those who want to become our friends for the first time because they've only seen our good side. They also include our old friends who don't know any bad things about us. We feel ashamed not only of shameful acts themselves but also of the evidence of those acts. For example, we're not just ashamed of engaging in sexual activities, but also of the signs of it. Similarly, we're ashamed not only of disgraceful actions but also of disgraceful talk.

We also feel shame not just in front of the people mentioned, but in front of those who might tell these people what we've done, like their servants or friends. And generally, we don't feel shame in front of people whose opinions we completely look down on as untrustworthy. No one feels ashamed in front of small children or animals. We don't feel ashamed of the same things in front of close friends as we do in front of strangers. In front of close friends, we feel ashamed of what we see as real faults, while in front of strangers, we feel ashamed of what are considered social faults.

The conditions that make us feel shame include having people in our lives who fit the description of those before whom we feel shame, as mentioned earlier. These people are those we admire, those who admire us, those whose admiration we seek, or those from whom we want something that we can't get if we lose their good opinion. These people might actually be watching us (like when Cydias told the Athenians to imagine that all the Greeks were watching how they voted), or they might be close enough to find out what we do. This is why we don't want to be seen by people who once wanted to be like us when we're in trouble—it reminds them of when they admired us.

We also feel ashamed when we're dishonoring actions or accomplishments that we or our ancestors are proud of. We feel shame before people for whose wrongdoings we would also feel shame, such as those we've mentioned before, those who take us as role models, those we've taught or advised, or others who are like us and with whom we compete. There are many things that shame in front of such people makes us do or avoid doing. And we feel even more shame when we'll be constantly seen by people who know about our disgrace. That's why, when the poet Antiphon was about to be beaten to death by Dionysius, and he saw the people who were about to die with him covering their faces, he asked them, "Why are you covering your faces? Is it because you're afraid these spectators will see you tomorrow?"

This is how shame works. To understand shamelessness, just think about the opposite of everything mentioned here.

Let's talk about Kindness now. Its definition will show us towards whom it is felt, why, and in what state of mind. Kindness is when someone helps a person in need, not to get anything in return, nor for their own benefit, but for the benefit of the person being helped.

Kindness is especially great when it's shown to someone who is in great need, or who needs something important and hard to get, or who needs it during an important and difficult crisis; or if the helper is the only one, the first, or the main person to give help. Natural desires make up such needs, especially strong desires accompanied by pain when they aren't fulfilled. These cravings include things like sexual desire and the urges that arise during injuries and dangers; because desire is active both in danger and in pain.

Therefore, those who stand by us in poverty or exile, even if they don't help us much, are truly kind to us because our need is great and urgent; like the man who gave the mat in the Lyceum. So, the help should ideally meet just this kind of need; and if not this kind, then some other kind that is as great or greater. Now we understand to whom, why, and under what conditions kindness is shown; and these facts must form the basis of our arguments.

We must show that the people helped are, or have been, in the kind of pain and need we've described, and that their helpers gave, or are giving, the kind of help described, in the kind of need described. We can also see how to remove the idea of kindness and make our opponents seem unkind: we might argue that they are being or have been helpful simply to promote their own interest—which, as we've stated, is not kindness; or that their action was accidental or forced upon them; or that they were not doing a favor but merely returning one, whether they know this or not—in either case, the action is just a repayment and is therefore not kindness even if the doer doesn't know the situation.

When considering this subject, we must look at all the categories: an act may be an act of kindness because (1) it is a specific thing, (2) it has a particular size or (3) quality, or (4) it's done at a particular time or (5) place. As evidence of the lack of kindness, we may point out that a smaller service had been refused to the person in need; or that the same service, or an equal or greater one, has been given to his enemies; these facts show that the service wasn't done for the sake of the person helped. Or we might point out that the thing desired was worthless and that the helper knew it: no one will admit they are in need of something worthless.

That's enough about Kindness and Unkindness. Now let's consider Pity, asking ourselves what things excite pity, for whom, and in what states of mind pity is felt. Pity can be defined as a feeling of pain caused by seeing some evil, destructive or painful, happen to someone who doesn't deserve it, and which we might expect could happen to us or a friend, and might happen soon.

To feel pity, we must be capable of thinking that some bad thing may happen to us or a friend of ours, and moreover, some such evil as we've defined or something similar. Therefore, pity is not felt by those completely ruined, who suppose that no further evil can befall them since the worst has already happened; nor by those who imagine themselves immensely fortunate—their feeling is rather arrogant pride, because when they think they possess all the good things in life, they believe that nothing bad can happen to them, which is one of the good things they think they have.

People who think bad things might happen to them include those who have already experienced it and have safely escaped from it; elderly people, due to their good sense and experience; weak people, especially those inclined to cowardice; and also educated people, since they can think ahead. Also, those who have parents living, or children, or wives; because these are close to us, and the evils mentioned above may easily befall them.

And those who are neither moved by courageous emotions like anger or confidence (these emotions ignore the future), nor by a disposition to arrogant insolence (arrogant people also ignore the possibility that something bad will happen to them), nor yet by great fear (panicked people do not feel pity because they are focused on themselves); only those who are between these extremes feel pity. To feel pity, we must also believe in the goodness of at least some people; if you think nobody is good, you will believe that everybody deserves bad fortune. In general, we feel pity whenever we are in the condition of remembering that similar misfortunes have happened to us or our loved ones, or expecting them to happen in the future.

That's enough about the mental conditions under which we feel pity. What we pity is clearly stated in the definition. All unpleasant and painful things excite pity if they tend to destroy or cause pain and ruin; and all such evils that are due to chance, if they are serious. The painful and destructive evils are: death in its various forms, bodily injuries and afflictions, old age, diseases, lack of food.

The evils due to chance are: being without friends, having few friends (it's a pitiful thing to be torn away from friends and companions), deformity, weakness, mutilation; evil coming from a source from which good ought to have come; and the frequent repetition of such misfortunes. Also, the coming of good when the worst has happened—for example, the arrival of the Great King's gifts for Diopeithes after his death. Also, when no good has come to a person at all, or when they can't enjoy it when it does come.

So, the reasons we feel pity are these or similar. The people we pity are those we know, as long as they aren't very closely related to us—in that case, we feel about them as if we were in danger ourselves. For this reason, they say Amasis did not weep at the sight of his son being led to death, but did weep when he saw his friend begging: the latter sight was pitiful, the former terrible, and the terrible is different from the pitiful; it tends to cast out pity and often helps to produce the opposite of pity.

Also, we feel pity when the danger is near ourselves. We also pity those who are like us in age, character, disposition, social standing, or birth; because in all these cases, it seems more likely that the same misfortune may befall us too. Here, we must remember the general principle that what we fear for ourselves excites our pity when it happens to others.

Furthermore, since it's when the sufferings of others are close to us that they excite our pity (we cannot remember what disasters happened a hundred centuries ago, nor look forward to what will happen a hundred centuries in the future, and therefore feel little pity, if any, for such things), it follows that those who enhance the effect of their words with suitable gestures, tones, dress, and dramatic action are especially successful in exciting pity: they put the disasters before our eyes and make them seem close to us, just happening or just past.

Anything that has just happened, or is going to happen soon, is particularly pitiful; so too are the signs and actions of sufferers—the garments and the like of those who have already suffered; the words and the like of those actually suffering—for instance, those who are on the point of death. Most pitiful of all is when, in such times of trial, the victims are persons of noble character: whenever they are so, our pity is especially excited, because their innocence, as well as seeing their misfortunes before our eyes, makes their misfortunes seem close to ourselves.

The feeling most directly opposed to pity is called Indignation. Feeling pain at someone's undeserved good fortune is, in one sense, opposite to feeling pain at someone's undeserved bad fortune, and comes from the same moral qualities. Both feelings are associated with good moral character; it is our duty both to feel sympathy and pity for undeserved distress, and to feel indignation at undeserved prosperity; because whatever is undeserved is unjust, and that's why we ascribe indignation even to the gods.

It might be thought that envy is similarly opposed to pity, on the ground that envy is closely akin to indignation, or even the same thing. But it's not the same. It's true that envy is also a disturbing pain caused by the prosperity of others. But it's excited not by the prosperity of the undeserving but by that of people who are like us or equal to us.

The two feelings have this in common: they are not due to something bad likely to happen to ourselves, but only to what is happening to our neighbor. The feeling ceases to be envy in one case and indignation in the other, and becomes fear if the pain and disturbance are due to the prospect of something bad for ourselves as a result of the other person's good fortune.

The feelings of pity and indignation will obviously be accompanied by the opposite feelings of satisfaction. If you are pained by the undeserved distress of others, you will be pleased, or at least not pained, by their deserved distress. Therefore, no good person can be upset by the punishment of parricides or murderers. These are things we are bound to rejoice at, as we must at the prosperity of the deserving; both these things are just, and both give pleasure to any honest person, since he cannot help expecting that what has happened to someone like him will happen to him too.

All these feelings are associated with the same type of moral character. And their opposites are associated with the opposite type; the person who is delighted by others' misfortunes is identical with the person who envies others' prosperity. Because anyone who is pained by the occurrence or existence of a given thing must be pleased by that thing's non-existence or destruction. We can now see that all these feelings tend to prevent pity (though they differ among themselves for the reasons given), so all are equally useful for countering an appeal to pity.

We will first consider Indignation—saving the other emotions for later—and ask with whom, on what grounds, and in what states of mind we may feel indignant. These questions are really answered by what we've already said. Indignation is the pain caused by seeing undeserved good fortune. So, it's clear to begin with that there are some forms of good whose sight cannot cause it.

For example, a person may be just or brave, or acquire moral goodness; but we will not be indignant with him for that reason, any more than we will pity him for the opposite reason. Indignation is aroused by the sight of wealth, power, and the like—by all those things, roughly speaking, which are deserved by good people and by those who possess the goods of nature—noble birth, beauty, and so on.

Also, what is long established seems similar to what exists by nature; therefore, we feel more indignation at those possessing a given good if they have only just gotten it and the prosperity it brings. The newly rich offend more than those whose wealth is long-standing and inherited. The same is true of those who have office or power, plenty of friends, a fine family, and so on.

We feel the same when these advantages of theirs secure them others. Because again, the newly rich give us more offense by obtaining office through their riches than do those whose wealth is long-standing; and so in all other cases. The reason is that what the latter have is felt to be really their own, but what the others have is not; what appears to have always been as it is, is regarded as real, and so the possessions of the newly rich do not seem to be really their own.

Also, not every person deserves any given kind of good; there is a certain appropriateness in such things. For instance, it's fitting for brave men, not just men, to have fine weapons, and for men of noble birth, not upstarts, to make distinguished marriages. Indignation may therefore be properly felt when anyone gets what is not appropriate for him, though he may be a good man.

It may also be felt when anyone sets himself up against his superior, especially against his superior in some particular respect— hence the lines:

"Only from battle he shrank with Aias, Telamon's son;

Zeus would have been angered with him, had he fought with someone stronger."

But also, even apart from that, when the inferior in any sense contends with his superior; a musician, for instance, with a just man, for justice is a finer thing than music.

Enough has been said to make clear the grounds on which, and the persons against whom, Indignation is felt—they are those mentioned and others like them. As for the people who feel it; we feel it if we ourselves deserve the greatest possible goods and moreover have them, because it is unjust that those who are not our equals should be considered to deserve as much as we have. Or, secondly, we feel it if we are really good and honest people; our judgment is then sound, and we loathe any kind of injustice.

Also, if we are ambitious and eager to achieve particular goals, especially if we are ambitious for what others are getting without deserving to get it. And, generally, if we think that we ourselves deserve something and that others do not, we are inclined to be indignant with those others concerning that thing. Therefore, servile, worthless, unambitious people are not inclined to Indignation, since there is nothing they can believe themselves to deserve.

From all this, it is clear what sort of people those are at whose misfortunes, distresses, or failures we ought to feel pleased, or at least not pained: by considering the facts described, we see at once what their opposites are. If, therefore, our speech puts the judges in such a frame of mind as that indicated and shows that those who claim pity on certain definite grounds do not deserve to receive pity but do deserve not to receive it, it will be impossible for the judges to feel pity.

Now, let's look at Envy: we can understand why we feel it, who we feel it towards, and what kind of state of mind we are in when we feel it. Envy is the pain we feel when we see someone else having good fortune, specifically the kinds of good things we've already talked about. We feel it towards people who are like us, not because we want what they have, but because they have it, and we don't. We feel envy when we consider someone our equal, and by "equal," I mean in terms of birth, relationships, age, personality, reputation, or wealth.

We also tend to feel envy if we fall just short of having everything we want. This is why people who are powerful and prosperous often feel envious—they think others are taking what should be theirs. We also feel it if we are especially known for something, especially if it's wisdom or good fortune. People who are ambitious tend to feel more envy than those who are not. The same goes for those who claim to be wise; they want to be seen as wise. In general, anyone who strives for a certain reputation tends to feel envy in that area. Small-minded people feel envy easily because everything seems big to them.

The types of good things that make people feel envious have already been mentioned. These include actions or possessions that bring respect, honor, and the desire for fame, and nearly all of them are things that can cause envy. This is especially true if we want the thing ourselves, believe we deserve it, or think that having it would make us a little better than others, while not having it would make us a little worse. It's also clear who we tend to envy—those who are close to us in time, place, age, or reputation.

This is why there is a saying: "Family members can be jealous of each other."

We also feel envy towards our competitors—people just like the ones we've been talking about. We don't compete with people who lived a hundred centuries ago, or those not yet born, or the dead, or people living far away. Nor do we compete with people we consider far below or far above us. Instead, we compete with those who want the same things we do—our rivals in sports or love, for example. So, it's these people we are most likely to envy.

Another saying goes: "Potter envies potter."

We also feel envy towards people whose success makes us feel like failures. These are people we see as our neighbors or equals because it feels like it's our own fault that we didn't get the good thing they have. This bothers us and makes us feel envy. We also envy people who have what we believe we should have, or who got something we used to have. This is why older people often envy the young, and people who spend a lot of money envy those who spend less but get the same thing.

People also feel envy when they don't have something, or haven't gotten it yet, and they see someone else getting it quickly. We can also understand what things and people bring joy to envious people, and in what states of mind they feel it. The states of mind that bring pain are the same ones that will bring joy when the opposite happens. So, if we ourselves are in an envious state of mind, and those who are asking for our pity or help are in the same position we have described, it's clear they won't get our pity.

Next, we'll look at Emulation, focusing on its causes, its objects, and the state of mind in which it occurs. Emulation is the pain we feel when we see someone like us enjoying good things that we also value and could have for ourselves, but don't yet. However, this feeling isn't caused by the fact that someone else has these good things, but because we don't have them. Therefore, emulation is a good feeling, felt by good people, while envy is a bad feeling, felt by bad people.

Emulation encourages us to work for the good things we want, while envy makes us try to take those things away from our neighbor. Emulation is more likely to be felt by people who think they deserve certain good things that they don't yet have. It's important to note that no one tries for things they believe are impossible to get. This feeling is common in young people and people with high ambitions. It is also felt by those who already possess good things that are fitting for people held in high regard—such as wealth, many friends, public office, and so on.

These people think that since they deserve to be honored, they should also get these goods. They are driven by emulation because they believe these things belong to people with good character. Also, we feel emulation when others believe we deserve something. We feel this way about anything for which our ancestors, relatives, close friends, race, or country are highly honored, seeing it as something we should have, too. Since all things that are greatly honored are objects of emulation, moral goodness in its various forms must be something people emulate, as well as any good thing that benefits others. People honor those who are morally good, as well as those who are helpful to them.

We also tend to emulate people who have wealth and beauty more than those who have health, because wealth and beauty can bring joy to others. It's easy to see who we tend to emulate. These are the people who have qualities like courage, wisdom, or public office. Generals, speakers, and others in high positions can do a lot of good for many people. We also emulate those we want to be like, those who have many friends, and those admired by others.

People of the opposite kind, however, are objects of contempt, since the feeling of contempt is the opposite of emulation. People who are able to emulate or be emulated by others tend to look down on those who have bad qualities that are the opposite of the good things we've mentioned. They despise them for this reason. We often despise people who are lucky when their luck seems undeserved because they don't have the qualities that should come with it.

This wraps up our discussion of the feelings that can be created or eliminated, and the ways these emotions influence persuasive arguments.

Let's now look at the different types of human character in relation to emotions and moral qualities, and how they match up with different ages and circumstances. When I say emotions, I mean things like anger, desire, and so on, which we've already talked about. When I say moral qualities, I mean virtues and vices, which we've also covered, as well as the things different types of people are likely to want or do. By "ages," I mean youth, middle age, and old age. By "circumstances," I mean birth, wealth, power, and their opposites—in other words, good and bad fortune.

Let's start with the character of young people. Young men are passionate and tend to give in to their desires without much thought. Of all their bodily desires, sexual desire has the most control over them, and they often lack self-control in this area. They are also changeable and inconsistent in what they want. Their desires are strong, but short-lived, like a sick person's sudden hunger or thirst. They are quick-tempered and often let their anger take over. This happens because they love honor and can't stand being disrespected. If they feel unfairly treated, they become indignant. While they love honor, they love winning even more. Youth is eager to prove itself and victory is one way of doing that.

They value both of these things more than money, because they haven't yet learned what it's like to live without it. This is why Pittacus once made a remark about Amphiaraus. Young men tend to see the good in things rather than the bad, because they haven't yet seen much wickedness. They trust others easily because they haven't been cheated very often. They are hopeful, their youthful energy making them optimistic like they've had too much wine, and they have had few disappointments so far.

Their lives are focused more on what's ahead of them than what's behind, as they have a long future and little past to remember. The further back they go, the less they have to recall, which is why they focus on what lies ahead. They are easily deceived because of their optimistic nature. Their tempers and hopeful outlook make them braver than older people. Anger reduces fear, and hope increases confidence. When people are angry, they don't feel afraid, and when they expect good things to happen, they feel sure of themselves.

They are shy, following the rules of society in which they were raised, and they haven't yet developed their own standards. They also have high ideals, as they haven't been humbled by life or learned about its limitations. Their hopeful outlook makes them believe they can achieve great things, which is another reason for their high ambitions. They would rather do what is noble than what is useful. They live more by their sense of right and wrong than by practical thinking, which is why they prefer noble actions over useful ones. They are more attached to their friends and companions than older people because they enjoy spending time with others and haven't yet come to value their friends for what they can offer.

They tend to go to extremes in everything they do. They don't follow Chilon's advice, overdoing everything—whether it's love, hate, or anything else. They think they know everything and are always completely sure of themselves, which is why they tend to go too far. If they wrong someone, it's usually because they mean to insult them, not because they want to cause actual harm.

Young people are also quick to feel pity because they assume everyone is as good as they are, or at least better than they actually are. They judge others by their own harmless nature and don't think anyone deserves to be treated badly. They enjoy having fun and are often witty, as wit is a form of well-bred mischief.

Now let's talk about older men, those who have passed their prime. Their character is mostly made up of traits that are the opposite of those of young men. They have lived a long time, been fooled many times, and made many mistakes. Life, for them, has been tough, so they are never sure of anything and do everything with caution. They 'think' instead of 'knowing,' and because they are hesitant, they often add 'maybe' or 'perhaps' to everything they say. They are cynical, always looking at the worst side of things.

Their experience has made them suspicious and distrustful, so they neither love deeply nor hate passionately. As Bias said, they love as if they will one day hate and hate as if they will one day love. They are small-minded because life has humbled them, and their desires are limited to just what they need to survive. They are not generous because they have learned how hard it is to get money and how easy it is to lose it.

Older people are more cowardly and constantly worry about danger. Unlike the hot-blooded nature of youth, their temperament is cold, making them more prone to fear. They love life even more as they get closer to death, because people tend to desire what they don't have. They are also more self-centered, which is another form of small-mindedness. They are driven more by practical considerations than by noble ones, as the practical is what benefits them personally, while the noble is good for everyone.

They aren't shy, but more shameless, because they care more about what's useful than about what people think of them. They have little confidence in the future, both because of their experience—since most things turn out worse than expected—and their cowardice. They live more in the past than in the future because they have little future left, and memory focuses on the past. This is why they tend to talk a lot, always discussing the past, as they enjoy remembering it.

Their anger is quick but weak. Their physical desires have either faded or become less intense, so they don't feel them much, and their actions are driven more by greed than by passion. This is why people often think older men are self-controlled, but the truth is their passions have weakened, and they are motivated by the love of money. Older men live by reasoning more than by moral feeling; reasoning focuses on practicality, while moral feeling focuses on goodness.

If they wrong someone, they intend to cause harm, not insult. Old men may still feel pity, but for different reasons than young men. Young men pity others out of kindness, while old men pity others because they see that anything bad that happens to someone else could happen to them too. This thought provokes pity. Older men are also more likely to complain and less likely to joke or laugh, as the love of laughter is the opposite of complaining.

These, then, are the traits of young men and older men. People always appreciate speeches that reflect their own character, and now we can see how to craft speeches that appeal to our audiences by reflecting both their character and ours.

Now, let's talk about Men in their Prime. It's clear that their character lies somewhere between that of the young and the old, without the extremes of either. They don't have the overconfidence of the young, which can lead to recklessness, nor do they have the fearfulness of the old. Instead, they show the right balance of confidence and caution. They don't trust everyone, but they don't distrust everyone either—they judge people fairly.

Their lives are guided by both noble and practical considerations, not just one or the other. They avoid being either stingy or wasteful, instead choosing what is appropriate for the situation. When it comes to anger and desire, they are both brave and self-controlled. The young are brave but lack self-control, while the old are cautious but often too fearful. To sum it up, the best qualities of youth and old age are combined in people who are in their prime, while the excesses or shortcomings of each are balanced by moderation and good judgment.

The body reaches its prime between the ages of thirty and thirty-five, while the mind matures around the age of forty-nine.

This concludes the discussion of the character types found in youth, old age, and middle age. Now, let's turn to the influence of Fortune on human character, starting with Good Birth. Being born into a respected family makes people more ambitious. Anyone who starts life with advantages tends to want to build on them, and good birth implies that their ancestors were important. People who are well-born often look down on others, even those who are just as good as their own ancestors. This is because we see far-off achievements as greater than those that are closer to us, and they are easier to boast about.

However, being well-born—meaning from a good family—must be distinguished from nobility, which refers to living up to the standards of one's family. Most well-born people lack this quality, and many of them turn out to be weak. Like crops from the earth, the quality of people varies from generation to generation. Sometimes, a good family line produces exceptional individuals for a while, but then it starts to decline. A family known for intelligence can give way to people with eccentric or even unstable characters, like the descendants of Alcibiades or the elder Dionysius. On the other hand, a family known for being steady can decline into dullness and laziness, like the descendants of Cimon, Pericles, and Socrates.

The character of people shaped by Wealth is easy for anyone to see. Wealthy people often become arrogant and rude. Their wealth affects how they think, making them feel as if they possess every good thing in the world. They begin to see wealth as the measure of everything else.

Book 3

When making a speech, you need to focus on three things: first, how to persuade the audience; second, the language or style to use; and third, how to arrange the different parts of the speech in the right order. We've already talked about the ways to persuade. We said there are three main ways to persuade:

1. by appealing to the emotions of the audience,
2. by making them trust the speaker's character, and
3. by proving that the speaker's statements are true.

We also discussed enthymemes and the sources of arguments for them, noting that there are both specific and general types of arguments for these.

Next, we'll look at style. It's not enough to know what you need to say; you also have to say it the right way. Good style helps make a speech more effective. The first thing we discussed was naturally how persuasion comes from the facts themselves. Now, the second thing is how to present those facts in a proper way through language. The third thing, which is also important, is the way the speech is delivered. Delivery plays a big part in how successful a speech is, but it's been neglected for a long time. Even in theater and epic storytelling, it took a while to become an art form. In the past, poets acted out their plays themselves. It's clear that delivering a speech is as important in oratory as it is in poetry. (In poetry, delivery has been studied by people like Glaucon of Teos.) Essentially, delivery is about controlling your voice to express different emotions—speaking loudly, softly, or somewhere in between; using a high, low, or medium pitch; and adjusting the rhythm to match the subject. A speaker needs to think about these three things: volume, pitch, and rhythm. Those who do this well often win prizes in dramatic competitions. In public life, actors are now more important than poets, due to flaws in our political systems.

No complete guide on the rules of delivery has been written yet. Even the study of language itself made little progress for a long time. Delivery is not considered a very high-class subject to study, and that's understandable. Still, because rhetoric is all about appearances, we must pay attention to delivery, even though it's not the most respected topic. This is because we can't succeed without it. Ideally, we shouldn't need to do more than avoid annoying our listeners, without trying to charm them too much. We should win our arguments based on facts alone, so nothing but the proof of those facts should matter. However, as I've already said, other factors do influence the result because of the flaws in our audience. The way we speak does have a small but real effect, no matter what we're talking about, because the way something is said affects how clear it is. But style doesn't matter as much as people think. Fancy language is just for show and meant to entertain the audience. Nobody uses flowery language when teaching math.

When the principles of delivery are fully developed, they'll have the same impact as performance does on stage. But so far, only a few people, like Thrasymachus in his "Appeals to Pity," have made small attempts to explain them. The ability to perform dramatically is a natural talent and is hard to teach in a systematic way. However, the principles of good diction can be taught, and that's why we have skilled speakers who win prizes for their ability, just like those who are good at delivering speeches. Written or literary speeches rely more on their style than on their ideas.

It was the poets who first started using elevated language because words represent things, and they could use the human voice to represent emotions, too. The voice is the best tool we have for that. This is how the arts of reciting and acting were developed, along with other arts. Poets seemed to become famous because of their fancy language, even when their ideas were simple, so orators began to imitate them. For example, Gorgias's prose had a poetic style. Even today, many uneducated people think that poetic language makes the best speeches. But that's not true—prose language should be different from poetry. This is proven by how things are today, as even the language of tragedy has changed. Just like iambic meter was adopted instead of tetrameter because it is the closest to natural speech, tragedy has dropped the flowery words used in the early dramas, which are still found in epic poems. So, it's silly to imitate a poetic style that even poets no longer use. It's now clear that we don't need to discuss the whole question of style in detail, just the part that concerns rhetoric. The poetic side of style was already covered in the work on the Art of Poetry.

So, let's start from the observations made there, including the definition of style. Good style should be clear, as we know from the fact that if a speech doesn't make its meaning clear, it fails to do what speech is supposed to do. Style should also be appropriate, avoiding both low and overly elevated language. Poetic language may avoid being low, but it's not suited for prose. Clarity is achieved by using common, everyday words for both nouns and verbs. To avoid sounding low and to add elegance, you can use the other kinds of words mentioned in the Art of Poetry. Using different kinds of words makes language sound more impressive. People don't feel the same about strangers as they do about their fellow citizens, and the same is true for language. So, it's a good idea to give everyday speech a slightly unfamiliar touch, as people like to be surprised by something different.

In poetry, this happens a lot, and it works well there because the subjects are often removed from ordinary life. In prose, this happens less often because the subjects are more down-to-earth. Even in poetry, fancy language isn't always right, like when it's used by a slave or a young person, or when the subject is something trivial. To be appropriate, the style sometimes needs to be toned down and sometimes raised.

It's clear now that a writer needs to hide their skill and make it seem like they're speaking naturally, not artificially. Naturalness is persuasive, while artificiality has the opposite effect. When people sense that you're being artificial, they think you're trying to trick them, like when you water down their wine. It's like the difference between the voice of Theodorus and other actors: his voice really sounds like the character he's playing, while theirs do not. We can hide our effort by using ordinary words, the kind people use every day. Euripides, a poet, was the first to show how this could be done in his plays.

Language is made up of nouns and verbs. The different kinds of nouns were discussed in the Art of Poetry. Unusual, compound, and made-up words should only be used sparingly and in certain cases, which we'll talk about later. The reason for this is that they go too far from what's appropriate. In prose, besides the regular words for things, metaphors are the only other useful tool. We know this because both regular words and metaphors are what everyone uses in conversation. We now understand that a good writer can create a style that is clear without being too fancy, which matches our idea of what good oratorical prose should be. Words with multiple meanings are mostly useful for sophists who want to mislead people. Poets benefit from synonyms—words that have the same general meaning, like 'advancing' and 'proceeding', both of which are common and mean the same thing.

The Art of Poetry, as we've said before, has definitions of these different types of words, a classification of metaphors, and explains that metaphors are important in both poetry and prose. However, prose writers should focus especially on metaphors because they have fewer resources than poets do. Metaphors give style clarity, charm, and distinction in a way nothing else can. But metaphors aren't something that one person can easily teach another. Like epithets, metaphors need to be appropriate, meaning they should fit the thing they describe. If not, their lack of fit will be obvious, and the mismatch will stand out. It's like picking the right clothes for an old man—he wouldn't look good in the bright red cloak that suits a young man.

If you want to compliment someone, use a metaphor that makes them sound better. If you want to insult them, use a metaphor that makes them seem worse. For example, since opposites are often in the same category, you could say that a person who begs is 'praying', and that a person who prays is 'begging', as both actions are forms of asking. Iphicrates called Callias a 'beggar priest' instead of a 'torch-bearer', and Callias replied that Iphicrates must be uninitiated, or else he would've called him a 'torch-bearer' instead of a 'beggar priest'. Both are religious titles, but one is honorable and the other is not. Similarly, someone once called actors 'followers of Dionysus', but the actors called themselves 'artists'. Both are metaphors, but one is meant as an insult and the other as a compliment. Pirates now call themselves 'suppliers'. In this way, we can describe a crime as a mistake or a mistake as a crime. You could say a thief 'took' something or that he 'plundered' his victim.

An example from Euripides' Telephus shows how a metaphor can be inappropriate: "King of the oar, on Mysia's coast he landed." Here, the word 'king' is too grand for the subject, making the metaphor stand out too much. A metaphor can also fail if the sounds of the words used in it are harsh or unpleasant. Dionysius the Brazen once called poetry 'Calliope's screech'. Poetry and screeching both involve sounds, but the metaphor is bad because screeching is harsh and unpleasant, unlike poetry.

When using metaphors for things that don't have a name, it's better to take them from similar things that are closely related, so the connection is clear as soon as the metaphor is spoken. For example, in the famous riddle, "I saw a man gluing bronze with fire to another man's body," the process described has no name. However, both this process and gluing are forms of attaching things, so it makes sense to call the use of a cupping-glass 'gluing'. Good riddles often provide good metaphors because a metaphor is like a riddle, and a good riddle usually has a good metaphor.

Additionally, the materials for metaphors should be beautiful. As Licymnius says, both the sound and the meaning of words can be beautiful—or ugly. There's also another consideration that disproves the false argument of the sophist Bryson, who said there is no such thing as offensive language because the meaning is the same no matter which words you use. This is not true. One word can describe something more accurately than another, bringing the idea to life more vividly. Different words can show the same thing in different ways, so one term can be more beautiful or uglier than another. Both words may express fairness or foulness, but not to the same degree.

Metaphors should be pleasing to the ear, to the mind, and to the senses. It's better to say 'rosy-fingered dawn' than 'red-fingered' or, even worse, 'crimson-fingered dawn'. The epithets we use can also have a good or bad connotation, like calling Orestes a 'mother-killer' or calling him 'his father's avenger'. Simonides once refused to write a poem for the winner of a mule race because he found it unpleasant to write about "half-donkeys." But after he was paid well, he wrote, "Hail to you, daughters of swift-footed steeds!" even though the mules were also daughters of donkeys. The same effect can be achieved with diminutives, which make bad things seem less bad and good things seem less good. For example, in Aristophanes' Babylonians, he makes fun by saying 'goldlet' instead of 'gold', 'cloaklet' instead of 'cloak', and 'plaguelet' instead of 'plague'. However, whether using epithets or diminutives, we must be careful and strike a balance.

Bad taste in language can show up in four ways:

1.   The misuse of compound words. For example, Lycophron talks about the 'many-faced heaven' above the 'giant-headed earth' and the 'narrow-shore path.' Gorgias uses phrases like the 'poor-poet flatterer' and 'breaking promises while keeping others.' Alcidamas says things like 'the soul filling with rage, and the face turning flame-red,' and 'he thought their enthusiasm would lead to success,' or 'success was the result of his words.' He also says, 'the dark-colored floor of the sea.' All these compound words sound better suited for poetry. So, this is one way bad taste can appear.

2.   Another way is using strange or unusual words. For instance, Lycophron speaks of 'the extraordinary Xerxes' and 'thieving Sciron,' while Alcidamas says 'a toy for poetry' and 'the foolishness of nature.' He also says, 'sharpened by the unbending spirit of his mind.'

3.   A third form of bad taste is using too many long or unnecessary adjectives. A poet can describe 'white milk,' but in prose, this kind of description may feel out of place, or if used too often, it makes the writing sound like poetry. Of course, we need to use some adjectives because they make the writing stand out and give it a certain quality. But we should aim for a balance, or the result will be worse than not trying at all. Instead of improving the writing, it can make it worse. That's why Alcidamas's use of adjectives seems so overdone— he doesn't treat them like seasoning for a dish but like the dish itself. For example, he doesn't just say 'sweat' but 'the wet sweat.' Instead of saying 'to the Isthmian games,' he says 'to the world-gathering of the Isthmian games.' Instead of simply 'laws,' he says 'the laws that rule the states.' And instead of 'at a run,' he says, 'his heart urging him to run fast.' He also doesn't say 'a school of the Muses' but 'the natural school of the Muses that he inherited.' He uses phrases like 'frowning care of heart,' and instead of 'gaining popularity,' he says, 'gaining universal popularity.' This kind of overuse makes his language seem absurd and unclear. When the meaning is already obvious, using too many words just makes it harder to understand.

The usual time to use compound words is when there isn't a simple term for something, and a compound can be easily made, like the word 'pastime.' But if you do this too much, the writing stops sounding like prose. That's why compound words are more common for writers of dithyrambs (a type of ancient Greek hymn) who like loud, booming words. Strange words are for writers of epic poetry, which is grand and lofty, while metaphors are best suited for iambic verse, the meter often used today.

4. The fourth area where bad taste shows up is in the use of metaphors. Just like other things, metaphors can be misused. Some are ridiculous, and that's why comic poets and tragic poets both use them. Others are too grand and theatrical, and if they're too far-fetched, they can be confusing. For example, Gorgias speaks of 'events that are green and full of sap,' and says, 'you planted a bad deed, and a terrible harvest you reaped.' That sounds too much like poetry. Alcidamas once called philosophy 'a fortress threatening the power of law' and the Odyssey 'a beautiful mirror of human life.' He also spoke of 'not offering such a toy to poetry.' These expressions don't work for the reasons I've mentioned—they don't connect with the listener.

Another example is Gorgias's comment to a swallow that had dropped something on him as it flew by. He said, 'Shame on you, Philomela.' He was making a joke, addressing her as the girl she once was, not the bird she is now. It was a good jab because, as a bird, the act wasn't shameful, but as a girl, it would have been.

A simile is also a metaphor; the difference is small. When a poet says Achilles 'leapt on the enemy like a lion,' it's a simile. But if he says, 'the lion leapt on the enemy,' it's a metaphor—he's calling Achilles a lion because they're both brave. Similes can be useful in both prose and poetry, but not too often, since they're more like poetry. You should use similes the same way you use metaphors, as they are nearly the same thing except for this slight difference.

Here are some examples of similes. Androtion said that Idrieus was like a dog let off the leash, ready to attack and bite. Theodamas compared Archidamus to Euxenus, who couldn't do geometry. This simile shows that Euxenus is like an Archidamus who can't do math. In Plato's Republic, those who strip the dead are compared to dogs that bite the stones thrown at them but don't touch the person who threw them. There's also a simile comparing the Athenian people to a ship's captain who is strong but a little deaf. Another compares poets' verses to people who are fresh and youthful, but once the freshness fades, the beauty is gone—just like verses that lose their charm when broken into prose. Pericles compared the Samians to children who take their food but still cry. He compared the Boeotians to oak trees, saying they were destroying each other in civil wars, just as one oak tree causes another to fall. Demosthenes said the Athenian people were like seasick men on a ship. He also compared political speakers to nurses who swallow the food themselves but smear the children's lips with spit. Antisthenes compared the skinny Cephisodotus to frankincense, saying that his thinness was enjoyable, just like frankincense.

All these comparisons can be made as either similes or metaphors. A good metaphor will also work as a simile, and a simile can be turned into a metaphor by removing the explanation. But the proportional metaphor must always work both ways. For example, if a drinking bowl is called the shield of Dionysus, a shield can also be called the drinking bowl of Ares.

These are the elements that make up speech. The foundation of good style is correct language, which can be broken down into five main points.

1. First, the proper use of connecting words and arranging them in the right order. For example, the connective 'men' (as in ego men) requires the correlative de (as in o de). You must introduce the second word before the first is forgotten, and not let too many other words get in the way. Avoid inserting

too many connectives before finishing the thought. For example: "But as soon as he told me (because Cleon had come begging and pleading), he took them along and set out." If too many words get in the way before "set out," the meaning gets lost. So, one key to good style is the proper use of connecting words.

2. The second point is to use specific names for things instead of vague or general ones.

3. The third point is to avoid being unclear, unless you want to be vague on purpose, like those who have nothing to say but want to seem like they do. These people tend to use this style in poetry. Empedocles, for example, uses long-winded phrases to impress his audience, much like fortune-tellers who use unclear language to sound wise.

Fortune-tellers use general statements because they are less likely to be proven wrong. It's easier to guess 'even' or 'odd' in a guessing game than to guess the exact number. In the same way, fortune-tellers have a better chance of being right if they say something will happen, without specifying when it will happen. This kind of unclear language has the same effect and should be avoided unless you have a specific reason for using it. (4) The fourth rule is to follow Protagoras' classification of nouns as male, female, or inanimate and use them correctly. For example: "When she arrived, she spoke and then left." (5) The fifth rule is to express plurality, fewness, and unity correctly. For example: "When they arrived, they struck me."

In general, written work should be easy to read and therefore easy to deliver aloud. This isn't possible when there are too many connecting words or clauses, or when the punctuation is unclear, like in the writings of Heracleitus. His work is hard to punctuate because it's not always clear if a word belongs with what comes before or after it. For example, at the beginning of his treatise, he says, "Though this truth is always, men understand it not," and it's unclear whether "always" goes with the first part or the second part of the sentence.

Another thing that causes mistakes is when you attach a third idea to two ideas that don't fit with it. For example, "sound" and "color" don't both work with the same verbs: you can "perceive" both, but you can't "see" both. Finally, confusion happens if you try to give too much information without first making your main point clear. For example, saying, "I meant, after telling him this, that, and the other, to set out," is less clear than saying, "I meant to set out after telling him; then, this, that, and the other thing happened."

The following suggestions will help make your language more impressive:

1. Instead of simply naming something, describe it. For example, instead of saying 'circle,' say 'a shape where every point is the same distance from the center.' To be concise, do the opposite—use the name instead of a description. When mentioning something ugly or offensive, use the name if the description is ugly, and use a description if the name is ugly.
2. Use metaphors and epithets, but be careful not to make it sound too much like poetry.
3. Use the plural form instead of the singular, like in poetry, where you might see something like "the Achaean havens" even though only one harbor is meant, or "the many-leaved folds of my letter."
4. Don't group two words under one article—give each word its own, like 'that wife of ours.' But to be concise, you can combine them, like saying 'our wife.' Use plenty of connecting words, but if you want to be concise, leave them out while still keeping the connection, like saying 'having gone and spoken' versus 'having gone, I spoke.' (6) Another useful technique comes from Antimachus, who described something by talking about what it's not. For example, he described Teumessus by saying, "It is a small, wind-swept hill." You can apply this technique to good or bad qualities, depending on what you're talking about. Poets use this device to create phrases like 'stringless' or 'lyreless melody.' A good example is calling a

trumpet sound 'a lyreless melody.'

Your language will feel appropriate if it matches the emotion and character of the subject. 'Matching the subject' means you shouldn't speak casually about serious matters, or use solemn language for trivial things. You also shouldn't use fancy adjectives for simple nouns—otherwise, it will sound ridiculous, like in the works of Cleophon, who wrote absurd phrases like 'O queenly fig-tree.' To express emotion, you should use the language of anger when talking about injustice, the language of disgust or reluctance when talking about impiety or something foul, and the language of joy when telling a story of glory. Use the right tone for each situation.

This kind of language makes people believe your story. They think you're telling the truth because people usually behave the way you describe when facing similar situations. As a result, they believe what you're saying, whether it's true or not. An emotional speaker often makes the audience feel the same way, even if the argument itself isn't strong. That's why many speakers try to overwhelm their audience with just noise.

This way of presenting your story also reflects your character. Each type of person, and each kind of personality, will have its own way of expressing the truth. By 'type of person,' I mean differences like age—whether someone is a boy, a man, or an old man. I also mean differences in gender, like being a man or a woman, or nationality, like being Spartan or Thessalian. By 'personality,' I mean only those qualities that shape a person's character, as not every trait does this. If a speaker uses words that fit a certain personality, they will bring that character to life. For instance, a rustic person and an educated person won't say the same things or speak in the same way.

Another way to impress the audience is by using a common tactic of speechwriters—phrases like 'Who doesn't know this?' or 'Everyone knows.' The listener may feel embarrassed about not knowing, so they'll agree with the speaker to appear knowledgeable.

All the different styles of speech can be used either appropriately or inappropriately. One way to counteract exaggeration is to include a small criticism of yourself. People will think it's fine for you to speak this way because it seems like you know what you're doing. Also, it's better if not everything fits together too perfectly because then your audience won't see through your speech as easily. For example, if your words are harsh, don't also make your tone of voice and facial expressions harsh—otherwise, your speech will seem too rehearsed. But if you mix things up by using one technique and not the other, you'll still be using skill, but no one will notice it. (However, if you express mild feelings with a harsh tone or harsh feelings with a mild tone, you'll be less convincing.) Compound words, frequent adjectives, and unusual words fit best in emotional speeches. People tend to forgive an angry speaker who describes something as 'colossal' or 'sky-high.' We excuse this language when the speaker has already won over the audience and stirred their emotions, whether through praise, blame, anger, or affection, as Isocrates does at the end of his Panegyric with phrases like 'name and fame' and 'in that they brooked.' People do speak like this when they are deeply moved, so once the audience feels the same, they naturally approve of the speech. That's why this kind of language works in poetry, which is inspired. It should be used either when emotions are high or ironically, like Gorgias and some of the passages in Plato's Phaedrus.

The structure of prose should have rhythm, but not be metrical. If it sounds too much like poetry, the audience won't trust it because it will seem too artificial. It will also distract them, making them focus on the rhythm instead of the message, just like how children interrupt with answers to questions before the speaker finishes. But if your prose has no rhythm at all, it will feel too loose and unfocused. While we don't want the restrictions of meter, we do need some structure, or else the speech will feel vague and unsatisfying. Rhythm, which comes from numbers, provides that structure. Meters are just specific kinds of rhythm. So, prose should have rhythm, but not follow a specific meter, or it will become poetry instead of prose. The rhythm should not be too exact either, just enough to be noticeable.

Of the different types of rhythm, the heroic rhythm has dignity but lacks the natural flow of speech. The iambic rhythm is closest to everyday conversation, so it shows up more often in casual talk. However, in a speech, we need more dignity and the power to lift the listener beyond ordinary life. The trochaic rhythm feels too much like lively dancing, which you can see in tetrameter verse, one of the trochaic rhythms.

The paean is the best rhythm for prose. It was first used by speakers in the time of Thrasymachus, though they didn't have a name for it yet. The paean is a third type of rhythm, closely related to the others. It has a ratio of three to two, while the other rhythms have ratios of one to one, or two to one. The paean is a middle ground between these ratios.

The other two types of rhythm should be avoided in prose because they sound too much like meter. The paean should be used instead because it doesn't produce a clear meter, so it stands out less. Right now, the same type of paean is used at the beginning and end of sentences, but the end should be different from the beginning. There are two types of paean: one starts with a long syllable and ends with three short ones, as in

"Dalogenes | eite Luki | an,"

and

"Chruseokom | a Ekate | pai Dios."

The other type starts with three short syllables and ends with a long one, as in

"meta de lan | udata t ok | eanon e | oanise nux."

This kind of paean creates a true ending. A short syllable doesn't give a sense of completion, so the rhythm feels cut off. A sentence should end with a long syllable, signaling the end through rhythm, not just a period or punctuation.

We've now seen that prose should have rhythm but not follow strict meter, and which rhythms work best for this.

The style of prose can either be loose, with only connecting words linking the ideas, like the preludes in dithyrambs, or more structured and balanced, like the strophes of old poets. The loose style is the older one, like in the opening of Herodotus's work: "Here is the investigation of Herodotus the Thurian." Everyone used this style in the past, but few do so now. By 'loose style,' I mean writing that has no natural stopping points and only ends because there's nothing more to say. This kind of style is unsatisfying because it feels endless. People like to see a finish line in front of them. It's only when they reach the end that they relax. When people see the end of the course ahead of them, they keep going. This is how the loose style works. The more compact style, on the other hand, is written in periods.

A period is a section of speech with a clear beginning and end that's small enough to grasp all at once. This kind of language is satisfying and easy to follow. It's satisfying because it's definite. The listener feels like they've understood something and reached a conclusion, while endless speech leaves them feeling lost. It's easy to follow because it's easy to remember. Periodic language can be counted, and numbers are the easiest thing to remember. That's why verse, which has a clear structure, is easier to recall than prose.

A period should only be complete when the sense is complete— it shouldn't break off suddenly, like in these iambic lines from Sophocles:

"Calydon's soil is this; of Pelops' land

(The smiling plains face us across the strait.)"

By splitting the lines wrong, the meaning becomes unclear, and you might think Calydon is in the Peloponnesus.

A period can be either made up of several parts or be simple. A period with several parts is a section of speech

1. complete in itself,
2. divided into parts, and
3. able to be spoken in one breath.

Each part is called a member. A simple period only has one member. Both the members and the whole period should not be too short or too long. If a member is too short, it can trip up the listener, as they expect the rhythm to continue but are cut off. If it's too long, the listener feels left behind, like someone walking past the finish line without turning back for their friends. A period that's too long becomes a speech or a dithyrambic prelude. The result is much like the prelude that Democritus of Chios made fun of Melanippides for writing instead of antistrophic stanzas:

"He who sets traps for others' feet
Is likely to fall into them first;
And long-winded preludes do harm to us all,
But the preluder suffers the most."

This applies to speakers with long, drawn-out periods. Periods with too short members aren't really periods at all, and they make the audience feel jarred.

The periodic style with multiple members can be of two types. One type is simply divided, like in the sentence: "I have often wondered at the organizers of national gatherings and the founders of athletic contests." The other type is antithetical, where each part contains opposites or contrasts, like "They helped both groups—not only those who stayed behind but also those who went along with them. For the latter, they gained new land larger than what they had at home, and for the former, they left enough land at home." Here, the contrasts are 'staying behind' versus 'going along,' and 'enough' versus 'larger.' Another example: "It often happens that the wise fail, and the foolish succeed." Or: "They were awarded the prize of valor immediately and gained command of the sea shortly after." And:

"They sailed through the mainland and marched through the sea, by bridging the Hellespont and cutting through Athos." And: "Nature gave them their country, and law took it away again." And: "Some perished in misery, others were saved in disgrace." And: "Athenian citizens keep foreigners as servants in their homes, while the city of Athens allows its allies to live as slaves." And: "To possess in life or to leave behind at death."

Someone once said about Peitholaus and Lycophron in a court case: "These men used to sell you when they were at home, and now they have come here to buy you." All of these examples use the structure I just described. This kind of speech is satisfying because the listener can easily grasp the meaning of the contrasts, especially when they are placed side by side. It also gives the impression of logical reasoning, as placing two opposing ideas side by side helps prove one of them false.

This is how antithesis works. Parisosis is when the two parts of a period are equal in length. Paromoeosis is when the first or last words of each part are similar. At the beginning, the similarity is usually between whole words, while at the end, it's between the final syllables or forms of the same word. Here's an example at the beginning:

"agron gar elaben arlon par' autou"
and
"dorhetoi t epelonto pararretoi t epeessin"
And here's an example at the end:
"ouk wethesan auton paidion tetokenai,
all autou aitlon lelonenai"
and
"en pleiotals de opontisi kai en elachistais elpisin"
An example with the same word form:
"axios de staoenai chalkous ouk axios on chalkou."
An example of the same word repeated:
"su d' auton kai zonta eleges kakos kai nun grafeis kakos."
An example of one syllable:

"ti d' an epaoes deinon, ei andrh' eides arhgon?"

It's possible for a sentence to have all these features at once—antithesis, parisosis, and paromoeosis. (The ways to begin periods have been fully covered in the Theodectea.) There are also false antitheses, like the one from Epicharmus:

"There once I as their guest did stay,
And they were my hosts on another day."

Now that we've covered the points above, let's talk about how to come up with lively and interesting sayings. The ability to invent them comes from either natural talent or lots of practice, but this guide can show the general approach. We can do this by looking at the different types of sayings. First, we should note that we all enjoy getting new ideas easily. Words express ideas, so the best words are the ones that help us understand something new. Strange words confuse us, and ordinary words tell us what we already know. It's through metaphors that we can best grasp something fresh. When a poet calls 'old age a withered stalk,' he's giving us a new idea by connecting it to something we already understand, like how a plant blooms and then withers. The similes poets use do the same thing, and if they're good similes, they can be very striking. A simile is just a type of metaphor, but since it's longer, it's not as appealing. It doesn't say directly that 'this is that,' so the listener isn't as interested.

We can see that both speech and reasoning are more lively when they help us grasp a new idea quickly. This is why people don't respond well to obvious arguments (ones that are so clear they need no explanation) or to ones that confuse them. People prefer arguments that give them new information immediately, or that their minds can almost understand right away. These two types give us a sense of learning something new. But obvious and confusing arguments don't teach us anything at all. So, these are the things that make an argument interesting in terms of meaning. In terms of style, the antithesis (contrast) is appealing, like in the phrase, 'thinking that the peace for everyone else was a war against their own interests.' Here, there's a contrast between peace and war.

It's also good to use metaphors, but they shouldn't be too far-fetched, or they'll be hard to understand, nor too obvious, or they won't have any effect. The words should also paint a picture in the listener's mind—events should feel like they're happening right now, rather than being described as something in the future. So, we should aim for three things: Antithesis, Metaphor, and Making Things Feel Real.

Of the four types of metaphor, the most appealing is the proportional metaphor. For example, Pericles once said that the young men who had died in war had left the country 'as if the spring were taken out of the year.' Leptines, when talking about the Lacedaemonians, said that he didn't want the Athenians to let Greece 'lose one of her two eyes.' When Chares was being examined for his part in the Olynthiac war, Cephisodotus was upset and said that Chares wanted to be examined 'while he still had his fingers around the people's throat.' The same speaker once urged the Athenians to march to Euboea, 'with Miltiades' decree as their food rations.' Iphicrates, frustrated at the truce between the Athenians and Epidaurus, said that the Athenians had given up their travel money for the journey of war. Peitholaus called the state galley 'the people's big stick,' and he called Sestos 'the grain storage of the Peiraeus.' Pericles urged his fellow citizens to get rid of Aegina, calling it 'the eyesore of the Peiraeus.' Moerocles joked that he was no more of a crook than a certain respectable citizen, 'whose crookedness earned him over thirty percent profit every year, unlike my ten percent.'

There's also the iambic line of Anaxandrides about how his daughters delayed getting married: 'My daughters' wedding days are overdue.' Polyeuctus once said about a man named Speusippus, who was paralyzed, that he couldn't stay quiet 'even though fortune had locked him in the prison of illness.' Cephisodotus called warships 'painted millstones,' and Diogenes the Dog called taverns 'the dining halls of Attica.' Aesion said the Athenians had 'poured their town into Sicily,' which is a vivid metaphor. The phrase 'until all of Greece shouted out loud' is another vivid metaphor. Cephisodotus warned the Athenians not to hold too many 'parades,' and Isocrates used the same word when talking about those who 'parade around at national festivals.' Another example comes from the Funeral Speech: 'It's fitting that Greece should cut her hair in mourning beside the tombs of those who died at Salamis, because her freedom and their bravery are buried together.' Even if the speaker had only said that it was right to cry when bravery was being buried, it would have been a metaphor. But linking 'bravery' and 'freedom' also creates an antithesis.

Iphicrates once said, 'The path of my words goes straight through the middle of Chares' deeds.' This is a proportional metaphor, and the phrase 'straight through the middle' makes it vivid. The phrase 'calling in one danger to save us from another' is also a vivid metaphor. Lycoleon, while defending Chabrias, said, 'They didn't even respect the bronze statue of him standing over there, which pleads for him.' This was a metaphor for the moment, but it wouldn't always apply. It's still a vivid metaphor, though. Chabrias was in danger, and his statue seemed to plead for him, like a lifeless yet living thing that reminded people of his service to his country. The phrase 'practicing every form of pettiness' is metaphorical because practicing something means you're getting better at it. So is the phrase 'God lit our reason like a lamp inside our souls,' because both reason and light help us see things. The phrase 'we're not ending our wars, just postponing them' is also metaphorical, because both war and postponement deal with future actions. The saying 'This treaty is a nobler trophy than those we set up on battlefields' is another metaphor. It means that while trophies on the battlefield celebrate small victories, the treaty celebrates our success in the whole war. The saying 'A country pays a heavy price when it's condemned by the judgment of the world' is also metaphorical, because 'paying a price' refers to deserved damage.

We've already said that liveliness comes from using proportional metaphors and making people 'see things.' We still need to explain what we mean by 'seeing things' and how to make this happen. By 'making them see things,' I mean using words that show things in action. For example, saying a good man is 'four-square' is a metaphor because both a good man and a square are considered perfect. But the metaphor doesn't suggest any action. However, saying someone is 'in full bloom' does suggest action. The phrase 'you must wander like a free, sacred animal' also suggests action. The line 'Then the Greeks sprang to their feet' is another example—'sprang' shows both action and a metaphor, suggesting quick movement. Homer often uses this technique to bring life to lifeless things in his poetry. For example, 'The boulder bounced downward into the valley,' or 'The arrow flew,' or 'The spear struck the earth, still eager to feed on the flesh of the heroes.' All of these examples give action to things that aren't alive. Homer attaches these ideas to things using proportional metaphors, like comparing a shameless man to the boulder of Sisyphus. In his famous similes, he also makes non-living things seem alive, as in 'Curving and crested with white, wave after wave followed each other without stopping.' Everything here is described as moving and full of life.

Metaphors should be taken from things related to the original, but not in an obvious way—just like in philosophy, where a sharp mind can see similarities between very different things. For example, Archytas said that both an arbitrator and an altar serve the same purpose because injured people seek refuge in both. You could also say an anchor and an overhead hook are alike, because one holds things down from below, and the other holds them from above. Saying a state is 'leveled' is another metaphor, as it connects the idea of a flat surface with equal political power.

Liveliness is especially created by metaphor, and by surprising the listener. When the listener expects something different, they're more impressed when they hear the new idea. It's as if their mind says, 'Yes, of course, I hadn't thought of that.' Epigrams are lively because they don't mean exactly what the words suggest, like when Stesichorus said, 'The cicadas will chirp to themselves on the ground.' Well-written riddles are enjoyable for the same reason—they present a new idea and use metaphorical language. The surprising phrases of Theodorus work the same way. His thoughts are striking because they don't fit in with what you already know. This is also the effect of burlesque words in comic plays. Even jokes that change the letters of a word can create surprise. This happens in both poetry and prose. The word that comes next isn't what the listener expected, like in the line, 'Onward he came, his feet shod with—chilblains,' where the listener expected the word 'sandals.' But the joke should be clear as soon as the words are said. Jokes that change the letters of a word work by suggesting something different from the usual meaning. For example, Theodorus once said about Nicon, the harpist, 'Thratt' ei su' (which means 'you're a Thracian slave') instead of 'Thratteis su' (which means 'you're a harp player'), making a surprising joke. But this only works if you know that Nicon is from Thrace. Another example is the phrase 'Boulei auton persai.' In both cases, the joke has to fit the facts.

This is also true of sayings like, 'To the Athenians, their control of the sea wasn't the beginning of their troubles, since they gained from it,' or the opposite argument from Isocrates, that their empire was the beginning of their problems. In both cases, the speaker says something unexpected, and the listener recognizes it as true. There's nothing clever about saying, 'Empire is empire.' Isocrates means something more and gives new meaning to the word. The first example denies that 'beginning' in one sense means 'beginning' in another. In all these jokes, whether they use a word in two senses or as a metaphor, they're effective if they fit the facts. For example, if someone is named Anaschetos (which means 'unbearable'), and you say 'Anaschetos is unbearable,' the joke works if the person is really unpleasant. Another example is the saying, 'Don't be a stranger, stranger than you should be.' Here, you're using one word in two different senses. Another example is the famous line from Anaxandrides: 'Death is fitting before you do something that would make death fitting.' This is another way of saying, 'It's right to die before you do something that makes you deserve to die.' The point is that the shorter and more balanced these sayings are, the more effective they become. Antithesis makes the new idea stand out, and brevity makes it more impactful. They should always have some personal relevance or a clever expression if they're to be meaningful without being boring—two goals that aren't always met at the same time. For example, 'A person should die without doing wrong' is true, but not interesting. 'The right man should marry the right woman' is also true, but not engaging. To be effective, a saying needs both qualities, like 'It's right to die before you deserve to die.' The more a saying has these qualities, the more lively it feels. For example, if it uses metaphor in the right way, is antithetical, and balanced, it will give the sense of action.

Good similes are also metaphors, as they compare two things in the same way proportional metaphors do. For instance, we might say that a shield is 'the drinking bowl of Ares,' or that a bow is 'the stringless lyre.' This is a more complex way of using metaphor than just calling the bow a lyre or the shield a drinking bowl. There are also simpler similes, like saying a flute player is like a monkey, or comparing a near-sighted person's eyes to a flame flickering with water dropping on it. Similes work best when they're like converted metaphors. For instance, you could say that a shield is like the drinking bowl of Ares, or that a ruined building is like a house in tatters. Or you could say that Niceratus is like Philoctetes after being beaten by Pratys, which is a simile made by Thrasymachus after Niceratus lost to Pratys in a recitation contest and walked around unkempt and unwashed. Poets fail most when they don't capture the right resemblance, and succeed best when they do, as in the line 'His legs curled up like parsley leaves,' or 'Just like Philammon battling with his punch ball.' All of these are similes, and as we've said many times before, similes are metaphors.

Proverbs are also metaphors, as they compare one thing to another. For example, if a man starts a project hoping to profit, but ends up losing, someone might say, 'He's like the man from Carpathus and his hare.' This refers to both the man and the person in the proverb experiencing the same misfortune.

We've now explained how liveliness is created and why it works. Hyperboles, when successful, are also metaphors. For example, the saying about a man with a black eye, 'You'd have thought he was a basket of mulberries,' compares his black eye to a mulberry because of the color. The exaggeration lies in the amount of mulberries being suggested. The phrase 'just like so-and-so' can introduce a hyperbole in the form of a simile. For example, 'Just like Philammon battling with his punch ball' is the same as saying, 'You'd have thought he was Philammon battling with his punch ball,' and 'His legs curled up like parsley leaves' is like saying, 'His legs were so curly, you'd have thought they were parsley leaves.'

Hyperboles are best suited for young men to use because they show a lot of passion. This is why angry people tend to use them more than others. For example:

"Not though he gave me as much as the dust
Or the sands of the sea...
But her, the daughter of Atreus' son, I never will marry,
Not though she were fairer than golden Aphrodite,
And more skilled with her hands than Athene..."

The Attic orators often use this kind of speech. However, it doesn't suit an older speaker as well.

Each type of rhetoric has its own style. The style used for written works is not the same as the style for speaking, and political speeches differ from legal speeches. You need to know both styles. Knowing how to speak well helps you communicate clearly, while writing well allows you to share ideas with the public.

Written style is more polished, while spoken style allows for dramatic delivery, which can reflect character and emotion. This is why actors look for plays written with this in mind, and poets look for actors who can deliver those lines well. But poets who write for reading are different, like Chaeremon, who wrote in a polished, professional style. Professional writers' speeches may seem weak when performed, while the speeches of orators may sound impressive but look less professional when read. This happens because orators write speeches suited for live delivery, full of dramatic touches that lose their effect without the performance and can seem silly when written down. For example, strings of disconnected words or repeated phrases are fine in spoken speeches but would be criticized in written ones. Speakers often repeat phrases for dramatic effect, like "This is the man who deceived you, who cheated you, who meant to betray you." Actors like Philemon would use this technique in plays to great effect. But if it's not delivered with skill, it becomes awkward.

Another example is repeating unconnected statements like "I came to him; I met him; I begged him." These need to be acted out with variety in tone and pitch, or they sound flat. They make it seem like a lot has happened in a short time, as if several statements were made at once. It's similar to how conjunctions connect ideas in writing. Without conjunctions, a single statement can feel like many. For instance, "I came to him; I spoke to him; I pleaded with him," makes each part seem more important. Homer used this trick when he wrote:

"Nireus likewise from Syme (three well-fashioned ships did bring),

"Nireus, the son of Aglaia (and Charopus, bright-faced king),

"Nireus, the comeliest man (of all that to Ilium's strand)."

By repeating his name, it feels like Homer is saying a lot about Nireus, even though he only mentions him once and never talks about him again.

Public speeches are like painting a scene for a large audience. The larger the crowd, the less important fine details become. In legal speeches, though, more detail is needed, especially when speaking to a single judge who can pay closer attention to the arguments. In these cases, the speaker needs to be more careful with the facts, as the judge can judge more accurately without distraction. This is why speakers don't usually succeed in all areas of rhetoric at once. The less detailed speeches require a strong, clear voice, while ceremonial speeches need more literary quality, as they're meant to be read. Forensic speeches (legal ones) come next in terms of literary quality.

Going further, some may say that style should also be pleasant or grand, but that's not as necessary as being clear and appropriate. Style should balance ordinary and unusual words, include rhythm, and be persuasive by fitting the subject. If the speech is too long, it won't be clear, but if it's too short, it can feel incomplete. A middle path works best. The right balance of words, rhythm, and appropriateness will make the style pleasant.

This wraps up our discussion of style, both in general and in how it applies to different kinds of rhetoric. Now we'll move on to how to organize a speech.

A speech has two parts. You must present your case and then prove it. You can't present your case without proving it, and you can't prove something if you haven't stated what it is. The first part is called the Statement, and the second is the Argument, just like in reasoning we distinguish between a premise and proof. The common way of dividing speeches is not very useful. For example, "narration" is only a part of legal speeches, not political or display speeches. In political speeches, there's no need for "narration" or responding to an opponent, and an epilogue isn't always necessary either. In short speeches or those where the facts are easy to remember, an epilogue may not be needed at all. So, the only truly necessary parts of a speech are the Statement and the Argument.

Other parts, like refuting an opponent or comparing your case to theirs, are just part of the argument, because you're still proving something. The introduction doesn't do this, nor does the epilogue, which just summarizes what's been said. Dividing speeches into too many parts is pointless unless each part is truly distinct.

The introduction is the beginning of the speech, like the prologue in a play or the prelude in music. It sets the stage for what's to come.

Musical preludes are similar to introductions in speeches meant for display, where the speaker can begin with any impressive thought before leading into the main topic. For example, Isocrates' introduction to his Helen doesn't have much to do with Helen. It's acceptable to begin far from the main subject to avoid being monotonous.

Introductions to display speeches often involve praise or criticism. Gorgias, in his Olympic speech, praised the people of Greece for starting the festival gatherings. Isocrates, on the other hand, criticized them for honoring athletes but giving no prizes for intellectual achievement. Another way to begin is by offering advice, like saying, "We should honor good people, so I'm here to praise Aristeides," or "We should honor people who are not well-liked but are not bad, like Alexander, son of Priam." Sometimes, introductions may ask the audience to be patient if the topic is unusual or difficult, much like Choerilus did in his lines:

"But now when allotment of all has been made..."

Introductions to display speeches can include praise, advice, or requests for patience, and they can be either connected or disconnected from the main speech.

Introductions in legal speeches work like prologues in plays or epic poems, where the audience is given a preview of the main theme to avoid confusion. In epic poems, the introduction often tells what the story will be about, like:

"Sing, O goddess of song, of the Wrath..."

Or:

"Tell me, O Muse, of the hero..."

Tragic poets also give a hint of the story early on, as in Sophocles' play when he begins with "Polybus was my father..." The same happens in comedies. So, the main purpose of an introduction is to show what the speech is about. When the subject is short or simple, there's no need for a lengthy introduction.

Other types of introductions are used to address the speaker, the audience, or the subject. They can help to remove or build up prejudice. A defendant may start by clearing away any negative feelings the audience may have, while a prosecutor may wait until the end to stir up prejudice against the defendant.

Sometimes the introduction is used to gain the audience's attention, whether to make them take the subject seriously or, in some cases, to distract them. Speakers may also make the audience laugh to lighten the mood. You might use different strategies to make your listeners interested, like showing that you have a good character or that the topic is important or surprising. If you want to distract them, you could suggest that the subject isn't important or that it's unpleasant.

But none of this has to do with the speech itself. It's just about how easily the audience is swayed by things that aren't related to the topic. When the audience is focused, all you need is a summary of the subject at the start to help them follow along. In fact, it's better to call for attention later in the speech if necessary. It's silly to ask for attention at the beginning when the audience is already paying attention. Save these appeals for points where the audience might lose focus, saying something like, "Now I need you to pay attention to this point—it's just as important to you as it is to me," or "I'm going to tell you something more surprising than anything you've heard before."

These types of introductions are meant for real-life audiences, not ideal ones. They're often used to stir up emotions or remove doubts, like when a speaker says, "My lord, I will not say eagerly..." or "Why all this introduction?" Introductions are useful when the case seems weak. In these cases, it's better to focus on something other than the main facts.

To sum up, introductions help to get goodwill from the audience or to create certain emotions. In display speeches, it helps if the praise somehow includes the audience or their values, as Socrates said in his

Funeral Speech: "The challenge is not praising the Athenians in Athens, but in Sparta."

Introductions in political speeches are rare because the audience already knows the subject, but sometimes you need to address yourself or your opponents, or adjust the importance of the topic. Sometimes an introduction adds elegance to the speech, as in Gorgias' praise of Elis, where he begins without any preamble, saying, "Happy city of Elis!"

When dealing with prejudice, one way to defend yourself is to get rid of false assumptions that people may have about you. It doesn't matter if these assumptions have been spoken aloud or not; this difference doesn't change how you should handle them. Another approach is to confront the issue directly. You can deny the accusation, claim that you didn't cause harm, or argue that the harm wasn't as bad as claimed. You can say that you didn't act unfairly, or that if you did, it wasn't significant. These are the types of arguments you can use to respond. For example, Iphicrates, when replying to Nausicrates, admitted that he had caused harm but argued that he hadn't acted unjustly.

Another option is to admit that you did something wrong, but to balance it with other facts. You could say that even if what you did hurt the other person, it was still honorable, or that while it caused pain, it was for their benefit. Another approach is to say that the action was a mistake, or due to bad luck or necessity. For instance, Sophocles responded to someone accusing him of trembling to appear old by saying he was shaking because he couldn't help it—he didn't want to be eighty years old.

You could also explain that your intention was different from the actual result. For example, you might say, "I didn't mean to hurt him; I intended to do something else," or "The damage was an accident. I'd be terrible if I had planned this outcome." Another argument is that the person accusing you has faced similar suspicions or situations themselves. You could also point out that others who were suspected for the same reasons were later found innocent, like saying, "Am I a bad person just because I dress well? If that's true, then so-and-so must be too."

If others have been falsely accused by the same person or have faced suspicion like you, but were later proven innocent, you can use that to support your case. Another method is to accuse your accuser in return by saying, "It's outrageous to believe this person's claims when you can't even trust them."

You can also argue that the matter has already been settled. A good example is when Euripides responded to Hygiaenon, who accused him in court of encouraging perjury with a line in one of his plays that said:

"My tongue has sworn, but my heart has not."

Euripides replied by saying that his opponent was wrong to bring this issue to court when it should be decided in a theatrical contest. He said, "If I haven't already answered for my words there, I'm ready to defend myself if you take it to the proper place."

Thank You for Reading

Dear Reader,

We hope this timeless classic has sparked your imagination and enriched your literary journey. Now that you've turned the final page, we want to share a vision for the future of reading—one where every classic you've ever wanted to explore is at your fingertips, in a format that best suits your life.

We'd like to invite you to gain immediate, unlimited digital & audiobook access to hundreds of the most treasured literary classics ever written—along with the option to secure deluxe paperback, hardcover & box set editions at printing cost. Together, we can spark a new global literary renaissance alongside our small, independent publishing house called "The Library of Alexandria."

Thousands of years ago, the Library of Alexandria stood as a beacon of knowledge—until it was lost to history. We aim to reignite that spirit of preservation and discovery right now, in the modern age—only this time, it's accessible to all, in every language and every format.

Picture a world where every timeless classic, novel, poem, or philosophical treatise is not only available to read but also updated for today's readers—modernized, translated into any language or dialect, and ready to enjoy in any format you choose, whether that is in an eBook, audiobook, paperback, or deluxe hardcover & box set version a printing cost.

By joining our movement to rebuild the modern Library of Alexandria, you become part of an unprecedented mission to offer:

- **Unlimited Audiobook & eBook Access to the Greatest Classics of All Time**

    Instantly explore thousands of legendary works, from Plato and Shakespeare to Jane Austen and Leo Tolstoy. All are instantly ready to read or listen to, giving you a complete literary universe at your fingertips.

- **Paperback & Deluxe Editions at Printing Costs:**

Purchase any title in a paperback, deluxe hardbound, or deluxe boxset edition at printing costs, shipped right to your doorstep. Curate your personal library of Alexandria with editions worthy of display—crafted to last, designed to captivate, and delivered straight to your door.

- **Modern translations for Contemporary Readers in all languages and dialects**

Discover a vast selection of classics reimagined in clear, current language—no more struggling with outdated phrases or obscure references. Next to the original versions, we aim to offer translations in as many languages and dialects as possible.

As we continue our translation efforts and add new languages, readers everywhere can connect with these works as if they were written today. By bridging linguistic divides, you're contributing to ensuring that these timeless stories become more meaningful, accessible, and inspiring for people across the globe.

- **Your Personal Library of Alexandria:**

Over the months and years, you'll curate a unique physical archive of classics—each volume a testament to your taste, curiosity, and love of knowledge. It's not just about owning books—it's about curating a cultural legacy you'll cherish and pass down for generations to come.

- **Join a Global Literary Renaissance:**

Your support fuels an ongoing mission: allowing us to reinvest in offering deluxe print editions (including special boxsets) at their true cost, broaden the range of available formats and translations, and extend the reach of these works to new audiences worldwide. By joining today, you're not just preserving a legacy of masterpieces; you set in motion a powerful wave of literary accessibility.

We are more than a publisher—we're a movement, and we can't do it alone. Your support lets us scale our mission, preserving and reimagining history's greatest works for tomorrow's readers.

Become a Torchbearer of knowledge.

Thank you for picking up this book and allowing us into your literary journey. As you turn the pages, know that you're part of something larger: a global effort to keep these stories alive, share their wisdom across borders and generations, and spark a true cultural revival for the modern era.

If this resonates with you—please consider taking the next step by visiting:

www.libraryofalexandria.com

With gratitude and a shared love of knowledge,

The Modern Library of Alexandria Team

Visit:

www.libraryofalexandria.com

Or scan the code below: